NECROMANCY
THE CALLBACK

DEBBIE HIBBERT

To Donna: the one who knows too much to be called just friend.

CHAPTER ONE

MY HOUSE: THE ROUGAROU

Not to brag, but my boyfriend's perfect. Soft blue eyes that shift through shades like me changing guesses on a multiple-choice test; unsure if glowing sapphire or bottomless navy is the right answer. His sexy smolder that puts Prince Charming, and all the Disney dudes, to shame. Thoughtful, funny, smart, not to mention the way he'd take a bullet for me, or — you know — a powerful magical attack from a desperate murderer. Which he did.

We sit on the couch in my front room, and a movie plays. A suspenseful flick about an undead army overtaking the city and the reluctant hero who races against time to stop them. But my attention wanders from the epic zombie showdown to the feel of Zach's fingers curled in mine. Warmth radiates from his touch, his magic coiling through my veins like an IV of sparkling hot sauce. There's something else too, though. A thicker, dirtier slither tainting the glow. A metaphorical coating of grease on my hands that's impossible to rinse off.

"The black magic is still here." Keeping my voice low, I glance to where my dad sits at the kitchen table. He pays us no mind, his full focus on a file, probably his latest case from the New Orleans Police Department. Usually, he asks for my unique skill set to help with his murder investigations. Not so much, lately. Something about the deep trauma from being forced to use magic, and how he wants me to focus on recovering and not jumping into talking to murder victims again, and yadda, yadda, yadda.

"You can feel it?" Zach asks, his low volume matching mine.

"When I brush your skin here—" I rub the underside of his wrist, his pulse line thrumming with more than the beat of his heart— "a little punch of it hits me."

Before drama camp—*was that only two months ago*— I hardly acknowledged my necromancy. Now I know it emits a distinct and palpable aura, as do all the different magics. Which is why I recognize the hint of oily darkness infecting Zach's power.

I rub his wrist again, like running my fingers over a scar. After I'd been force-fed black magic by my dad's former partner, I became well acquainted with the darkness. Detective Rivera tried to bring his wife back from the dead, and he needed me, a reluctant necromancer. Luckily, we foiled that frightening venture—without an epic zombie showdown.

"Hmm." He removes his hand from mine and puts his arm around my shoulders. The stirring of our magic dims without the skin-to-skin contact. It's something he's done more of lately, withdrawing his touch so I can't sense the oiliness. "Are you craving it? Wanting more?"

The questions serve as a reminder of the dangerous, addictive nature of black magic. And Zach is determined to keep me from falling into it, even taking a personal hit to save me from its influence.

"No, not even close. I'm worried about you. How long will it take for it to..." I fumble to find the right word. *Fade?* No, because even a slight trace of black magic pollutes everything. A small drop of inky poison spreading. "Heal," I settle with.

"I don't know. Does it bother you?" He tips his head, his blue-eyed gaze studying my face like it's the pre-test for the chemistry final.

"It's not that." I lean into him, my cheek against his shoulder, my breath whispering in his ear. "I hate that you have to live with this. If it weren't for—"

"No," he cuts me off, softening the interruption by rubbing his chin on the top of my head. "You have nothing to feel guilty about."

"But—"

"Shh." He leans away, silencing the same old debate.

That debate being:

Me: *I totally made you save me, using the black magic you're addicted to.*

Him: *It was my choice, and I would make the same one again. Every time.*

Me: *But if you spiral and crave the darkness, and fall into a pit of despair, ruining your life for a cheap fix, forgetting me and your family, I will send dead people to haunt you.*

At that, he usually silences me with a kiss. Which flusters my mind. Steals my words. Sends *me* into a spiral where only our lips exist. Well, lips and glancing touches. His fingers brushing my cheek. His arms pulling me into the snug zone, the perfect place where my head nestles in the crook between his neck and shoulder.

We both think about it, his method of ending the debate, and the look in his eyes turns my internal burner to high. *Click, click, click, flame.* Just that fast. Finding alone time (aka, time for kissy face) has been a challenge. Between friends, his work schedule, and my dad who won't allow Zach around without his supervision, we sneak moments when we can. And it's been four hundred years since the last meeting of our lips. My eyes lower to his mouth, staring with intent.

He leans forward, an incremental inch. "Since you brought up magic, we need to work on your plane."

Disappointment, thy name be magical plane. Not only is it interrupting potential smooch sneaking, but I CAN'T DO IT. To build a mental supernatural landscape, detail by detail, barely touches the surface. Sending my spirit there to engage in multi-plane mysticism is the real purpose. Which I can barely describe, let alone do.

"I've been trying." My whole body melts into the couch. Shoulders sagged, muscles liquifying.

He smiles, the curtain parting to reveal the glorious gift of dimpled perfection. To describe the dimples would be an insult to poetry. An attack to metaphors everywhere.

Simply put, get this girl a tall drink of water because his face dents are making me thirsty.

"You're getting distracted," he needlessly says. Because yeah. He smiled.

"No, I'm not."

"Magical plane, CeCe."

"Right." Ugh. Why can't he just accept my failure at this? But I close my eyes, bringing my space to mind.

According to Zach, it helps to form a world with details

not normally found in nature. A bit of imagination to create something individual and unique.

First comes the turquoise sky, an aqua rich enough to make a billionaire jealous. A perfectly still, extremely thin layer of water stretches across the ground. A reflective pool mirroring the sky above. Then the clouds roll in, fluffy puffs matching the color of my hair: cherry-dipped rose gold.

"Do you see it?" he asks.

"Yes." The peaceful oasis extends in front of me. Beautiful...and empty.

"Picture yourself there. Listen for your cicadas." His soft, encouraging voice flows over me. But those stubborn bugs stay silent. "Now pull your spirit."

Oh, we're just moving right along. "Yep. Pulling. Go spirit. Go now."

Nothing.

"CeCe." Dad interrupts, and I jump. Not figuratively, but a literal jump that lands me a football field away from Zach, closer to cuddling the arm of the sofa than enjoying the snug zone. Zach bites his lip to keep from laughing at my teleportation.

"Are there other magical...uh...things out there?" Dad asks.

He pays no attention to me (and the disruption of my nearly, almost, kind of stepping onto my plane). Instead, he stares at a photo. A few different ones that he flips through from the manilla NOPD folder.

I clear my throat, hoping to sound normal. "What kinds of things do you mean?"

He grunts. "Things that would help this case make sense. Unbelievable things."

Now that he mentions it, this case has seemed particularly preoccupying. Fewer grunts, longer stares, less dates with his "sort of" girlfriend, Gina.

We met Gina when she stepped in to help us, our friendly local sketch artist. Between Dad's gooey eyes and her nervous glances, I wasn't surprised when he asked her out. Two months and many dates later, they approach making it official. But Dad worries about moving too fast.

I'm happy for him, though. Thrilled, really. Barring a few awkward interactions where Gina continues to think I have psychic abilities (and no idea about my necromancy), she fits into our world.

"It sounds like a weird one," I say. "Do you need me in the morgue?"

"No, baby girl. Not this time." A deep breath blows from his cheeks, and he continues to focus on the pictures.

I know he's not ignoring me. I'm used to this behavior. Daddy hails from Louisiana, a deep south boy who talks when he has something to say. A man of few words and no need for superfluous expressions. He'll get back to me when he's good and ready. While I wait for him to gather his thoughts, I subtly scooch closer to Zach.

Magic things? He mouths, his eyebrows raised.

I shrug and reach to take his hand, but he tucks me next to him, his arm resting on my shoulder. The onscreen explosions dazzle, but I pay them no mind. Leaning back, I roll my head to watch Zach. The corner of his mouth rises, a sexy smirk letting me know that he knows I'm enjoying the view.

Just as I get into the ogling of the most adorable dimples known to mankind, my phone rings. My bestest best friend's picture lights up the screen, and my stomach roller-coaster swoops as I answer, hoping for good news. Dreading the worst.

I skip the cordial basics and fly right to the point. "Did you get it?"

Silence greets me, and I pull the phone away to make sure I actually answered. Yep. Screen glowing, timer ticking the seconds since I swiped. I press the cell to my ear again. "Portia?"

A high-pitched scream assaults my hearing, and I fumble the phone, bouncing it in my hands a few times before settling it back to my cheek.

"...can hardly believe it." The conversation picks up mid-sentence, but the jubilation in her voice tells me she got the part.

A local play, *Voodoo Bayou*, premiers in four weeks at Le Petit Theater. Sort of a Phantom of the Opera meets New Orleans vibe. Portia desperately wanted the lead. The countless hours she spent perfecting her audition piece for Kate— the young college student entranced by the mysterious man living in the swamp— paid off. At least if her squealing excitement is any indication.

"Because of the accelerated schedule, rehearsals start Monday and there's so much to do. I just got the script, and I'll be living, eating, breathing the words until I know it better than the Gap summer sale." The thoughts hit rapid fire, one on top of the other. "I haven't even met the male lead yet, but I hope he's amazing and that we have good chemistry like you and Zach, because, yes, we're going to have a stage kiss. More than one, actually."

"Be careful. Those stage kisses can leave a lasting impression." I glance at *my* said lasting impression, and his slow wink bubbles my insides. Carbonated soda fizzing in my stomach.

"Don't get my hopes up. Now that things are over with Devin, I'm ready to, as my diva Ariana says, *thank you, next.*"

"Maybe you should avoid the co-star dating this time around." After Portia's traumatic role as kidnappee and bait in Rivera's resurrection plot, she broke things off with her drama camp hook-up, Devin. He had no interest in supporting her through the inevitable tears and sleepless nights. And she had no interest in a useless boyfriend.

"Yes, mother," she says with a dose of audible eye-roll. "But I won't complain if the male lead causes my pheromones to firework."

I give her a solid *mmm hmm* because who doesn't want a sexy co-star? "In other news, dot, dot dot..." I leave the thought hanging, drawing out the suspense. An urge to laugh, or cheer, or break into a dance routine with lots of jazz hands rises in me.

"What?"

"Zach's mom has worked with the music director before, and he reached out for help to set up the jazz quintet. Specifically, a guitarist."

"Shut your face." She's back to shrieking, and I put distance between my ear and the phone. "Are you going to play on *Voodoo Bayou*?"

"Meet the newest member of the band." We whoop it up together, which consists of laughing, cheering, and me waving one jazz hand. "And that's not all. Zach's on piano."

"I didn't even know he played!" At this point of her screechy exclamations, my hearing might need to undergo a tympanic transplant.

I open my mouth, ready to tell her about Zach's surprising musical skills, but Dad grunts to get my attention. He moves next to the couch, focused on me. Clearly his thoughts are now gathered.

"Portia, I need to call you back. Sherlock has a question."

Dad gives a small, exasperated sigh at my nickname for him, but he waits for me to say my goodbyes. It involves several congratulations, giggling like a flock of loons, and a back-and-forth battle of who's the most amazing (obviously her). Hanging up, I toss my phone on the couch and look at Dad.

"Werewolves," he says. No lead in. No other words. Just that.

"Um...what?" My mind wanders back to our earlier conversation. "Are you asking me if werewolves are real?"

He grunts, one nod, his chin dipping down and then up.

All that waiting for a question about... *werewolves?* A laugh bursts out of me, and I lean forward, my hands pressing into my knees. "Humans who transform into violent, furry creatures during a full moon? Yeah, fiction."

I chuckle until I realize no one else joins in. In fact, Zach's lips pinch together, his forehead scrunched, warning me of an impending revelation. One that will shake the foundation of what I think I know.

I'm far too familiar with earth-altering information these days. Things like magical planes, spirit kidnappings, and—oh yeah—my mom might be a murderer.

"CeCe," he starts cautiously, glancing between me and my dad. "You've heard of the Rougarou, right?"

"Hold up!" I lift my hand, wielding it like a stop sign. "You're talking about the urban legend? The whole '*don't go out at night, kids, or else the Rougarou will get you.*' That thing?"

"All stories are based on pieces of truth. Like zombies, Miss Necromancer." He gives me a pointed look because, yes, I understand how the origins of the walking dead have been greatly exaggerated.

"Fair, but...the Rougarou?" Tales of the Louisiana werewolf span generations and households, the versions as different as the people spouting them. Some say it kidnaps misbehaving kids. Others claim it lurks around the bayou, killing at night and living in the shadows.

Dad moves closer, sitting on the coffee table in front of us. "What part of it is real?"

"Most of the legends, actually. The Rougarou lives in the bayou, hunting in the forests and marshes. The full moon part is fiction, they can change whenever, and it lasts one-hundred-and-one days." Zach shrugs. "But they don't take kids, as far as I know, and it's not a disease or anything. You don't get it from being bitten."

"Then how does it happen?" I ask.

His eyes meet mine, and the roller-coaster swoop strikes, the speedy downhill dread gripping my insides. "It's a black magic curse. Unbreakable. It's been around for centuries, and I've heard it passes through certain families."

Black magic. Why does it always come to this? My inescapable, recurring nightmare.

"What families? Can you give me names?" Dad pats his pocket, looking for his notebook.

Zach shakes his head. "I don't have names. People don't really talk about it. Just whispers of rumors."

"Even a rumor could give us a lead." Dad blows out a breath, rubbing the back of his neck. "We might have a rogue Rougarou. But it's not hunting in the bayou." *Rogue Rougarou, come on, say that ten times fast!* His tongue twister barely registers before his next words: "This one's killing in the heart of the French Quarter."

The French Quarter. Home of Bourbon Street, Jackson Square, and the Le Petit Theater. The very theater Portia, Zach, and I will be working on *Voodoo Bayou* for the next two months.

Of course.

CHAPTER TWO

LE PETIT THEATER: THE CO-STAR

Taking a deep breath, I fill my lungs with hints of dusty velvet, fog machine residue, and please-don't-let-me-forget-my-lines sweat. No matter what auditorium I step into, be it at my school or at Le Petit, the scents are always the same. The nostalgia stirs my adrenaline, and I bounce with nervous energy.

The show director and the music director decided to hold simultaneous, pre-rehearsal meetings. One at the front, close to the stage, where Portia and the rest of the cast gathers. And one at the back of the auditorium for Zach, me, and the other musicians.

Since the production is sponsored by Tulane University Youth Programs, all the cast and musicians are between the ages of sixteen and twenty. Only the directors are older, which makes the atmosphere feel a little like a school classroom.

Zach and I sit next to each other on the back row. The jazz quintet for *Voodoo Bayou* is here, ready to collect music, meet each other, and get our rehearsal schedule. Pretty standard stuff. But the music director, Chance, paces behind us, talking on his phone. He started introductions, and before the saxophone player said his name, Chance took a call. The five of us wait in awkward silence for him to finish.

I pull out my own phone and look at the *recents* log. The top entry reads *MM(17)*. Seventeen calls I've made to the contact known as Maybe Mom. All of them unanswered. Glancing at Chance, I click the button, figuring I have time to bring my count to *MM(18)*. I hate odd numbers anyway.

The line rings. Four times. Five. And then a message kicks on: *I'm sorry, the person you are trying to reach has a voicemail box that has not been set up yet. Please try your call again later. Goodbye.*

The line goes dead, and I sigh, pulling up my one-sided text conversation to her. A series of bubbles trails down the screen. Seeing the lack of response doesn't stop me from adding another plea.

> ME: I have so many questions. Please talk to me.

Zach reads over my shoulder, his leg jiggling. "Still no answer?"

"Radio Silence." I put my hand over his bouncing knee, the buzz of magic an oily shimmer. "She's totally vanished. Poof."

He's been a trooper, supporting me through my journey of frustration and self-doubt. Do I keep reaching out? Calling until my phone log reads *MM (100)?* Dad told me to move on and leave Mom in the rearview. But I want answers, information about my magic, her magic, why she left. Why she continues to ignore me.

Zach's eyes crinkle in sympathy. "I'm sorry she hasn't responded, but...there must be a reason."

"Obviously. She killed a person, stole their heart, and went underground." All true. *Allegedly.* So why do I even try to contact the woman who gave birth to me?

At the front of the theater, the play director claps her hands, getting the attention of the actors. Being a smaller cast, only a dozen or so people gather there. Portia plays with her dangly, silver earrings, looking through the packet handed to her. To anyone else she might seem bored. But I recognize the truth.

She's nervous. Really nervous.

Chance's conversation goes the distance, so I lift my phone and send a quick text to my bestie.

> ME: Stop trying to twist your earlobes off.
> Why the gut boulder?

Her earring mangling pauses as she pulls out her phone. Reads. Glances at me, glances at the door, before typing out a response.

> PORTIA: He's not here yet.

> ME: Who?

> PORTIA: Beau.

Not "beau" as in the old-fashioned word for a guy you're super into. But the character name of "Kate's" love interest, "Beau." Portia's co-star. The one who she will share stage kisses with.

> PORTIA: He better be worth the stress.

My texting reply is cut short by the conclusion of Chance's phone call. "Sorry about the interruption. Thanks for your patience." He pulls a small bottle of hand sanitizer from his pocket and rubs it on. "Where were we?"

"Uh, introductions." The sax-playing guy, whose name we still don't know, speaks up.

"Right." Chance hands out packets of music, using the sanitizer again when he finishes. *Germaphobe much?* "As a quintet, it's essential to have a bond to make the playing flawless. Let's go ahead and get to know each other. I'm the conductor, Chance."

Which we learned because he already introduced himself before his phone call.

In short order, we meet Lovelie Delva, who plays the double base. She looks about my age, maybe a pinch older, and she slouches in her chair, knees poking from ripped jeans, her hair twisted in Bantu knots. Our petite drummer, Aubree Bloom, has shoulder-length blond hair, blue eyes, and a personality that reminds me of pink bubblegum. Zach and I introduce ourselves as the pianist and guitarist. And just as the sax player opens his mouth, a side door swings open, stealing my attention.

A tall guy in a black tank top walks in. Although *guy* is an understatement, and *walk* is the wrong word. This hunky hunk strides. Swaggers. His long legs eat up the aisle like a bottomless stomach at an all-you-can-eat buffet. Dark skin, dark hair, dark eyes, and — dare I say — dark aura. A mysterious air floats around him, a captivating fog that forces my eyes to follow his journey to the front row.

"Mr. Etienne, you're late." The play director shoots him an annoyed glare.

"My apologies, ma'am." His deep bayou drawl covers the air in a sweet M&M candy coating.

"Well"—she adjusts her glasses, a soft blush tinting her cheeks—"I hope it won't happen again."

"You and me both." He grins, a lop-sided smile that has half the room falling instantly in love. But the smooth smirk feels deliberate to me. Calculated.

Chance talks to our quintet, and I ignore him in favor of watching the newcomer. Hunky Hunk grabs an information packet and looks for a seat, his gaze stopping on Portia. His eyebrow lifts and he mouths the word, *Kate?* At her nod, he puts a hand on his chest saying, "Beau," and moves to sit next to her.

Oh no! This is Portia's stage kiss partner. The stranger in the swamp who entrances the naïve Kate. And the way her eyes pass over him, I worry about life imitating art. *Mayday, Mayday, abort the attraction,* I attempt a telepathic message to my BFF. But his mouth inches up into a full, flirty grin, and I watch as Portia's shoulders squee.

Not good.

Zach leans closer to whisper in my ear, a difficult task with an armrest between us. "I've met him before."

Wait, what? My boyfriend somehow knows the tall, dark, enigmatic co-star of Portia? "Where?"

"At Black Wren," he says.

Apparently the new guy shops at Zach's mom's voodoo store. *Interesting.*

"What did he buy?" Pheromone spray? Magnetism charms?

"He was looking for herbs. I remember him because he made a scene when we were out of wormwood." His muscles coil, tightened springs filled with tension. "You seem pretty interested in him."

"I am. Did you see how he looked at Portia?" My bestie

currently stares with hearts in her eyes. "She just broke up with Devin, and the new guy's giving her palpitations."

He glances over his shoulder at the co-star of questionable origin. "I don't like him."

Yeah. The dark aura thing. There are other words to describe what Mr. Etienne has going on: scoundrel, rebel without a cause, forbidden fruit. The bad boy vibe radiates off him like catnip. And Portia eats it up.

"He's probably a decent guy." At least I hope.

"You and Portia need to steer clear," Zach's voice rises enough that the acoustics catch hold. Chance notices we aren't fully engaged in his enthralling speech. Something about how he places the cogs in the musical clock that creates harmony.

"Am I interrupting your private conversation with my important instructions?" Chance snaps at us, both with words and literal finger clicking.

"Sorry," we say, hunkering back in our seats, and the lecture (err...inspirational pep talk) continues.

A paper rips and I glance to see Lovelie tearing a square from her notebook. She's been quietly writing this whole time (doodling? Copying everything Chance says word for word?). With the note hidden in her palm, she reaches across the seat between us, hand extended.

Even though her arm stretches toward me, I still point at my chest, the international symbol for, *me?* She dips her chin, the international symbol for, *who else would I be giving this to? You're the only person within reach.* I blow out a breath, the international sound for, *sorry, you're right. I'm just distracted by the strange new guy, and my boyfriend's reaction.*

At least, I *think* that's the right international sound.

Taking the paper, I open it. The small letters scrawl across the top of the page.

I've worked with Chance before. He's ALL ego. But I'd like to work with the guy who just walked in. Do you know him?

Curiosity about "Beau" abounds. She must have overheard pieces of my whispered conversation with Zach.

Digging in my small bag, I pull out a pen and write a response on Lovelie's note. I could go basic and simply say no. Instead, I offer a little more since she threw me an olive branch about our music director who gives main character energy.

Never met him, but my best friend will be sharing the stage with him.

I subtly pass the note back and watch as her eyes look over what I wrote. She nods once and tucks it away, returning to her doodles.

Chance continues to talk about himself. How he deserves accolades for all his work but always gets looked over. I think he wants us to be impressed, but my second-hand embarrassment kicks in, and I fight the cringe.

With a few minutes to spare, or years at Chance's rate, I conjure a landscape of turquoise sky and pink clouds. I try everything Zach taught me, *just pull your spirit there* — as if that actually helps. And I end up with my usual result. A pretty and *empty* daydream.

An eternity later, Chance ends the meeting with,

"Remember, the music makes the magic," and we collect our things to leave. Portia's meeting ended before ours, and she lingers, talking — i.e. flirting and giggling — with Mr. "Bad Boy" Etienne himself.

I make my way to the front of the theater with Zach behind me, and he tugs my T-shirt to keep us from getting separated. The stack of music in my hands ruffles as I walk down the aisle, and I hug it close to my chest. Chance, the man of verbose speeches and snapping fingers, will have a meltdown if I ask for any replacement sheets.

Portia spots us approaching and squeals. "CeCe! Come meet Luc. He's playing Beau."

She grabs my elbow and places me right in front of Luc. His gaze passes over my face, and this close, I see the color of his eyes. Imagine being in an amusement park and going on a haunted house ride. That moment between leaving the outside world and slinking into the darkness...that's the exact shade. A little thrilling. A lot terrifying.

Zach wedges next to me, close enough our arms rub, and our power sings. That slight hint of black magic in him slicks my skin. Standing between the two guys, the air thick with oil and aura, heightens my awareness. The something-strange-is-afoot radar pings. Breathing through the odd strain, I introduce myself.

"I'm CeCe," I say, and glance over my shoulder. "And this is my boyfriend Zach."

"Hi." Zach's stony expression could be carved from, well, stone.

"Nice to meet y'all." Luc barely tips his head in acknowledgement.

"Luc's on his gap year and decided to audition. Lucky us, he got the part." Portia squees again, her dreamy sigh all for her co-star.

"Lucky us." I smile, trying to minimize the awkward. The whole meet and greet is uncomfortable and formal. Zach keeps silent, and Luc observes, a stiff, hyper awareness reminiscent of my detective dad.

He stands about an inch taller than Zach and tucks his hands into his pockets. While I've never considered myself an expert on shoulder definition, Luc Etienne makes me want to become one. The shape. The tightened skin. The way his tank top accentuates his...what are the shoulder muscles even called? I'll name them: Thor and God of Thunder.

Yes, the way his tank top accentuates Thor and God of Thunder.

But not to lose sight of my extremely attractive and perfect boyfriend, I shift to take Zach's hand. The papers in my arms slip from my grip, and despite my scramble to hold on, several float to the ground. Zach and Luc both bend to collect the loose sheets.

The next moment happens so fast. Zach's hand brushes against Luc, and both of their eyes go wide. In a flash, Luc grabs Zach by the arm and yanks him to stand.

"You better watch out. You're on my radar now." The sweet M&M coating voice turns sour Warheads. "If I find out it's you, we're gonna have trouble."

"I don't know what you're talking about." Zach's fists clench, and my loving boyfriend who has been nothing but gentle and sweet, shoves Luc, making him release his arm.

A surprised yip leaves Portia's mouth at the same time I yell, "Zach!" I step forward, unsure if I need to defend him or stop him.

We all freeze. Pistols at high noon as music plays and tumbleweeds blow by. Waiting for someone to move and jump-start us into motion.

Luc breaks the standstill by tucking his hands into his pockets. With a smirk, he turns his attention to Portia. "See ya next time, darlin'."

And with that, he walks away.

Wide eyed, I stare at Zach. He rolls out his shoulders and shakes his head, a deep breath heaving from his lungs.

"Is it me, or did Luc get more hot?" Portia asks, fanning her face.

Seriously. Catnip.

CHAPTER THREE

JACKSON SQUARE: THE FORTUNE TELLER

"What just happened?" I ask.

The production excitement and nostalgic theater scents fade as uncertainty replaces everything else. I replay the scene in my mind, super confused. Arm yanking, threats uttered, a manly display of manliness. That about sums it up.

"Let's talk at Café Du Monde." Zach lifts his chin, gesturing to the people still lingering in the theater, a few of whom watch us. Probably because of the charged show-down of clenched fists and bunched shoulders. At least we can pass it off as practice for the play.

"He called me darlin'. Did you hear that?" Portia seems unaffected that my boyfriend nearly came to blows with her co-star.

"Come on." I tug Portia by the hand and walk, Zach right behind us.

As we leave the theater, the blinding mid-afternoon sun

stuns like a flashbang grenade. The balcony overhead shades us from the direct light, but the terra cotta colored stucco of Le Petit's facade practically glows.

I ate lunch before the musicians meeting, but my mouth salivates at the thought of Café Du Monde. They offer coffee, hot chocolate, and most importantly, beignets. Delicious slabs of fried dough smothered in powdered sugar. A delight to the tastebuds, and to the soul.

The narrow street, blockaded by buildings on either side, opens as we cross to Jackson Square. Thin clouds wisp across the sky, and the humidity simmers, the air a thick soup. The temps edging into the high 90's force people to dart into the shops for some air-conditioned relief. While summer in the French Quarter is a slower season, especially after the hubbub of Mardi Gras, plenty of tourists still brave the heat.

We pass a spray-paint artist with a full display of brightly colored canvases, a veiled fortune teller, and a busking brass band that plays *Sweet Caroline*. Right as the trombone hits the famous three note sequence, everyone, including our trio, shout "bum-bum-bum." It's not a choice; it's the law.

The music draws us in, and we pause to listen. Of all the street performers flooding Jackson Square, I'm a sucker for the bands. The deep timber of the tuba, the clear ring of the trumpet. And who doesn't love some classic Neil Diamond.

An unavoidable smile curls my lips as I enjoy the unique flavor of New Orleans. Dozens of trees fill the area. Tall live oaks. Magnolias with their waxy leaves. Flowering Crape Myrtles, the bright pink blossoms bursting.

The band approaches the chorus again and Zach looks at me. "CeCe, I'm sorry for what happened at the theater."

Bum-bum-bum.

His shoulders ease, the tension drained out. My Zach is back, the easy going, lovable guy who snuggles with me on the couch and gives me dimple when I fail another magical plane attempt.

"Yeah, I still want an explanation, though." I give him my best *I-still-want-an-explanation* smirk.

At the final *bum-bum-bum,* I throw a dollar in the open guitar case laying on the pavement. A gloved hand grabs my outstretched arm, and I gasp, lifting my eyes to see the fortune teller we passed earlier.

"You wear the mark of betrayal!" She speaks in a heavy accent, something Eastern European, and obviously fake.

A purple chiffon veil covers her hair, and another piece stretches across her face, leaving a gap from mid-forehead to the bridge of her nose exposed. Her hazel eyes, more green than brown, stare directly at me, and green jewels extend from the corners to run down her cheekbones like tear drops. With her features mostly covered, it's hard to distinguish age. But if I had to guess, I'd place her in the middle-age to older category. The long-sleeved purple dress covers her from head to foot and my sweat glands weep in sympathy. Silver and gold beads dangle from her outfit, clicking with her movements. I catch a scent drifting around her. *Maybe sage?*

"Not interested." I attempt to wrench my arm from her grasp, but she digs in. At least her satin gloves protect my flesh from her nail indentations.

In her other hand, she holds a rectangular paper, and she waves it around. "The cards show it, CeCe. You need to listen."

Hearing my name from a complete stranger gives me pause. At least until I remember Zach said it as we walked by earlier.

"Amateur move, Zach," Portia mutters, obviously thinking about the same thing; placing emphasis on *his* name as payback.

Important lesson for the Square: never speak your name out loud. The fortune tellers will pounce on any opportunity to deceive for a dollar. Last summer, Portia and I walked loops, calling each other by different, and increasingly bizarre things to mess with the seers and psychics. When a man with a handheld crystal ball shouted that he had a message for Methuselah Honeysuckle, I nearly peed my pants.

So just because this veiled lady uses my name means nothing.

"I'm out of money," I say, a sure tactic to scare away the buskers.

"No charge. A warning. Your aura cried out to me, and I drew a card." Her fingers tighten, and she lowers her voice. "The storm is brewing, CeCe."

I want to shrug off the heavily accented fortune teller as an eccentric money grubber. But my mood shifts, her words casting a sense of foreboding. A creepy, horror-movie anxiety builds in tempo like the *Jaws* theme. Or maybe I'm still recovering from the trauma of a crazy person stalking me, kidnapping my spirit, and stealing my blood without consent.

My friends both look wary, solidifying my growing creep factor. They glance between me, the fortune teller, and her grip on my arm. I pull from her grasp, freeing myself.

Zach bumps my foot with his. "Come on—"

"No! Don't ignore the signs," she cuts him off. The beads at her wrist jangle as she waves the paper again, and her eyes meet mine. Serious. Sincere.

"Ohhhkay," I draw out the word. "But I'm really not paying."

Instead of acknowledging my comment she displays what I now see is a tarot card. "The Seven of Swords."

Tarot cartomancy is beyond my box of knowledge, but I appreciate the artistry of what she holds. The image on thick, rectangular paper, around the size of a three by five card, is hand-illustrated. It shows a person in a white hoodie, a backpack thrown over his shoulder. In the bag are four "swords" represented by black feathers. Another one floats to the ground, and two are left behind. At the bottom, an open-mouthed crow shrieks, and the title, "7 of swords," glares in white.

"This represents deceit. The thief"—she points to the hooded figure—"steals strategically and silently, believing he's gotten away with something. But the crow sounds the alarm. It's only a matter of time before the betrayal will be revealed."

"Betrayal? What are you talking about?" The *Jaws* theme picks up speed. She is a fake psychic selling fortunes, so why does my heart beat faster? Why does my mind conjure blinking caution signs reading, *danger ahead?* Zach puts his hand on my lower back, and I'm so distracted I don't even think about the sweat pooling there. Much.

"This is your warning. Someone around you is lying. It could be him"—she points to Zach—"or her." She points to Portia.

The proper protocol to acknowledge someone accusing my best friend and boyfriend of deceit escapes me, and I offer a solemn head nod. "Right. Thank you."

She tucks the card away in the folds of her dress and takes a few steps back. "When you're alone, follow the glow of the silver moonlight. Find the truth."

"Wait—what did you say?" I ask, but the fortune teller disappears into the crowd.

Follow the glow of the silver moonlight. Thoughts swirl in my head, new questions confusing me even more. First and foremost, how does she know that phrase? I've read it before. Hundreds of times. The words more familiar than the lyrics to any Taylor Swift song.

And I love her music.

The first time my eyes passed over, *follow the glow of the silver moonlight*, I was eight, going through my necromancy guide to understand my magic. Mawmaw somehow found it during the early struggles to figure out my new power. That book stays in regular rotation anytime I have questions.

It's as much a mystery now as it was back then. Yet a random fortune teller in Jackson Square quoted it like it was her truth to give.

"That was interesting." Zach tucks his hands into his pockets.

"She's good, I'll give her that. The whole mystical mumbo jumbo at the end. Woooo." Portia sings a ghostly warble and meets my gaze. "Hey, don't get sucked in, okay?"

"I won't." I try to shake off the creepy vibes, which, let's be honest, vibe with excessive creepiness.

"So...beignets?" Zach asks.

I nod my approval. "Definitely."

As we walk, I feel like someone watches me. The trees, which I appreciated for their sturdy beauty earlier, now create dark pockets of the unknown. Shadows of branches stretch across the pathway, gloomy fingers snaring me in their traps. My nerves work double time, and I imagine a person behind me, catching up. Like turning off the lights and sprinting down a dark hallway, even though no one is there.

I spin around, and from the corner of my eye, I notice someone ducking behind a tree. I mean, we're in a popular place, surrounded by a decent sized crowd. Even still, the odds of the quick movement coinciding with my turn seems unlikely. Squinting, and raising a hand to block the sun, I focus on the spot. A chill prickles down my spine.

"CeCe?" Zach touches my shoulder. "Everything okay?"

"Do you think the fortune teller might be following us?" I ask.

"No way." Portia glances at the shady knoll. "Girl's gotta earn her living. Already chasing a sucker with a full wallet, I'm sure."

"You're right. I just thought..." I look away from the trees and continue walking. "Never mind. Let's get beignets."

No need to spew my paranoia like a stomach-full of bad crawfish. At least not when delicious slabs of fried dough smothered in powdered sugar await.

The music of the brass band fades as we cross to Café Du Monde. A heavenly aroma fills my nostrils, the distinct perfume of oil-saturated yeast and café au lait. We order and take our paper bag filled with deliciousness to find a seat.

It is a truth universally acknowledged, that a person in possession of a beignet cannot eat and stay clean. I take my first bite, powdered sugar coating my fingers and dusting down my shirt. Brushing it off only seals the streaks in place, the gluey adhesion smearing on my cotton tee. But the pillowy dough melts in my mouth and all is right in the world.

Except...it's not.

Zach leaves his beignet untouched, drumming his powdered-sugar-free-fingers on the table. His nerves have returned, his jaw clenched and his shoulders tight. *Explanation time.* The conversation about Luc Etienne looms, and I rip off the Band Aid. "What happened at the theater?"

Running a hand through his hair, he glances at Portia, who splits her attention between him and her beignet.

"That Luc guy has magic. Dark magic," he says.

I lean in, lowering my voice. "Black magic?"

"No. Something else. Something I've never felt before." His leg jiggles under the table, wriggling with restlessness. "When you use black magic it feels..."

"Dirty?" I fill in.

"Yeah." He pinches his eyes shut, a slight shake of his head. "But Luc's magic is heavy. Oppressive. Dark."

"Why did he grab you?" Portia waves her beignet hand, and powdered sugar dusts the table like drifting dandelion puffs. "Do magic users always start fights when they meet?"

He shakes his head. "No, but our power...clashed."

"What does that mean?" I think of the first time Zach and I touched, how our magic melded. His warmth to my cold. Definitely no clashing. More like dancing.

"He's looking for something. His magic gave me a pat down. I felt...searched." He runs a hand through his hair again, clutching the strands. "Stay away from him. As much as you can."

"That should be easy." Portia rolls her eyes. "Maybe we can blow kisses to each other from across the stage. Or text lip emojis."

"Don't flirt with him and ask about his gap year—" Zach starts, but my phone rings. In the hustle to pull it from my pocket, my knee bashes under the table, rattling everything on top, and silencing the conversation.

"Sorry," I mutter, distractedly.

In the brief seconds between my cell ringing and checking the screen, fireworks light up my belly, and I wonder if Maybe Mom finally decided to call me back.

Nope. Just Dad. I slide my finger across the screen to answer.

"Hi, Daddy."

"Baby girl." An exhausted grunt follows his greeting. "There was another murder."

"What?" I straighten in my seat and slash my finger across my throat, giving Zach and Portia the international sign for a person was un-alived. "Is it the same...method as the others?"

That method being something resembling a werewolf attack.

"Same method," he confirms. "As much as I don't want you involved, we need to go to the morgue tonight. It's time for you to talk to the victim."

Dad finally opened the door for me to join an investigation. Something I've asked about over the last two months, wondering when we'll get back to our Sherlock and Watson tag-team.

And now that he asked, my stomach roils. Curse you, fried dough! My first time using necromancy since the night Rivera almost un-alived me.

I take a deep breath. I can do this.

CHAPTER FOUR

THE MORGUE: THE VICTIM

Summer Break. A magical escape from the daily grind of school. The reason for carefree days, tan legs, and uncontrollable sweats from the ghost pepper sun. Also, a time when late nights at the morgue can be used as a bargaining chip for sleeping in.

"11:00," I say, hoping for 10:00, but okay with 9:00.

Dad glances at me, not slowing his pace as we make our way down the echoing hall. Cold seeps through me, the humming air conditioner keeping the morgue at negative four thousand degrees. At least it feels that way since I forgot a jacket.

"9:30," Dad says, and I respond with a quick, "sold" before he changes his mind. Better than the normal 8:00 a.m. wakeup call. Yes, every day of summer.

We step into the mortuary fridge room, and I take short, choking breaths as the scent of formaldehyde stings my nose. The acidic aroma burns my throat and lays on my tongue like an extra-potent pickle. I pull supplies from my magic bag and set them on the floor: candle, lighter, grave-yard soil, water, penknife, and salt. I go through the motions, forcing back the anxiety bubbling below the surface.

Panic at using necromancy again? Nah. Heart palpitations? Never heard of them. Sweat rolling down my back despite the sub-zero chill? Pffft, non-existent.

Unexpected tears blur my vision and I blink them away, clearing the nightmare memories. And the pit of dread sitting heavy in my gut.

Blink, blink. I'm totally fine.

"Her name's Mary Mosley," Dad says. Normally, he hands me a police file, which includes cause of death, physical descriptors, that type of thing. Tonight, he skips the routine.

"Why no file?" I ask.

"It's bad. *Without* reading it." He sighs, the sound so hopeless it throws me off balance. Dad rarely strays from his business-as-usual detective façade.

"I've seen bad before," I reassure him.

"Not like this. The evidence doesn't add up. There's fur, wolf fur, but the wounds are too high and deep for any kind of wolf. And too intentional." His shoulders droop, the weight of the world crushing. "It's the third victim, and we have nothing. Feds will engage any day. You're my last hope, but I hate asking you to do it."

Three victims, and he's just now bringing me in? It must be bad.

"Dad, it'll be okay. I've got this."

His reluctance is so easy to read, he might as well hold a sign that says, "Worst father ever." But he steps back, letting me get to work.

It always takes a few minutes to adjust to the morgue,

the odor and the chill, but the cold is extra tonight. Without my jacket, I full-body shake. So much so, that as I light the green candle, my trembling hand skips around the wick like the best game of dodge-flame, until it finally catches.

A sudden warmth shrouds my shoulders, Dad dropping his suit coat over me. His unique scent of cedar and soap smells far better than preserved dead people, and I bury my nose deeper in the collar. I slide my arms into the sleeves, rolling the fabric to free my hands, grateful for the borrowed heat, and for the comfort only he offers. The subtle reminder that Sherlock is also Dad.

I grab the pouch of graveyard soil— not just any dirt will do, but soil taken from sacred ground, sanctified for the dead. I pinch a small amount and mix it in my palm with a few drops of water, forming a paste. It covers the scar that still itches from time to time, where two months ago an open wound pulsed and thrummed with black magic. Sometimes I wonder if the oily traces lurk below the surface.

Blink, blink. Everything is great.

The gliding sound of Dad rolling the table from the fridge reverberates in the small room. Then the hissing of metal tines as he lowers the zipper of the body bag. I approach the victim, my heartbeat loud in my ears, my feet clomping like cinderblocks. Of all the times for the fortune teller's words to repeat in my brain, now seems like the worst. And yet, they whisper through me like a bad omen. *The storm is brewing. Someone around you is lying.*

Dad stands in my path, blocking my progress. His fingers wrap around my upper arms. "Are you okay, baby girl?"

The quarter-sized circle of muddy paste paints my hand, and traces of magic tingle. My scar irritates me, and I want to scratch it. Wash my skin free of the building power and go home. But Dad needs my help, and I'm the only one who can do this.

Blink, blink.

"I'm fine." I curl my fingers over my palm, hiding the mud.

"This was a bad idea." He stares me down, his green eyes searching mine.

I blow out a breath. "We're already here. Let's get it over with."

Studying me a few seconds longer, he nods, moving aside to let me approach the table.

And I get my first glimpse of the victim.

The body bag opening only uncovers the top of the head to the top of her lip, a deliberate move from Dad. Even through the small gap, I see signs of why he asked about werewolves. Deep, jagged canals gouge the left eye and down the cheek, glances of white bone contrasting to the dark puckered skin and torn flesh. The scratches trail below the black material, and I'm grateful the zipper closes off any further damage. There's also something wrong with the head, and it takes me a few seconds to realize she's missing an ear. Her tightly coiled brown hair hides most of the damage, but beneath the strands, deep claw marks scar the space where the appendage should be.

Her remaining ear has an earring, a little guitar, and I wonder if she played. Did she spend time on The Square in a pick-up band, smiling when the crowd joined in on *Sweet Caroline?*

A shiver takes hold as I spread the muddy paste across her closed eyes. Her torn skin snags on my fingertips like un-sanded wood. But the sanctified graveyard soil connects our vision together through death magic, and I can't skip this part of the ritual, as much as I want to.

I think through the list of instructions in my necromancy book. A simple, step-by-step recipe to bake the perfect magical ceremony. No need to worry about Rougarou attacks. Or anxiety. Or the fact that I might have residual trauma from what went down with Rivera. My hands shake, my heartbeat so loud it pulses in my neck and wrists.

I upgrade that *might* have trauma to *definitely*.

Dad watches me with a careful expression, one with a hint of wariness and a dash of regret.

So I smile to put him at ease. "Don't forget to stand in the circle. We don't want to risk another haunting."

With a grunt of agreement, he shuffles a little closer. Neither of us wants a repeat of the nightmare that followed an awakened corpse touching Dad.

Grabbing the canister of salt, I pour, walking a short route in the small space. Then, for good measure, I take a second loop, doubling the salt. I pick up the green candle, dripping hot, melted wax into my hand.

Dad clears his throat. "Third—"

"Quarter." I finish up. Following the lunar phase never mattered to me before. But after Rivera, I don't want to get caught unaware again, and now I fervently follow the moon cycle.

The wax cools quickly, and I form a crescent-shaped moon token. The weight of my pen knife comforts me, and I turn the handle to trace over the engraved words: *Death is good for the soul.* Thinking of my Mawmaw, I open my knife and poke my index finger, the sting quick and sharp. Blood seeps from the puncture, and I slick it across the hardening paraffin. Stepping over the salt, I move to the table and place the token on her forehead. Then I pluck out a hair and go back inside the protective circle to sit cross-legged on the floor.

"Are you ready?" I ask.

"Are you?" He usually responds with a grunt, and his question gives me pause. I look at him over my shoulder, his concern etched on the wrinkles between his eyes.

"I...think so?" Stop. Center myself. Dredge up some confidence. "Yes."

"We can leave. Just clean up and go." He gives me an out. An all-expense paid trip to retreats-ville. Or maybe Escape Town. Avoidance Valley? But I need to do this. Because if I don't, it'll be harder to try the next time, and harder the time after that. Until I stop trying.

An important lesson I learned recently is that pretending I don't have magic doesn't make it true. It will overtake me. Just like Jeff Goldblum muttered the iconic line in Jurassic Park, "Life finds a way," the same is true of my necromancy. Magic finds a way.

"I'm ready." The loose strand of hair fizzles as I drop it in the candle, and the flame turns blue. Closing my eyes, the cold ices my veins in a painful pulse. It's never hurt like this before, and I clench my teeth to keep Dad from noticing. "Mary Mosley, show me your killer and you can rest."

Wind shrieks in the room, an unholy banshee wail. Power fills me, floods me, as if a full moon fuels my energy, even though I know it's a third quarter. Mary jolts against the table, the body bag writhing. Rattling metal clangs like an emergency siren as she violently shakes. The moon token holds her in place, and she can't rise, but in all my experiences talking to the dead, they've never reacted in such a turbulent way. I cover my ears, hunching close to my crossed legs. Struggling to remember the next part of the ritual.

"CeCe." Dad puts a hand on my shoulder, alarm growing in his voice. "What's happening?"

"I don't know." *Think, think, think.* Place the moon token, burn the hair, talk to the dead. Sometimes they resist and I exert more force into my tone. *Right. More urgency.*

"Mary Mosley," I shout over the banging table. "Show me your killer."

A powerful whoosh fills the room, my breath halting in my lungs, and Mary's body goes still. I see her in my mind, a place from her past, before the missing ear and body bag. Hovering from above, I watch her movements. She hustles down a sidewalk in an area I recognize. A spot not far from Jackson Square. Her small duffle thuds against her leg and she stops to adjust, shuffling the things inside. A few small canvases, cans of spray paint, brushes.

The tools of an artist.

She pulls off the scarf wrapped around her hair and shoves it in the bag. Then she fast-walks again, dodging around the few people out, her flip flops slapping her heels. Turning on a quiet street, she takes a dozen or so steps before her pace slows. Her shoulders stiffen, and I hear what she hears.

Growling. A fierce rumble like an approaching storm.

Her eyes search the darkness, and she keeps moving. I smell her building fear, skin slick with sweat, clothes moist and sticking. An elevated crack in the concrete stubs her toe and she stumbles, the heavy duffle slinging forward. It nearly catapults her to the ground, but she gains her balance.

"Ouch," we both mutter, our voices one. Hers from the

past, mine from my observation on the hard floor of the morgue.

Another loud growl thunders. Deep, guttural, wet, and close. Terror prickles, our hearts beating faster.

There's another noise behind the animalistic rumble. Something faint. I strain my ears, trying to make sense of it. The steady cadence hums in the background. Tuning out the snarling and the slap of flip flops, I focus on the melodic whisper. It's someone speaking in rhythm. Or a group of someones. Words I don't understand in another language. It reminds me of Gregorian chanting, hooded monks all in sync, but heavier and more compelling.

The sound calls to me, strangely familiar. Hypnotic. Just as I fade into the tempo, almost forgetting Mary and the morgue, a dark shadow lurches from a side street. I barely register what I see, barely feel the horror, my magical connection to the moment buried under the lull.

The creature pounces on Mary, grabbing her under the arms and lifting her feet off the pavement. Its hulking shape stands easily over six feet tall, with a muscular, man-like body and a wolf-like head.

The Rougarou.

Mary and I both open our mouths to scream, but the long snout rips out her throat, silencing our cry. One hand continues to hold her up and the other flashes razor-sharp claws which slice her chest, tear her face. Her ear falls in a quiet splat, landing in the blood pooling on the sidewalk. The beat of her heart fades. Slower and fainter, *thump... thump...thump...*until it stops.

A long howl pierces the night, the Rougarou tipping back its head and wailing at the moon. The super-bright moon highlighting sprays of red staining the fur, all along the muzzle and down the chest. *Wait!* It's a third quarter, so how can it be this luminous?

But more importantly, why am I still here? The vision always cuts when the victim dies. This is Mary's memory, her lived-in experience.

The Rougarou releases its hold and her body slumps, a lifeless heap left like a pile of garbage. Its shaggy face lifts, staring right at the spot where I hover above, seeming to meet my gaze. I know it can't see me. My presence intrudes in something that already happened. This moment in time has passed.

It steps closer, sniffing the air, a wet snuffle grazing my shoulder, my cheek. I recoil at the slimy muzzle as it tastes my skin. A smooth tongue licking me along my throat. This should not be happening. It's impossible. And yet, my physical body sits in a different place while my spirit feels the moisture.

The rhythmic chanting starts again, growing in volume, puffs of wind stirring my senses. What I thought of as hypnotic turns haunting. Instead of focusing on the sound, I try to shut it out. I picture the morgue. My dad standing inside the salt circle with me. Mary on the table, my moon token on her forehead.

With a gasp, I open my eyes. Cold surrounds me. The pungent scent of formaldehyde bites at my nostrils. The artificial fluorescent lights glare above. Back to myself, in my body. Dad stands next to me, his lips turned in a frown.

"You okay?" he asks.

Touching my neck, I rub the spot where the Rougarou's tongue lapped. "It was there. I saw it." My voice drops to a whisper. "The Rougarou."

The self-recrimination is there on his face, but a spark of curiosity lifts his expression. "So it's real?"

"Very real."

"Did you see anything else? Anything useful?" he asks.

"It's over six feet tall, dark fur, and it hid in the shadows. And it watched her, with glowing red eyes."

"How am I supposed to capture that kind of monster?" His eyes adopt the far away gaze of thought.

It's a rhetorical question, but I answer anyway. "With my help."

"No." He shakes his head. "I'm sorry, baby girl. I never should have asked you to do this."

"But Dad, this is magic. It's what I do." Why am I negotiating to be in on this horror show? Because Sherlock needs his Watson. "The moon was extra bright. Something is going on."

"Let me handle it." He blows out a breath, tucking his hands in his pockets. "Why don't you finish up?"

Though I disagree with his Lone Ranger approach, I need to close the necromancy ritual.

"Mary Mosley, you can rest now. It's over." I lean forward and blow out the candle. Knowing full well it's not even close to over.

CHAPTER FIVE

MY HOUSE: THE CONFESSION

I start a CeCe To Do List, first item up: talk to Zach. Hopefully he knows how a Rougarou could sniff me out through a memory and taste my neck like a human flavored popsicle. Or at least help me determine where to start looking for answers.

But before calling him, I endure the necro-shivers, full body shakes brought on from using my power, the cost of death magic. The intensity, though, is leveled up. Maybe because I'm out of practice?

As Dad and I drive home, I roll down the sleeves of his suit coat, which I still wear, and huddle under a blanket. He turns the heat on high, aiming all the vents in my direction. Even though the temps outside linger in the mid 80's.

Welcome to summer in New Orleans. Where nighttime offers no relief from the oppressive heat.

We pull into the garage, and I keep expecting my necro-shivers to ease. They usually putter out a block from our house. But I continue to tremble, the cold a living thing icing my insides. With quaking fingers, I grab my bag of magic supplies and slip from the car, clutching Dad's jacket around me.

"Good night, baby girl," he says leaning his head against the seat, his eyes half-closed. Poor Daddy. This case is rough.

"Night." My slightly unsteady feet manage to carry me in the house. Fatigue drags every muscle, the persistence of the shakes leaving me depleted.

The familiar smell of vanilla candle and pear lotion greets me as I enter my bedroom. I sit on the bed, waiting out the shivers, unable to stop the replay of what happened. Mary thrashing against the metal table. The hypnotic chant brain-worming me. And then the Rougarou. Violence. Blood. I rub my neck, wanting to wipe away any traces of the memory. But it lives rent-free in my mind.

The trauma builds and the relentless cold chills my bones. I need somewhere to dump all the excess. *My magical plane!*

Sitting on my bed, I test it out. Sky, clouds, blah, blah, blah. The picture forms in my mind, an almost perfect image.

"Come on cicadas. Talk to me."

Still nothing. Stubbornly, annoyingly silent. Maybe they don't like the landscape I conjured. *Should I give them a tree?*

I strain to hear, strain to step onto the plane. The reflective pool stretches across the ground as far as the eye can see, an endless horizon. My breathing slows, the chills calm. Not to brag, but I think I'm getting my zen on.

Go, spirit. Don't you want to be in the oasis?

The sky shudders. My clouds grow thin, their color turning gray like wisps of smoke.

My eyes flash open and I jolt from another failed attempt to enter my plane. Maybe turning it into a magical landfill isn't the right approach.

My shaking finally eases to a slight tremble. I'm not ready to take off Dad's jacket though, so I bunch up the sleeves to free my hands. Smears of blue streak my fingertips like I dipped them in a paint named "coastal wind" or "frozen pond." A cold color that has no place in a Louisiana summer. I wipe my bedspread, trying to clean them off. But the icy azure stays, and my fingers tingle with numbness.

Weird.

More questions for Zach. Digging through my bag, I pull out the used moon token and my cell. Glancing at the screen, I see a text from my bestie.

> PORTIA: Call me when you're done. We need to talk.

Words every person loves to hear. Telling Zach about the morgue will have to wait.

Hitting number one on my favorites, I listen to it ring as I plug in the wax melter on my desk and stick the moon token on top. Soon it will liquify, and Mary Mosley will be completely free of my magic. Something I look forward to with this one.

After three rings, Portia answers. "Hey, CeCe, how were the dead people?"

"Dead *person*," I correct. "A little more lively than I would have expected. The corpse shook the table."

"Ew. Creepy."

"Totally. What's up? Why the midnight call?" I slump in the chair at my desk, watching the third quarter melt.

"I gotta get something off my chest." A door closes, probably her isolating in the closet. She shares a room with her thirteen-year-old sister, Presley, who's a light sleeper. "I wasn't going to say anything, but after the psychic, I knew I should."

The psychic? It takes my brain a full minute to catch on. So much has happened since the fortune teller on Jackson Square. *Was that really this afternoon?*

"Okaaaaay." I draw out the word, wondering where this is going.

"I'm not lying to you, but I am kind of hiding something. Especially after the way Zach acted." Her tone carries a worry not typical of our normal. "Plus, besties before the resties, am I right?"

"Always. So spill."

"It's about Luc."

The shoulder-bearing, darlin'-uttering rebel who almost got into a fight with my boyfriend. Just hearing his name sends an apprehensive thrumming in my pulse.

"What about him?" I ask, my question drowned out by a loud knock on Portia's closet door. Then Presley's voice, *"Portia, why are you in there?"*

Portia covers the mouthpiece, but I hear her muffled response, *"Go back to sleep."*

"But what are you doing?"

"I promise to take you for ice cream if you leave me alone and go to bed." Ooh, Portia must really want to talk because she jumped into dangerous territory: sugared dessert. Mrs. Landry recently went on a lifestyle change and banned everything with sugar, sweeteners, and flavor. There is no forbidden fruit in their house; just forbidden fudge. Which leaves Pres begging for Portia's crumbs when she goes out.

"Pleasure doing business with you," Presley says.

"Sorry." The speaker rumbles as Portia adjusts. "Mom will kill me if she finds out about the ice cream."

I groan. "Don't tell me. I want plausible deniability."

"No way. When one of us commits a crime, the other buries the body." She laughs. "Besides, it's just one hot fudge sundae."

"The gateway treat. It starts with one sundae. Soon she'll be in dark alleys, buying mint brownies out of the back of a van." I find my first smile since going to the morgue, my feet returning to normal ground.

Until she speaks again. "So…about Luc. He asked me out, and I said yes. Beignets before play practice tomorrow." Her assertive tone takes no prisoners. "I know Zach thinks he's dangerous, but *I* think Zach is wrong."

"Portia—"

"This isn't up for debate, and I don't want to hide it from you either," she says. "Luc is adorable. Super dreamy eyes. And did you notice those shoulders?"

Thor and God of Thunder? Yes, we met. "You just ended a relationship with Devin."

"And I'm ready to move on. With Luc, who could read a textbook and make it sound interesting. Who invited me to Café Du Monde tomorrow." She has no trepidation in the face of sexy packaging. No healthy fear of the unknown.

Apparently, that's my job.

I take a deep breath. Blow it out. "Then I'm coming."

"What? No!"

"Non-negotiable. He has magic, Portia. Dark magic." I slash my hand through the air even though she can't see it. "Let me and Zach double with you. We'll sit at a different table and avoid eye contact. But I'll be there. Just in case."

Something bothers me about Luc Etienne. A niggling disquiet that he may not be what he seems.

Yep, I'm going.

She huffs an annoyed breath. "Fine. Then tell Zach no fighting."

I answer with an exasperated sigh. "Fine. Then tell Luc no instigating."

"Fine."

"Fine."

The silence holds for three seconds. Then a muted giggle from her. A short chuckle from me. We both burst into laughter, and it feels good to let out the tension.

"The two Amigos?" She offers me an olive branch. Asking me to forgive her for the almost secret.

There was never a question about it. "Always."

We hang up and I have a smile on my face as I unplug the wax melter. The moon token liquified into a dark-green puddle, and the extra distance from Mary Mosley boosts my comfort level. Even my fingertips seem to agree, the color closer to living flesh and less like zombie decay. The numbness has eased to a pinprick of tingling as I send a text.

I still need a conversation with Zach.

ME: You awake?

While I wait to see if he responds, I fortify the protective circle around my bed. My new every-night habit developed after the Rivera incident. The salt hisses from the canister as I fill the gaps, closing any vulnerable spots. No more spirit kidnappings on my watch, and no more black magic seeping in. The filthy, invasive power nearly destroyed me, stripping me of the ability to think clearly. I ended up trapped in my own home, plagued with feelings of hopelessness and loss.

A shudder runs through me at the memory.

My phone vibrates on the desk just before I finish with

the salt, and I note at least one more gap to fix later. But for now, I put the horrors of black magic and spirit kidnappings aside.

ZACH: Yep. Wide awake.

ME: Can you talk?

My phone rings.

"Hi, beautiful girlfriend." The smile in his voice sends a happy breeze flowing through me. I want to stay here, coasting on the carefree cloud of contentment with my perfect sweetie who loves me. And yeah, I love him too.

"Hi, cute boyfriend."

"How was the morgue?" he asks.

"Terrifying. Weird stuff happened." I lay on my bed and tell him the tale, starting with the rush of excessive power. Moving on to the chanting. And then finishing it off with the Rougarou. "The necro-shivers lasted forever. My fingertips turned blue. Crazy, right?"

"This chanting...you said it was hypnotic?" Of all the things he could focus on (I mean, a Louisianan werewolf slurped my spirit body) he chooses the monk song.

"At first. But then something changed. It grew louder. Closer." The haunting whisper rings in my eardrums, reminding me of the rhythm. "Maybe I'm imagining things, but I can almost hear it now."

"Does it feel like sound magic, CeCe? Like how Rivera's drums affected you?"

I *hate* thinking about anything Rivera related, but it's impossible to forget the lull of his drums. They drew me in, overwhelmed my senses. The dirty power frightened me with its hammering intensity.

The chanting grows louder, and I slam a metaphorical

door closed, shutting out the noise. My heart beats wildly, the past and present colliding in a way that makes all my muscles tense. "It could definitely be sound magic."

His breathing reverberates on the line, but otherwise he stays quiet.

"Zach?"

"I'm here. Hold on."

My phone rumbles with an incoming FaceTime call, and I sit up, tucking my legs close and resting my chin on my knees. Small tremors rattle my limbs, but not from necro-shivers.

I meet his deep navy gaze as I answer. "Hey."

"Hi, beautiful girlfriend." He sits on the edge of his bed, the phone braced on his nightstand. The corner of his mouth quirks for a brief second before melting into a somber expression. "I need to tell you something."

The tone in his voice warns me of an incoming revelation. I'm really starting to hate those.

"What?" An uneasy clamminess sticks to my skin.

"Remember when I lost my phone?"

"You mean the one I threw in the dumpster?" RIP Zach's phone. I discarded his instead of mine, hoping Zach would read the texts Rivera sent me and uncover his heinous plan. "Sorry about that."

"No more apologies." He clears his throat and runs a hand through his hair. His obvious nerves feed into mine. "When I got a new phone, an unknown number kept calling. I should have told you about it, but by the time you and I worked things out, I didn't want you to worry."

"Worry about what? Who was calling?"

He pauses, folding his arms, and his fingers tap against his bicep. *Tap, tap tap.* "Constance."

My mom. The one who instructed him in black magic.

Forced his addiction. Bonded them together with a nearly unbreakable spell. The one who killed a person and took their heart for Rivera.

Allegedly.

She ignores my every phone call and text.

But she called my boyfriend. And he didn't tell me.

CHAPTER SIX

MY BEDROOM: THE LIAR

My stomach skydives, my whole world slowing to this moment. This discovery. We stare at each other, me holding my phone, him a couple of feet away from his where it's propped next to his bed.

"You talked to my mom?"

"Yes." His fingers continue their rhythm on his arm. *Tap, tap tap.*

"After I cried because she vanished, you never thought to mention it? I wondered if she had died!" I shift on my bed, the mattress squeaking below me as I lean against the headboard. Dad's suit coat bunches around my shoulders and I shrug it off, tossing it to the floor. The phone juggles out of my grasp, and he says something, but the words muffle in my blanket. I pick up my cell, cutting him off.

"I've called her twenty times in the past month. Double that in texts. All unanswered. But you've been in contact." My voice rises, and I grit my teeth to calm down. "Did she say anything about coming back?"

As soon as I ask, I want to bite my tongue. My mom left when I was six years old. Initiated zero contact until two months ago when I barely survived a powerful and dark attack from a murderer. Her text simply said, *your magic didn't disappoint. I'll be in touch.*

But apparently not with me. With Zach!

"No, she didn't," he speaks softly. Carefully.

The denial lands a direct hit to a part of my heart that should be dead. "So, do you talk to her daily? Weekly?"

"It's not like that. We had one phone call, and she told me someone might be looking for you, someone I couldn't allow to find you." He adjusts, his body fidgety with nervous energy.

"Wait, I'm confused. Constance — my MOM — called and said not to let an anonymous person find me?"

"Now that Rivera exposed your necromancy, there are others who will come after you. It's such a rare gift. And I think, maybe, this thing with the chanting sound is the person trying to track you down." His eyes shimmer with determination. "I won't let it happen."

I laugh without humor. "How are you supposed to stop it?"

"By shielding you." He scootches in, bringing his face closer. "Constance gave me a spell. Something I cast nightly to camouflage your ability for anyone looking."

Alarm bells ring in my head. The pieces of the puzzle click into place, and I feel. So. Stupid. Everything adds up: the lingering oiliness in Zach's power, his reluctance to touch skin on skin, his jittery restlessness.

My vision blurs as I hold my breath. "A black magic spell?"

His weighted silence answers for him.

Tears well in my eyes, the hurt a jagged stab to my

chest. I hold a hand over my heart, the pain tangible. "Please tell me it's not true."

"I need to do it to protect you. To hide you."

"You have to stop." Emotion clogs my voice, and I swallow it down. "I went to your magical plane. I saw the battle you fight against the addiction."

"If it keeps you safe, I'll use it again and again." His wall of justification stands tall and strong, impenetrable to my plea.

"Last time you ended up linked to my mom. You had to magically stalk her to cut the connection." I rise from my bed to pace around the room. "What if it's a trap? This is exactly what happened with Mason. She tricked you, and he ended up in a wheelchair."

Zach flinches like I slapped him. His brother will live the rest of his life paralyzed from the heavy cost of using black magic. That dark power requires a sacrifice, and the person casting doesn't always get to choose the offering.

"It's not that kind of spell."

"How do you know?" My foot shuffles through salt, making another gap that needs to be fixed. Later, after I calm down enough for steady hands.

"Look, it's a simple spell, no linking capabilities." He picks up his phone from the nightstand to join me in pacing. "You take a hair from the person you're trying to hide, a drop of the caster's blood, a small, poured circle of black oil, and set it on fire."

"What? Zach, have you been taking my hair?"

His eyes pinch closed, and he tips his head back. "I'm not pulling it out. Just collecting loose pieces. Don't make this into a big deal."

"This is a *very* big deal. Why didn't you tell me? If you said something, we could have searched for a solution together." Like ask his mom and Aunt Lucy. They run Black Wren Voodoo and work with all kinds of magic. "We can still figure it out. If you stop—"

"It's too late for that. Things are escalating." His breathing grows rapid. Erratic. "They'll find you if I stop now."

"You believe this based on something my mom said? The most untrustworthy person in my life. Even Rivera told the truth. But my mom is a liar." Starting with the first *I love you*, down to *I'll be in touch.*

"What happened at the morgue proves it's real. But they can't find you if I keep casting this spell." He leans close to the phone, his eyes pleading. "Listen to me. Please. I would do anything for you."

"But what about you? It's time to talk to your mom. Or Aunt Lucy." Tears pool over my lashes to run down my cheeks. I swipe them away. "I'm not going to be your excuse."

"It's not an excuse. I love you."

"Do not say that right now. You're into black magic again. Stealing my hair." I clutch my phone so tight my fingers turn white. "You should have told me."

"I wanted to. Believe me. I'm so sorry." His voice wavers, but I ignore his pain in favor of my own.

"The fortune teller said I wear the mark of betrayal." My lip trembles as her prophetic words haunt me. *The storm is brewing. Someone around you is lying.*

"No, CeCe." The conversation slips through his fingertips, and he desperately grasps at the threads.

"It's my turn to protect you. We can't see each other. No coming over." If we don't have contact, he can't collect my hair to perform the spell.

"Seriously? For how long?"

"As long as it takes. I'm doing this because *I love you.*" My chest caves in, my heart crushed. I see the long days ahead of no kissing. No snug zone. No sitting on the couch, pretending to watch a movie when we're really watching each other.

"CeCe…"

I almost back down, weakened by the anguish in his voice. But I stay strong. "I refuse to be the reason you're trapped in black magic. Please get help. Goodbye, Zach."

I disconnect the call and set my phone down. It immediately starts buzzing on my nightstand, but I ignore it. Instead, I close my eyes and remember Zach's magical plane, the place he created to dampen the effects when he practices black magic. But even in his space, I witnessed the pull of addiction calling to him, an endless tide dragging him deeper. An insatiable temptation drowning him in darkness.

And he's using again.

I'm drowning too. Swallowed by waves of anger and hurt. Unable to see how to move forward. Too many things tow me under, Zach and black magic, my mom, the Rougarou, Portia and Luc.

Portia and Luc! I forgot about the double date tomorrow. But I won't be asking Zach. Not after the revelations of tonight. Guess I'll go by myself and play the role of third wheel. Because friends don't let friends date potentially dangerous guys without backup.

And girlfriends don't let boyfriends fall into dangerous magic without fighting to free them. Even if that means opening myself to the stranger hunting me down.

CHAPTER SEVEN

THE DREAMSCAPE: THE STRANGERS

It takes a million years to get comfortable in my bed. A million more to fall into a restless sleep. Every time I close my eyes, I see the memory of Zach's magical plane. The odd beach with sand in shades of bruises and the foreboding blood-colored sky.

In my dream, I walk along the shore. The churning water swells higher, lapping over the crumbling levy. The cawing of crows rises in the distance—Zach's sound magic. My ears strain to hear the screeching birds as I spin, trying to pinpoint the noise. I murmur under my breath, *find Zach, tell him to stop,* over and over, the mantra endless in my mind. Until I realize that's not actually what I'm saying. It's something different. Words I don't understand in a language I don't speak.

The chanting.

On and on, it continues, until I find myself on a different beach, my toes digging into the sand as the monotonous tones become waves. The rhythm ebbs and flows, water washing closer, almost touching me, until it pulls back into the depths of the ocean, fading to a quiet hush.

I stare at a black sky, devoid of stars or any hint of illumination. All the light is swallowed by the moon, concentrated into a bright spotlight which moves erratically, like an eye searching for something. *Searching for me?* The moon has always been my ally, the source of death magic. A reliable power to draw from to perform necromancy. But tonight, in this dreamscape, it feels corrupted. Malevolent.

Ducking away from the luminous beam, I put distance between myself and the waves. The chanting grows louder, an urgency strengthening the cadence, and I break into a run. The shifting sand slows my movement, and I stumble over unsteady ground. I change my direction, trying to dodge the heightening swell. Except it chases me, nipping at my heels.

Just as I think there's no avoiding the haunting sound and scouting spotlight, I notice an unusual radiance emanating from the moon. A shimmer reflecting off a graveled path.

Follow the glow of the silver moonlight.

The words from my necromancy guide, spoken by the fortune teller, resonate in my mind, and I turn toward the metallic glimmer. As I approach the pebbled trail, soft sand becomes sharp rocks. They stab the bottom of my bare feet, and I hobble along the walkway to a grove of trees.

Where did those come from?

The massive live oaks tower above me, the wide trunks far too big to reach around, the limbs extending in an ancient highway of giant arcs and meandering twists. Spanish moss hangs from the branches, and I push it aside, like searching the folds of a theater curtain for the opening.

It brushes my head and face as I continue forward slowly. Steadily. Lost in the dark expanse of the sheltered wood.

The space has a familiar feel to it, like maybe I've been here before. Though I know I haven't. The persistent sense of déjà vu follows me, and I finally connect why. This is a magical plane. A plane within a plane, actually.

Could it be Zach's protection spell?

A gap opens at the end of the trees, and I spot the silvery moonlight on the ground ahead. Staying focused on the glimmering patch, everything else around me fades. A group of people in the clearing draws my attention.

Five of them sit around a campfire, chanting the now familiar rhythm I first heard at the morgue. They all wear wooden face-shaped masks. The black enamel base has a white diamond painted on the forehead, and concentric stripes ripple out to cover the front. I watch from my spot, safe in the wooded haven.

There are two symbols etched into the ground, and I take a few hesitant steps forward to see more clearly. A crescent moon, and something else. A light bulb shape, wider in the neck and circles drawn like eyes.

Then it hits me. A skull. A moon and a skull. Recognizable symbols of necromancy.

I've been spirit kidnapped. Again!

A few more steps forward, and I observe those in the circle, taking in as many details as I can, daughter-of-a-cop style. The different hair, different clothes. I search for any identifying marks.

One of the people stands, ripping off the mask and throwing it to the ground. He's an older man, white haired with a short-trimmed beard, weathered hands that clench into fists. "Why can't we pull the girl here?"

The girl. He's talking about me.

"Constance is hiding her," one of them says. A male voice.

"She's not stronger than all of us. So how can she keep protecting the necromancer?" The old man kicks a clump of dirt into the flames, and they hiss. "We can watch her all we want. But we need to trap her on the magical plane."

Getting caught by that man...very bad. A spark of fear ignites inside me. I don't know what they want with my magic, but experience has taught me it's nothing good.

The thought barely touches my consciousness before the cadence grows louder, more forceful, and the moon spotlight scurries around the gathering. I shuffle backwards, looking to my sanctuary, surprised at how far I walked from it. The beacon zips dangerously close, and I pivot, racing for the grove. But the beam cuts off my route.

"She's here," someone says. A female voice. On her wrist she wears a bracelet, the bright red-orange stones reflecting the firelight.

"Find her!" The old man sits in the circle, and the chanting resumes.

The waves reappear, washing near my feet, the voices surrounding me in stereo. In a panic, I zig zag from the water and the spotlight, unsure how to escape.

Then I see the silver glow. Making a break for it, I run to the glimmer, sprinting to the trees. The searching beam catches my arm, and the light becomes fingers, wrapping around my bicep, pulling me back toward the masked strangers. I struggle against the tight clamp, fighting to free myself.

A presence stirs behind me, and I turn my head to see the old man. "I've got you."

Reaching blindly, I grasp a branch of a live oak and drag myself to the trees. Spanish moss tickles my skin, the thin tendrils peeling away the spotlight's grip. I feel the old man's panic, his anger that I slip from his hold.

I dive into the grove, landing on a layer of grass and dried leaves. Hugging my knees to my chest, I curl under the thicket and stay hidden from the strangers. Their chants murmur near my sanctuary, unable to break in, hovering just outside where I hole up. I don't know how long I wait. Listening. Lingering. But eventually their whispers fade, and I'm alone.

CHAPTER EIGHT

CAFÉ DU MONDE: THE DATE

The buzzing of my phone transports me from the dreamscape, waking me up. Sunshine streams in my window, and I blink against the brightness searing my eyeballs.

I swipe to answer the call, and a groan leaves my mouth. Something between a non-verbal zombie hungry for flesh and a bear waking from hibernation.

"9:30," Dad says. "Time to get up."

"I'm up," I croak, stretching the tightness from my muscles as my body pops and creaks. *What am I, an eighty-year-old?*

The thought conjures an image of the white-haired man. Age lines etched around his eyes and across his forehead. His scratchy voice filled with rage as he yelled, *find her!*

What does he even want?

Uneasiness clenches in my core, a solid gut punch of fear. Forget heights and spiders. Acrophobia and arachnophobia have nothing on being-chased-in-a-strange-magi-cal-plane-by-chanting-strangers-phobia.

"CeCe." Dad startles me, and I remember the phone gripped in my fingers. "Out of bed."

"Yes, Daddy." I swing my feet over the edge of the mattress and notice the smudged salt circle. No wonder I struggled last night. I left myself vulnerable.

We say goodbye and hang up. I go to call Zach, ready to fill him in on the weird night. But then I see two missed calls and 4 texts from him and remember we aren't on speaking terms.

> ZACH: I'm so sorry. Can we please talk.

> ZACH: Call me.

> ZACH: This is serious.

> ZACH: I'll come to your house tomorrow.

My heart breaks all over again, his betrayal undiminished by the night of sleep. Or not-sleep. Doubt sneaks in, an unwanted visitor, lounging in my brain space, reminding me of his attraction to black magic. How he pursued a relationship with me only after the oily touch of it slithered under my skin.

What if his addiction is stronger than his feelings for me?

The heavy weight of everything rolls in like a storm cloud. What happened at the morgue with Mary Mosley and the Rougarou. The chanting strangers. My mom's lies. Zach's lies. All of it rains down and dampens my mood.

I ignore his messages and text Portia.

ME: Can you pick me up? Zach can't come.

PORTIA: Y no Z?

It's too much to deal with, definitely too much to text, and I sum up the devastating downpour.

ME: We had a fight.

PORTIA: Be there in 20.

The idea of watching Portia and her new, potentially dangerous crush, makes me want to crawl back into bed. With a long sigh, I tuck the stress away, stuff it into the emotional junk drawer with the other things I can't find space for.

After a quick shower, I throw on a pair of denim shorts and a turquoise tee that says, "Not today." Which feels about right. A swipe of moisturizer and a ponytail later, I look out the front window. Portia's Fiat idles in my drive-way, sunlight glinting off the red paint like the fire of a thousand suns.

One day I'll get my own car and drive freely. Until then, I squeeze myself, and my emotional baggage, into the front seat.

It's a tight fit.

Portia attempts to lighten my mood. Instead, I tell her that Zach talked to my mom and kept it from me. I ignite her anger with my boyfriend. With men in general. At the world. *Smash the patriarchy!* But I don't mention Zach's been using black magic. My hurt about that is too raw to share.

By the time I finish recounting my night spent in the

morgue, then the dreamscape, hiding from the strangers, she takes my hand, clutching it in hers.

"CeCe, I'm so sorry." Her car stops for traffic as a group of pedestrians cross the street.

Tears prick my eyes, and I take a breath to keep the exhausted waver from my voice. "Why can't I just be normal?"

"Some people are meant to stand out. Oh!" She gasps, releasing my hand to point. "Speak of the devil."

I follow her gaze to see Luc Etienne crossing the street in front of us. He wears black again, but this time it's a tee that covers Thor and God of Thunder. A loud blare startles me—Portia honking her horn—and he lifts his eyes, spotting us. A slow smile curls his lips, a wolfish grin that makes me think we should build a house of bricks and hide.

Portia goes into full squee, my problems pushed aside by a cute face. And a great set of shoulders. And a rebel vibe that erases common sense. "He is *so* hot."

"Downright sweaty." I'm back to wishing I never left my bed.

Once he crosses the street, and traffic clears, Portia finds a place to park. Checking her reflection in the visor mirror, she fluffs her curls and puckers her vibrant pink lips.

"How do I look?" She turns to face me.

"Amazing." As always. Her blue and white striped shorts tie at the top with a bow, and her snug white shirt buttons up the front, leaving the bottom few undone. A patch of bare skin plays peek-a-boo in the gap every time she moves.

"Hey, we're going to figure things out. No matter what that psychic said, you're not alone." Leaning across the seat, she gives me a hug.

At first, I don't return the favor, annoyed by her excitement over Luc while I drown in dilemma. But then I remember this is Portia. Trustworthy, optimistic. The hot fudge to my vanilla. She was kidnapped and used as bait because of me, and she recovered from that trauma, still willing to be my friend. Loyal doesn't begin to cover it.

I wrap my arms around her, that pesky moisture dotting my lashes. Running down my cheeks. "Thanks."

"It's going to be okay. We'll make a to-do list. I know how much you love those."

A wet chuckle snuffles from my nose. "It's called having a plan."

"Sure. Everyone yearns for an over analyzed, color-coded system." She gives me one last squeeze and pulls back. "Now, let's get some beignets."

"You go ahead. I'll catch up." I flip down the visor to check my cry-face. "I need a minute."

She tosses me the keys to her car to lock it. "Okay, but don't be too long or I'll have to leave my very cute date to retrieve you."

"Deal."

The door slams shut, and she saunters away, her walk all hips. Gratitude for her changes my tears from frustration to appreciation. No matter how many boys try to intervene, she lifts my spirit in a way that only Portia can.

I take the time to get Zen. Or at least partially Zen. Wipe my eyes. Wipe my nose. Prepare myself for appearing in public.

On the short walk to the café, I relax the tension in my muscles, my sense of peace closer to the surface. I can make a plan, color-code it if I have to, and deal with the lingering problems.

The CeCe To-Do list now includes: visit Black Wren Voodoo for a non-black magic protection spell, help Zach through his addiction, find the Rougarou and help Dad stop the killings, and figure out who the strangers are. All before music rehearsals for *Voodoo Bayou* begin in a week.

Doable? Probably not. But at least it's something.

The smell of deep-fried oil greets me as I walk under the famous green and white striped awning of Café Du Monde. *Delicious!* My mouth waters, the Pavlovian response to the celestial donut as natural as a Taylor Swift breakup song. Despite the crowded tables, I spot Portia and Luc immediately. He holds a can of root beer in one hand and a beignet in the other. She also partakes in the pastry tasting, and suddenly her choice of a white shirt impresses me. What a queen to wear something that hides the free-roaming powdered sugar.

I almost laugh at Luc's black shirt until I realize it stays clean. Not a drop or dab of white stains his impeccable tee. It's abnormal. If I didn't already suspect Luc of having dark magic, this would seal the deal.

Walking closer, I get near enough for a more thorough inspection. Powder sprinkles Portia's hands, the table, and the paper bag used to serve beignets. But nothing on him.

"Luc, do you remember CeCe?" Portia lifts her eyebrow at my odd, lurking behavior.

My cheeks heat at getting caught hovering like a stalker. "Hi."

"Of course I remember." He rises, a true Southern gentleman, and pulls out a chair for me.

I go to sit down, nodding my thanks. But as I slide into the seat, his charming expression changes, his smile fading into a fierce frown. He leans forward, nose close to my neck before I lurch back, the metal chair screeching on the floor.

Did he just sniff me?

"What are you doing?" I ask.

"We need to talk," he says, motioning Portia to stay. "We'll be right back."

"I don't think—"

He takes my hand, lifting me to stand, and my vision goes black. A picture floats to my mind, clear and vivid. I see a dark expanse with a bright full moon—not the corrupted light of the strangers' vision—but beautiful and pure. The crisp, clean cold I associate with necromancy passes over me, and something else appears. A symbol, superimposed over the moon.

The top is a diamond-shaped eye, and below that, a triangle, pointing down. At the corners, holding the shapes together, are two round swirls. I stare at the winding circles, hypnotized by the spinning sensation. The silvery image shimmers, like a reflection off the water.

The place disappears and I'm back at Café Du Monde, holding Luc's hand, the restaurant busy, the world carrying on. But *what in the unsweetened tea was that?* Did Zach experience the same thing when his magic "clashed" with Luc's?

He jerks his hand away, blinking his eyes, his breaths quick. We both start talking at the same time. Me asking what just happened. Luc saying something about...

"Hold on. Would you repeat that?" I shake my head, wondering if I heard what I thought I did.

He grinds his teeth, his words a gritty whisper. "You've been marked by the Rougarou."

Yeah. That's what I thought he said.

CHAPTER NINE

LADY OF NEW ORLEANS STATUE: THE THIRD
WHEEL

The fortune teller said I wear the mark of betrayal. Luc told me I've been marked by a Rougarou. Pretty soon, I'll need to start a color-coded list to keep track of all the targets on my back.

"What do you know about the Rougarou?" I lower my voice, and my gaze darts to see if anyone watches us. But the crowd carries on, oblivious.

"Not here." He reaches for me, and I pull back, cradling my hand like he burned it. Which, oddly, makes him laugh.

"It won't happen again, honey." A smirk quirks the corner of his mouth, the smooth charm returning. "Our *gifts* were just gettin' acquainted that first time."

Portia stands, entering the fray. "Can someone clue me in here?"

"Does she know...?" He leaves the rest of the sentence unspoken, and I mentally multiple choice the possibilities.

About magic. About the Rougarou. About my secret diary where I write future acceptance speeches for an Oscar.

A, B, or C, doesn't matter — the answer is, "Yes."

"Come on." Picking up his root beer, he moves to the back of the restaurant. Portia and I follow, but not before she grabs the green and white bag holding the final beignet.

Again, what a queen.

He leads us to the long pedestrian walkway stretching behind Café Du Monde, and we search for a quiet spot. A tall, vine-covered wall runs along one side, obstructing our view of the Mississippi River, and the backs of the stores block us on the other side.

The humid air covers me like a blanket and the pavement sizzles, heat simmering through the soles of my flip flops. Summer glitter, aka sweat, glistens on my skin. Because of the heat, most people duck under the Café Du Monde awning or stay inside, leaving the pedestrian path nearly empty.

After a quick look around, Luc stops at "Michelle," the bronze Lady of New Orleans statue. The life-sized sculpture reclines on the lip of the half-circle fountain. Her legs extend into the walkway (hello tripping hazard), and a beautiful painted mural sets the scene behind her.

"This'll do." A grim expression flattens his lips. Despite the deserted path, he speaks softly. "I need to know what happened with the Rougarou. Where you saw it. When. How you got away without a scratch."

The flirty bad boy is gone, replaced by this super serious bloodhound on the trail of a scent.

"Who are you?" I ask.

His scoff sounds loud compared to my whisper. "*What* are you?"

A stare off ensues, and I refuse to blink as his dark eyes

bore into mine, the color so deep, it could absorb all the light shining from the sun.

"I feel like we need a why. Like, why am I out here, losing my body weight in sweat, while my date and best friend lock gazes?" Portia breaks the tension and reaches for his shoulder. Do her fingers give an extra squeeze? Carefully check the contours of The God of Thunder? Yes. "Obviously we have some trust issues going on, but I trust you both, and that should be good enough. So, let's play the honesty game. Each of you"—she steps between us, looking us both in the eye—"needs to spill one truth."

His smile slowly spreads. A full blown, rebel special that makes fathers hide daughters and mothers clutch pearls. Add to that the way he ducks his head as he runs a hand over his close-cropped hair, and I practically hear my Mawmaw say, *I do declare!*

"Alrighty, I'll go first." He relaxes his posture, arms loose at his sides. The switch to easy-going feels strategic, like he's playing us. "Let's just say I have a vested interest in the Rougarou. I'm...huntin' it."

Hunting?

"Like a Big Foot chaser?" Portia asks.

He laughs. "You could say that."

I try to imagine him listening to conspiracy theories, searching websites for sightings. Nope. Can't see it. "And your goal is to, what, get a picture? Prove it's real?"

Impossibly, his eyes darken. A chill passes over me, and I wonder if this is how Little Red Riding Hood felt, seeing something not quite right. A Big Bad Wolf in a person disguise.

"Oh, I know it's real," he says. "Catchin' it is the problem."

Portia juts her chin, pointing it right at him. "Messing

around with a creature that could chew off your face seems like a bad idea."

"Don't worry about me, darlin'. I know what I'm huntin'." Another grin oozes, a wink at her, and then he turns his attention to me. Serious Luc is back. "Your turn. Tell me where you saw it."

"It's complicated." In an I-don't-know-you-well-enough-to-trust-you kind of way. Not to mention Portia's well-documented history of putting faith in delectable guys over dependable guys.

"Honey, whatever you're hidin', it's better to just tell me. You're messin' with a danger you don't understand." Tipping back his head, he swallows the rest of his soda and crushes the can. The crunch of aluminum reverberates, and I flinch as he tosses it in the garbage.

Portia lifts an eyebrow, silently urging me to speak. Breaking off a piece of beignet, she pops it in her mouth, her stare promising me the rest if I cooperate. Shrugging, I throw him a bone. "I saw it through someone else's eyes. In a memory type thing." *Also known as a necromancy ritual.*

"A memory type thing?" he asks, and I nod.

"Then why do I smell it on you"—he leans in—"right here." His index finger trails down my neck, through the moist, summer glitter. I jerk away, lifting my hand to cover the spot he grazed.

"It licked me. I mean, not *me,* me. But my...spirit?" It comes out sounding like a question. I'm off balance by his touch, wondering *how* he can smell it. Wondering what kind of magic he has. Because something more than blood flows through his veins.

He folds his arms and studies me. I fold my arms and study him. A self-assured air surrounds him, one that consumes my confidence, leaving me nervous and unsure.

"That mark needs to be removed. The Rougarou won't attack in broad daylight, but come night, all bets are off. And it's marked you for the hunt," he finally says. "Luckily, Baba Geaux can do it."

"Who?"

"Baba Geaux. A witch doctor workin' around Jackson Square. He'll remove the mark." He dips his head toward me, taking a deep whiff. "Unless you wanna be Rougarou bait. I can work with that too. But you better decide quick."

"No. She's not going to be bait." Portia leans in, her forehead practically touching mine. "Right?"

I rub my temples, a headache building. "Where do we find this witch doctor?"

"We'll just walk around The Square. With the way you smell, he'll find us."

"Hold on." My head spins at everything Luc says. *Before sunset, Baba Geaux, Rougarou bait.* Do I trust him? No. But he knew the Rougarou marked me, touched the exact spot where I felt its moist tongue. So I can't risk ignoring him. "Zach's mom owns a voodoo shop. We could go there."

He wags a finger at me. "This isn't store-keeper voodoo. You need a witch doctor. Trust me, you want Baba Geaux."

"But I *don't* trust you."

He shrugs Thor and God of Thunder. "Suit yourself. I'm gonna catch the Rougarou one way or another."

"CeCe, I think we should go with him." Portia's worry pushes her to take his side.

I desperately want to call Zach, to ask him about witch doctors and Rougarou marks. He'd know what to do. "What kind of magic does this Baba Geaux use?"

"The kind that keeps you from bein' hunted."

Hunted like Mary Mosley. I think of her sad, lone guitar earring and touch my neck, right over the mark.

"Fine, let's go." I turn around, heading under the covered alley dividing the rows of shops. The pathway leads to Decatur Street and, more importantly, Jackson Square.

"Good choice, honey," he calls after me, his voice echoing in the tunnel.

The concrete arches overhead, and heavy lanterns hang above. The temperature cools by at least ten degrees in the shade, my flip flops no longer melting to the pavement. Portia walks next to me, and she rips off two pieces of the beignet, one for her and one for me. I unapologetically shove it in my mouth, needing the deep-fried fortification.

"I hate being the third wheel on my date." Her tone sounds less annoyed and more anxious, since she recognizes that the supernatural is a diva, upstaging everything else. Which has been trending in our friendship lately. "At least we have beignets," she says.

"They never make someone feel like a third wheel." I snag another piece. Delicious.

"Beignets understand." She eats the last bite, savoring the taste. "And I've never been stalked, kidnapped, or let down by God's gift to pastry."

"Amen."

As we exit the tunnel, no sound trails behind us, and I glance over my shoulder to see if Luc follows. He walks close enough that he probably overheard our conversation, and his sideways smile suggests he did. "Relax, darlin'. Our next date will be better."

"If there is a next date," Portia tosses back, eyebrow raised. Strutting forward, her hips sway better than any supermodel, all proud female who doesn't need a tall, dark, enigmatic co-star's attention. His eyes follow with more than just attraction. An expression of admiration softens his gaze. It makes me grudgingly like him.

Except he's not a normal guy pursuing a normal relationship. With the way he moves, his silent footfalls and easy grace, I wonder about his magic again. Specifically, the shimmering image I saw.

What is it?

I pause on the sidewalk at Jackson Square and face Luc, linking my arm through Portia's for moral support. The shade from a large oak covers us, shadows keeping the sun at bay. "Tell me about the symbol. The one from our…gifts getting acquainted."

"Symbol? What symbol?" His back straightens, and the charismatic mask slips.

"The diamond eye with the triangle."

His eyes widen the tiniest bit. If I hadn't been staring, I would have missed the reaction. Confidence still radiates in his stance, but I shocked him.

"What is it?" I ask.

"You shouldn't have seen that. Seein' is my gift, not yours," he drawls, a dark note entering his tone. The silence ticks between us, seconds on a clock. Or a timer on a bomb. His breathing slows, his body completely still. "Did it look like this?"

His fingers curl around the bottom edge of his black tee, and he inches it up. Past his belly button. Past his ribs. Portia pants beside me as the temperature rises to H-O-T. The look in her eyes tells me she's ready to do laundry. By hand. On a darkened bronze six-pack washboard. Suddenly that second date seems much more likely.

"Hell-o," she whispers softly.

I do declare!

The moment of ogling is interrupted when I realize what he shows me. A tattoo on his chest, right over his heart. A black and blue inked replica of the image.

I clench my fingers, resisting the urge to reach out and trace the design. Something about it speaks to me, like a captivating work of art. "Exactly like that. What does it mean?"

He drops his shirt, allowing the temperature to return to normal. "It's a sigil from La Siréne, the Voodoo Loa of sea and song."

"Oh." The answer surprises me.

Zach explained the difference between voodoo magic and practicing the religion. Some are born with a natural gift, the ability to draw from ancestors and convert that into power to perform spells. But not all have magic. Others call on the Loa, intermediary spirits between humans and the supreme creator. These spirits offer help in the form of protection, healing, direction, anything the worshipper seeks.

But Luc's magic doesn't feel the way Zach's mom's voodoo does. His power rippled, carrying a heaviness like the pressure of being deep underwater. Zach's not wrong when he called it dark magic. "Do you practice Voodoo?"

"When it suits me. I asked La Siréne for a favor, and she gave me the gift of sight." A slight shrug almost hides the secretive sideways glance. "Wanna know what I saw from you?"

"No," I say, and Portia throws an elbow in my ribs.

"Yes," she says.

He ignores the mixed messaging. "A bright crescent moon, too bright, a skull, and blood red Rougarou scratches."

A moon and a skull. The same symbols the strangers etched into the dirt. Necromancy symbols.

He keeps talking. "But more than what I saw is what I felt. You don't make sense. Flooded with moon power and enveloped by death." He shakes his head. "So, what are you?"

"My sandals are melting to the pavement." Portia changes the subject, saving me from answering, lifting one foot and then the other. "Are we gonna find this witch doctor?"

"Sure. Let's move." Luc leads the way around the corner to psychic row. The St. Louis cathedral towers above us on our right, the building looking like something straight out of a fairy tale. The iconic triple spires touch the sky, and the white granite shines starkly in the sunlight.

Music carries from a jazz quartet playing on the other side of The Square, and the din of tarot readers and charm sellers makes conversation difficult. But Luc's last unanswered question echoes in my mind.

What are you?

I don't even know anymore. A traumatized necromancer who falls apart at the morgue. A failed traveler of magical planes. A girlfriend who doesn't recognize her boyfriend struggles with addiction. Also...Rougarou bait.

We approach an empty stand with a cheap folding TV tray, black tablecloth and a small, gold umbrella providing a little shade. Plastic Mardi Gras beads in shades of purple, green, and gold hang down. A hand-drawn cardboard sign props against a metal chair, the words *World Famous Witch Doctor Baba Geaux*, written in bold black.

None of that grabs my attention. At the next table over, sits a woman. No chintzy signs of self-proclaimed greatness announce her presence. No beads decorate her table. But I know her. She wears a purple veil and distinct green jewels trail from the corners of her hazel eyes.

The fortune teller.

"It's the psychic," Portia whispers.

Since my recognition radar already pinged, I nod.

"CeCe, I've been waiting for you." She stands and takes the veil off her mouth, showing her soft smile. "Sit. It's time to talk about who you really are."

Holy spot on, Inner Thoughts. It's like she read my mind. Like a real psychic.

CHAPTER TEN

JACKSON SQUARE: THE CARDS

L uc gives a nod of greeting. "We're lookin' for Baba Geaux, Simone. Is he around?"

Simone. The fortune teller has a name.

"He'll turn up," she says, her accent suspiciously missing. "Why don't you and your date take a walk while I talk to CeCe?"

"How do you know we're on a date?" Portia juts her chin, a challenge thrown down, her skepticism clear.

Somewhere along the line, my previous skepticism shifted to curiosity. Between Simone showing me the Seven of Swords and now, my interest is piqued. Her prediction of betrayal was on point, and I wonder if she wants to warn me about betrayal again. Or maybe something new this time. What other relationship of mine could she crush?

"Portia, you *are* on a date," I remind her, and she rolls her eyes, like I spoiled the big reveal.

"It doesn't take a psychic to figure it out." Simone gestures to the two of them, standing shoulder to shoulder, both ridiculously attractive, a magazine ad for *cool people everyone envies*.

"But you are psychic. Right?" Portia lifts a doubtful brow.

"Come on, darlin'." Luc chuckles and throws an arm around her. He's like a lazy bear holding a fierce chihuahua. "We'll look for Baba Geaux. Holler if you need us."

They walk away and I sit in the chair across from Simone, wondering how to start a conversation with a psychic. *What's up?* Too casual. *Long time no see?* Too trite. *Tell me everything?* Too desperate.

I go with, "What happened to the accent?"

"The tourists prefer it," she says, in a voice more bayou than Romanian mafia. "I always use it when The Square gets busy."

Fake. Just like I thought.

An awkward silence ensues. Her eyes pass over my pink hair, studying my face, intent enough I turn away, uncomfortable with the inspection.

Simone runs a thumb along the edge of her tarot cards. "There's some things you need to learn, necromancer."

Her pronouncement steals my breath, the way my secret identity — *necromancer* — casually left her mouth. No one calls Peter Parker by Spiderman. Or points at Tony Stark and yells, *superhero!*

"How do you know about that?"

Instead of answering my question, she draws three cards from her deck and places them face down on the table. "I'm going to tell you the two secrets of necromancy. The ones only learned from knowledge passed down."

"Who passed the knowledge to you?" Because last time I checked, she exchanges fortunes for ten dollars. Two for fifteen.

A coy smile lifts her lips as she flips the first card. On the bottom, in a shimmering lake, it reads, "The moon," and at the top, a big, glowing orb shines. A river splits the middle, a dog on one side, a howling wolf on the other, with twin pillars in the background. In the pool of water, a girl sinks into the depths. Her pink hair floats around her, and she clutches a crawfish in her hands.

Yes, pink hair. My stomach sinks like the girl in the water, and I wonder who made the card with me in mind. I shift in my seat, casting a furtive glance around because I feel watched. Seen.

"There are three natural magics." The beads on Simone's dress jingle as she flips the next card. The Sun. Another pink-haired girl, this one with arms outstretched, and head tipped to the sky. A giant sun takes the whole background, and rays of it reach to cradle her. Two tall sunflowers bloom on either side, bright yellow petals fully opened. "Life, death, and voodoo. Each draw from a different source."

"Sun, moon, and ancestors." I jump in, ever the good student.

"Correct." She turns the final card, The Magician. Another girl with — *shocker* — pink hair. She floats cross-legged, and one hand points to the sky, the other points to the ground. A golden bow ties her hair back and it forms a perfect infinity symbol above her head.

"Some wield one—" she puts a finger on the magician card— "Some may wield two—" she adds a finger to the sun— "and only one can wield all three."

Simone stares laser beams at me, and I look over the cards again, at the girls who bear a striking resemblance to yours truly.

"Can we skip the whole cryptic tarot reading and just

talk straight?" It feels like I'm trying to empty Lake Pontchartrain, one teaspoon at a time. But each measly spoonful of information turns into rainstorms of more questions.

"This is the first truth of the necromancer, you can use all three magics."

"No way." Frustration bubbles up, all my memories of failure swimming at the surface. "I barely function in this world. I can't even get to my magical plane."

"You've been using them all this time without realizing. You wield the voodoo passed from your ancestors. Listen to them, they will guide and give you knowledge. Some call it intuition, but it's much more."

My cicadas! They've guided and given knowledge. *Could they be my ancestors?* But if so, then... "What happens if my guide goes silent?"

"Keep searching. They'll find you." She taps the sun card. "Life magic, the power of the sun, sustains you and allows you to not only communicate with the dead, but to unite with their essence. This brightness keeps the darkness at bay. Allow the sun to embrace you, and don't believe the lies your self-doubt tells."

"Well, I don't have any problems with that." And maybe if I say it enough, it'll be true.

"Hmm." She leans forward, her chest nearly touching the table. "Your death magic enables you to raise the dead. You may feel most acquainted with this magic, but death is never simple. It's a blessing, a curse. It can be peaceful or violent. A release or a thief."

Like Rivera's wife dying so young — thief. Or Mawmaw who believed death is good for the soul. Or me, able to help Dad. Mom may have left, but death magic connected me to

Dad in a way that made me feel needed. Our family unit of two, relying on each other.

Simone slides the moon card forward a couple of inches "There are two sides, one that is tame and controllable, represented by the dog, and then the side of the wolf, which is wild and untenable. Everything is a mirror of the other, and your struggle will be distinguishing truth from deception."

She rotates the card upside down, changing the perspective. Now the moon looks like a reflection on the water, and the girl lays on a beach, her hair splayed on the sand. "Sometimes the sinking girl is an illusion. When she surrenders her fear, she gains clarity and control and learns to swim."

"Is that supposed to be helpful?" I ask.

Swim. Through the morgue trauma. Into the magical plane. *How fast does a Rougarou swim?*

"It's still true, even if you don't understand it yet." She taps the cards, one by one. Magician, sun, moon. "Having all three magics is why you're sought after. There are those who want to trap you on the magical plane so they can access your power."

Like the old man from the dreamscape.

Will this be the rest of my life? Always faced with the next person who wants to spirit kidnap me and put me in a cage. My power a constant magnet attracting the maniacal, desperate, and ambitious.

"Someone's trying to trap me now," I tell her.

"I know. I'm sorry." She removes her purple gloves and sets them on the table, then pats my hand. As soon as she touches me, the easy vibration of voodoo hums on my skin. I should have known she has actual magic. More than a tourist trapper peddling fake fortunes for a few dollars. "And now for the second truth."

My mind whirls, the info dump real. And now she wants to tell me something else. "Okay...?"

"There's only one natural necromancer, one every three generations. It can't be passed until the previous holder crosses into the next life. And it's only passed on the female line."

"So...the necromancer is always a girl?"

"Yes. Many try to imitate the power with black magic, but they're limited. Black magic is a forgery, a hollow imitation of true ability."

The sound of shuffling feet steals my attention, and I turn to see Portia and Luc making their way to us. Apparently, their walk is over. She looks happy, though. Big, bright smile. Shoulders locked in *squee* position. Luc tucks her close, she leans in, and now they look like an ad for *#couplegoals*.

"How was the talk?" Portia's fierce Chihuahua has been tamed to cuddly kitten.

"Good?" I say it as a question. Because...was it good? Maybe informative would have been a better description. "How was the walk?"

"Hot," she says. The amount of innuendo in that word turns my cheeks pink.

"Did you find Baba Geaux?"

"He was surprisingly unaccounted for." Luc winks at Portia, giving her a little extra squeeze.

"Take this card." Simone holds the moon in her outstretched hand. "Constance wants you to have it."

"Wait, who?" Luc asks.

"Constance. CeCe's mom. Keep up." She throws him a playful elbow.

"You know my mom." Statement. Not a question. Forget swimming. Anytime my mom comes up I sink all over again.

"Cher, we all know your mama. She runs this place." A booming voice explodes behind me, and I stand from the chair and whip around.

"Baba Geaux." Luc inclines his head, nodding at the witch doctor.

The man's face is painted white, with black circling his eyes. A tall, top hat rests on his head, decorated with a brim of yellowed teeth. His long dread locks reach past his shoulders, and small bones weave into the strands. Multiple necklaces layer over his otherwise bare chest, long and short, chunky beads and wooden medallions. On his shoulders he wears an off-white feathered shawl, and his black pants, more like capris, have rough edges. To add some ick to his ensemble, his feet are bare on the hot pavement, his long, jagged nails extending far beyond the tips of his toes.

"Hold up...you're saying my mom runs Jackson Square?" I ask.

"Not the actual Square. The people. Card readers, fortune tellers. All the magic." Simone circles her finger in the air, indicating the block of psychic row.

Portia lifts her hand. "CeCe's mom controls a magical mafia syndicate? That's so cool."

Simone waves the card and waits until I take it. "Her message is there. Read it."

Since no words, other than "the moon" are written, I assume she means tarot cartomancy. Which...not my specialty. But I stuff the card in my purse.

Baba Geaux sticks his face next to my neck and inhales a deep whiff of air. Holding it. Savoring it. "What a delicious prize."

Okay. That's weird.

"I told you he'd be able to smell you." Luc lifts a knowing brow.

The varied necklaces around the witch doctor's neck clack and clatter. He curls his toes against the pavement and his long talons scratch like nails on a chalkboard. I cringe at the way they bend, almost to breaking, the concrete serving as a natural file.

"Do you realize what we have?" Baba Geaux hoots, a boisterous *hoo hoo* heard across The Square.

Luc looks side to side, clearly confused. "She was marked by the Rougarou."

"Don't I know it! The possibilities, Lou." He calls him Lou. Not Luc, which I gather means he knows him, but not well. Or maybe well enough for a nickname? *Shrug.*

"She just needs the mark removed. Nothin' more." Luc's syrupy drawl slows to molasses.

"That'll cost ya a pretty penny. Cures are cheap compared to this." He rubs his hands together.

What does he mean by cures?

"How much are we talking?" I think over the contents of my purse which includes six dollars, a moon tarot card, melted Chapstick, and a couple of gum wrappers.

"Triple. Three hundred to remove the mark."

My mouth loses the ability to stay closed. "Three hundred. As in dollars?"

"I have a hundred with me." Luc trails off, glancing at both me and Portia.

"Don't look at me." Portia points to herself. "Pretty, but poor."

"Well, that's alright. I'll take the hundred." His voice drops, any hint of levity gone. "And a favor."

"No." Luc closes the distance between him and the witch doctor. "We're not playin' your games."

Baba Geaux's nostrils flare. A fierce frown creases his features, his whole demeanor turning venomous. An argument ensues, in Cajun French, Baba Geaux yelling and Luc responding in a perfect, fluent tongue.

"Do you understand any of it?" Portia whispers in my ear. "Two years of French are failing me."

"What's the point of taking a language in high school? I understand zero." I listen for context clues, the angry tone of Baba Geaux, the unbending stance of Luc. *Why are they even arguing?*

One more weird piece in the weird puzzle that is my weird life.

"Let me ask her myself." Baba Geaux switches back to English, his eyes straight on me.

Luc sighs, shifting to put me in his sight. "Be specific. Askin' for a favor is too broad. No one is foolish enough to agree to that. Right CeCe?"

"Uhh, right."

Baba Geaux's smile stretches wide, too wide. Creepy. "I'll take off the mark if you agree to talk to someone for me."

Talk to someone? What an odd request. "Who?"

"Someone on the other side. You can't say no when the time comes." His toe clawing picks up speed, the *scratch, scratch, scratch* sending chills down my spine. Maybe he could scrape a fork across his teeth or squeak some Styrofoam for the trifecta of horrid sounds.

"Luc, is this a trick?" Portia asks.

He walks the two steps back to us, his tone dropping to a whisper. "He's a witch doctor. Not to mention he's slicker than a catfish. Be careful what you agree to."

Careful. Sure. My choices are being Rougarou bait or agreeing to necromance for a catfish. I think of what Simone told me about the moon card, the difficulty of distinguishing truth from deception.

"Okay. I'll talk to someone for you if you remove the mark," I reluctantly agree, hoping I haven't made a huge mistake.

"Come along, Cher. Step into my office." He gestures to one of the metal chairs tucked at the edge of the table, and I sit. The hot, black metal singes my flesh, my thighs taking a quick dip into molten lava. I yelp, scooting forward, and a howling laugh bursts from his lungs.

"Gets 'em every time," he says. "Now, let's work on that mark."

CHAPTER ELEVEN

BABA GEAUX'S OFFICE: THE CURE

Grabbing a bag from under the tablecloth, Baba Geaux dumps the contents out, rummaging through different herbs and stones. Muttered words flutter from his mouth, some in English, some in French, none of them making sense.

"I'll help." Simone lowers into the other chair, her long purple dress guarding her legs from the fires of sun-drenched metal. Shuffling through the baggies, she grabs a small, fabric pouch, stuffing in herbs that Baba Geaux hands her.

Luc and Portia both hover over my shoulder.

"I'm keepin' my eye on you." Luc throws out the warning.

"Same." Portia wraps her fingers around the back of my chair, leaning in.

Baba Geaux waves them off, unconcerned with their presence. "Who'd'a thought I'd have Constance's daughter sittin' with me, marked by the fake Rougarou." A dark gleam enters his eyes, and he lowers his voice to a whispered growl. "Now she owes me a favor."

Luc jumps in. "Not a favor."

"A specific task." Portia finishes. One walk together, and they're finishing each other's sentences.

I'm stuck on the gigantic news drop he casually tossed down. "*Fake* Rougarou?"

"You been livin' under a rock?" Baba Geaux laughs low in his throat. "Bad things are happenin'. Someone hijacked the Rougarou curse and now the real one can't transform."

Looking over my shoulder, my eyes meet Luc's. Even with his arm around Portia, a heavy intensity weighs his gaze, his stillness unsettling. *Does he know the Rougarou is an imposter? Is that why he's hunting it?*

I mentally smack my forehead. Of course he knows.

"The balance is off." Simone grips one of the baggies, her fingers white-knuckled.

"My mom's all about the balance." I talked to Zach about it once, and the memory gut punches me. The anger hits first — I need him here. And the sorrow swells after — I miss him already.

"We all should be," Simone says.

"Why?" My pretty but poor friend asks the same question I have.

"The magic is affected. Everyone's magic." She finishes up the sachet, tying it off, and setting it on the table.

"But the Hijackers are targeting The Square. Maybe I should leave the mark, let them come after you so they leave our people alone." He sneers, his yellowed teeth on display. "They want you. Don't know why they're killin' us."

"The bargain's already been struck," Luc warns.

"Yeah, yeah."

While Luc and Baba Geaux glare at each other, an image of the dreamscape pops in my head. The masked strangers and chanting rhythm. The old man with his bearded face, clawing to keep me in the vision.

Now I have something to call them. The Hijackers.

"It's ready." Simone hands a jagged hunk of charcoal to Baba Geaux.

He rubs the black rock over my neck, then scrapes the surface of the charcoal with his thumbnail. Little flakes sprinkle off, falling to land like pencil shavings on an empty plastic baggy. His magic vibrates against my skin, similar to the voodoo I've felt from Zach's mom, but thicker and colder. His humming buzzes in the air, the tune surprisingly like the rhythm of the chanting strangers.

The process repeats, color my neck, scratch off a layer, over and over again. Until a full body shudder passes through me, dizzying in its intensity.

"That oughta do it." He sets the charcoal down and carefully picks up the bag, keeping all the dust on top. In his other hand he holds a small, plastic vial half-filled with salt. Curling the edges of the bag, he sifts the flakes into the container.

His necklaces rattle as he corks and shakes the vial. The black and white mix together to make gray salt, and he passes the bottle to me.

"Sprinkle it in your bathtub, then rinse it down the drain. Make sure you get it all down. Then you gotta take a bath with this. It's a cure." He gives me the white sachet, which looks like a pouch of potpourri, stuffed with different herbs, some dried, some fresh.

"And that's all?" I lift the sachet to my nose, inhaling the strange perfume of dirt and spice cupboard before putting it, and the vial of gray salt, in my purse.

"No, that's not all. I lifted the mark, but the Rougarou still wants you. Better stay on your toes." His rancid breath invades my nostrils. The white makeup highlights his forehead and the bones in his cheeks, giving the illusion of a skull overlay. "Don't flaunt that magic around."

"Sure. Under the radar," I say.

"Better yet, don't use it at all." The mood shifts, a darker tone entering his voice. A sinister smile creases his cheeks, puckering the paint on his face.

He begins humming again, the same tune as before. But slower. Louder. The melody winds around me, a slithering snake. It takes me a few seconds to recognize the oily feel to the air, but as soon as I do, I abruptly stand, knocking into Portia.

Black magic.

"You smell better now." Luc puts himself between me and Baba Geaux. "We're done here."

The witch doctor keeps his eyes on me, barely acknowledging Luc's presence.

Portia threads her arm through mine and tugs me back a step, then another, uprooting my planted feet into motion. The solid wall of Luc stays put.

Baba Geaux slams his hands against the table, and I flinch. Several of the little baggies slide to the ground. The black magic slides away as well, leaving the air more breathable. "Don't let the Lou ruin our fun."

I tip my head, confused with what he said. Not just Lou. But *The* Lou. It seems strange, and the words tumble in my mind as I watch Simone slouch to pick up the mess on the ground. As I listen to Luc scold Baba Geaux for trying something slick.

"Maybe my two years of French aren't a waste." Portia's

breath tickles my ear as she whispers, "but why did Baba Geaux call Luc *the wolf*."

Loup, pronounced Lou, French for... "The wolf?"

Baba Geaux hears me over Luc's rant, and his lips curl in a look far more nefarious than a smile. "That's right."

Luc either didn't hear or chooses not to acknowledge my exchange with Baba Geaux. But I feel like the tarot card, turned around, my perspective flipped. The clues click into place. The fake Rougarou killing people. Luc on the hunt, searching for the imposter. *The Loup*. It all adds up to one conclusion.

The guy who will costar in *Voodoo Bayou* and kiss my best friend, the one standing up to Baba Geaux and acting weirdly protective is the real Rougarou.

A desire to run pumps through my legs, but I try to separate Luc from my shared memory with Mary Mosley. Our vision of the tall beast with piercing red eyes. The thick scent of fear as the clawed hands gripped under her arms and lifted her. Dangled her. Blood spattering the pavement as its snout tore into her throat. Luc wouldn't do that.

Would he?

"We need to go." I tighten my arm around Portia, who hasn't yet caught the implication of what The Loup might mean. Forget Baba Geaux and his knack for black magic.

With my fingers firmly wrapped around Portia's bicep, I take two steps before Simone stops us. She reaches for Portia's hand and flips it to stare at her palm. A curious look pinches her forehead, and she traces the lines on Portia's skin.

"Who are you?" she asks.

"Oh, you don't need to know me. I don't do the whole magic scene." Portia yanks her hand back.

"There's something in your future. An ominous path

ahead..." She presses her fingers to her forehead, squinting her eyes. "I see a connection between us. Let me read for you."

"Pass." Portia twists her earring, keeping her palm guarded, visibly bothered by the fortune teller.

Simone tries to argue, but Portia cuts her off, yelling to Luc. "We're gonna be late for practice. Let's head."

Luc pays Baba Geaux, and the witch doctor hands something to him. I'm too far away to see what it is, but Luc tucks it into the pocket of his shorts, drug deal style.

As he comes closer, I step back, my heartbeat drumming, the memories of Mary Mosley too fresh. The whisper of his dark magic lingers, like the scent of Baba Geaux's breath. I force my feet to stop their retreat and face him. But Luc's focus narrows on his co-star.

"Sorry darlin'. It's been a most unusual first date."

"It's fine, but we need to go." She's already moving, putting distance between herself and the fortune teller.

Simone watches her with curiosity, pulling a tarot deck from the depths of her robe. The cards whoosh as she shuffles her thumb down the edge, pausing to pull one from the middle. A shiver passes over me as I glance at the one word on the card she drew.

Death.

Keeping her gaze on Portia, she says, "it doesn't mean what you think it means."

No matter the spin you put on the tarot card, the word *death* connected to my best friend freaks me out. Especially when paired with her crushing on the (maybe) Rougarou. I don't wait for Simone's explanation; I hustle to catch up to her and the guy who may or may not turn into a savage beast.

We stay quiet as we walk, all simmering in thought. Luc

clenches and unclenches his jaw, his hand jammed into the pocket that holds the mysterious item Baba Geaux gave him. Portia's fast pace and zoned-out stare speak to her distress.

I stew on what I know about Luc, from the tattoo on his chest to the way he throws out charm like beads in a Mardi Gras parade. Is he capable of killing? Of ripping out a person's throat?

It takes rounding the corner from Chartres onto St. Peters before my breathing comes easier. Before my thoughts coalesce into a plan. Not even a fully formed plan, but something to get through the next few minutes.

"We're going to play the honesty game again, one truth each," I say, stopping a few feet from the entrance to Le Petit Theater. "But if you lie or betray the integrity of the game, Portia will think of new and unusual ways to exact revenge. Got it?"

Amusement ripples behind his eyes, but he nods. "Fair enough."

I fill my lungs with air, then blow it out, preparing for the leap of truth. I don't willingly spill my tea. If I learned anything in the last hour, it's that my secret identity is best kept secret. And yet, here I go.

"I'm a necromancer. I talk to the dead. That's how I knew about the Rougarou."

"I kinda figured somethin' like that. After seein' your magic, and hearin' the favor from Baba Geaux, it's the only thing that fits."

"Your turn." I say, getting in his face and poking him in the chest. "Are you the Rougarou?"

"No way." Portia scoffs, shaking her head. "We're talking about an ugly, vile beast. And Luc's...definitely not that."

He licks the corner of his lip, and I practically see the wheels spinning in his head. But I want the truth, and I poke him again, harder. "Honesty game."

He rubs the spot where I jabbed. "Not currently."

"What?" Portia says, her eyebrows lifting.

A guy walks by us, another member of the cast, and he gives a head nod as he enters the theater. The door squeaks, a ghostly shriek of sound. The oppressive heat bakes us, and I feel like a lit candle, dripping wax from every side.

I resist poking him again and settle for a *don't lie to me* tone. "Not currently because the ability was stolen?"

"Because it's not my phase." He speaks through gritted teeth, but his annoyance isn't directed at me. Or Portia. Or the random dude who just walked into the theater.

"What does that mean?" Portia mangles her earrings, her nerves hovering somewhere around merge-onto-a-busy-freeway level.

"I can't tell you," he says, and I open my mouth to interrupt with a reminder about the honesty game, but he holds up a finger. "It's not just my story, there are other people involved. I promise that I'll give you what I can, but you should know we're on the same side. You can trust me."

"Can we? Because apparently you're a werewolf." Portia juts her chin and steps close to me, practically drawing a line in the sand. "You better not do anything to hurt CeCe. I promise there isn't a hole deep enough for you to hide from me."

He raises his hand, slow and steady, the gesture as serious as a vow. "I swear that I won't hurt either one of you."

"What did Baba Geaux give you?" I keep pressing, not allowing the conversation to end, afraid the sanctity of the honesty game will die when we finish talking.

He pulls out a white sachet, like the one in my pocket. "It's a cure for my sister. She's sick."

"Your sister?" Portia's tone softens at the mention of his family. "Is she...okay?"

"No." He stuffs the cure back into his pocket. "Your turn, Portia. What's your truth?"

"Me? I'm not a part of this game."

"I did say one truth each." I smile, expecting Portia to steer the conversation into something lighter. A little levity after all the revelations.

"Fine." She rolls her neck from side to side, loosening the tension. "Sometimes I feel useless and left out. Not having magic."

"Seriously?" The most capable, self-assured person I know feels useless. Left out. "But you're funny and amazing. And your sense of fashion is a superpower. Plus, you've put up with me and my neuroses, which must be some kind of magic."

She doesn't smile, doesn't react to my encouragement. Instead, she shrugs, and her brown eyes glisten with emotion. "That's my truth."

CHAPTER TWELVE

THE FRENCH QUARTER: THE BOYFRIEND

I can't believe my best friend feels useless. How long has that been going on? How could I let it happen? She's Portia. My amigo. The little confetti sprinkles in our Funfetti cake. There is no cake without the sprinkles. At least not a good one.

My perspective flips again. Back to sinking.

Since the quintet doesn't start practice until next week, I head to Black Wren Voodoo, hoping to catch Zach's mom at the shop. Now that I have a need to learn more voodoo, she's the perfect guide. Also, she needs to know about Zach. Hopefully, he told her about the back magic. But if not, I will. Because I love him, and I want him to get better.

With a heaping dose of my day spent baking in the sun, my clothes hang heavy, a layer of sweat weighing down the fabric. My heart hangs heavy too. First Zach, now Portia.

Flyaway strands of pink hair cling to my neck and on my cheeks. I swipe under my eyes, sure my non-waterproof mascara smears, the dark circles helping me fit in with the regular vampire crowd.

Yes, the vampire crowd in New Orleans. Are they real vampires? Maybe — I have no idea — but probably not.

Then again, I'm a necromancer hanging around a possible werewolf, so who am I to judge?

Regretting I forgot my sunglasses at home, I lift my hand to shade my eyes from the scorching ball of fire in the sky. I check my phone and see several missed notifications, all from Zach. Call, call, text, text, text, call.

ZACH: Pls answer so we can work this out.

ZACH: CeCe! Stop being so stubborn.

ZACH: Sorry, I just need to talk to u.

A heavy pressure builds in my chest, the weight of Zach's lies caving in. I slow my pace, my feet dragging on the pavement, my phone heavy in my hand. *Should I respond? Keep ignoring him?* My thoughts scatter like powdered sugar from a beignet, all over and uncontrolled. But through the mind sugar, a distinct sensation intrudes. Shivers down my spine. Prickling on the back of my neck.

Someone is watching me.

Could it be Simone? Have the Hijackers found me?

I spin around and search the street, unsure of what, or who, to look for. The person I spot dodging into a shop, trying to avoid my gaze, surprises me. Someone so far off my radar I march a quarter of a block back to confront her, without a plan of what to say.

Julie Jolley. I catch my nemesis ducking behind a rack, jamming a sparkly NOLA hat on her head.

During drama camp, we both entered the dramatic

monologue competition, a contest she came out on top of with the first-place prize. In the end, I hoisted the plaque for the grand prize, winner of The Exhibition, the most coveted award of the whole camp. So maybe I came out on top after all.

But our nemesis-ery goes way back before that.

"Julie Jolley," I say.

A shrill *meep* flies from her mouth, and she starts digging in her bag. "Stay back."

"Why are you following—"

"Get thee hence!" she yells, emptying the contents of a vial at me. Liquid splats from my forehead to my chin, mixing with my sweat, which stings my eyes. At least I hope it's the sweat and not some weird concoction she chemistry-ed.

"Julie!" Using the collar of my shirt, I wipe my face. "What's wrong with you?"

She hisses at me, like a territorial cat. "That's holy water. You won't taint me with your corruption."

"Are you okay?" At the risk of putting a chink in our bitter rivalry, I can't help but notice Julie seems...off. Not only did she splash me with "holy water," but she wears no makeup, something I've never seen, and several crucifixes hang around her neck like Mardi Gras beads.

"Don't play nice. I'm on to you," she says.

"It was you stalking me the other day. At Jackson Square." The creeping sensation of being watched makes sense now. It was her. "But why?"

"Come on. Zombies breaking out from the wall vaults was a prank? I don't think so. That was witchcraft. You did something that night, you and Zach. Something"—she lowers her voice to a deep whisper—"unnatural." Ah, the zombies. Looks like our cover-up of *a fun drama camp prank,* fell short of believable.

A group of us performed a fake séance, but Rivera hid behind the scenes, attempting to magically connect with me. Some fleshy skeletons animated, Julie got grabbed by a decomposing hand, which luckily only touched her hair, not her skin. Otherwise, she would have been haunted. An incident I witnessed once when a murder victim touched my dad, and I hope to never see again.

"It was just a prank." I double down on the explanation.

"Lies! I know what you are." She tries to fling more water, but only a few drops splash out.

"I'm going to regret this, but"—I cross my arms and adopt a bored expression—"what am I?"

"Evil."

Ouch. Julie and I have done our fair share of slinging insults, but that one stung. A huge chasm separates a dig like *talentless hack* to a condemnation of *evil.* I think of Mawmaw, who always helped me see necromancy as a gift. Not something to be ashamed of.

"Seriously?" I check my tone, trying to hide the hurt.

"I'm watching you. I won't let you snare another victim." She shoves past, shouldering me so hard I knock into the shelf and send souvenirs tumbling. The plastic snow globes plunk to the floor, several landing with a rolling thud.

"Come on," the clerk shouts, but Julie storms from the store, the bell on the door jingling behind her.

Scrambling to pick up the kitschy mementos, I rush to put them back, and the clerk growls in a low rumble. I give an apologetic wave as I run out.

A few tourists stroll down the street. Music blasts from one of the shops, a Rolling Stones classic pumping loud enough to cover ambient noise. I search the sidewalk, look back and forth across the street. No sign of Julie. Between the dozens of stores, many side alleys, and regular chaos of the French Quarter, it's like hunting for a gator in the water; zero chance until she decides to surface.

A frustrated breath blows from my lungs. I need to convince her not to follow me, that nothing "unnatural" happened the night of the fake séance. Danger stalks me like a horror movie villain, around every corner and hiding in the shadows. Hijackers, murders, and Rougarous, oh my! To add in Julie Jolley's meddling gives me heartburn.

At school, she and her posse, the J-Crew, try to embarrass me, and generally make my life miserable on the regular. But it's summertime. My escape from them.

Putting a pin in the Julie Jolley problem, I make my way to the voodoo store. It carves out a spot along Royal Street between an antique shop and a place filled with brochures that sells tours. Above me, a classy, unobtrusive sign hangs, a simple white circle with the silhouette of a Carolina Wren. Over the bird, in black print, it reads *Black Wren Voodoo.*

The cool air conditioning surrounds me as I enter, the temperature relief immediate. I blink my eyes several times, adjusting to the dim interior. Incense burns, a musky perfume too heavy to breathe in comfortably.

"CeCe. I knew you'd show up."

I almost turn around and leave at the sound of that voice. A voice I've been avoiding since last night. Zach.

"What are you doing here?" My panic rises. I'm not ready to see him yet. It's too soon.

He moves from behind the counter, his slow steps approaching. "We need to talk."

"No, I came to see your mom." My stupid heart beats

faster, and my gaze catalogs everything about him. The way his brown hair falls over his forehead, a little messy from his fingers running through it. His gray tee tight across his chest and shoulders. The adorable freckles dotting his nose.

The snug zone calls to me, the cozy space where trouble and stress melt away. I long to move in, tuck my head into the alluring nook, and forget everything else but the comfort of his touch.

"CeCe, please. I can't do this without you." His fingers grip my shoulder. "I promise to give it up. I won't do it anymore."

I bat his hand away, my heart aching. "Have you told your mom yet? What about Lucy?"

"If I have you, I don't need to involve them. All I need is us." His fingers graze my cheek, as he tucks my hair behind my ear.

My hair!

The betrayal floods me, and I move out of his reach. He stole my hair, talked to my mom. He knew I'd show up, and he planned for this rendezvous, even after I told him we couldn't see each other. I notice the red rimming his deep navy eyes. Register the greasy vibration of magic where our skin met. A pang stabs my chest at the physical reminders of him using black magic.

Zach's phone dings, and we both ignore it, locked in our confrontation.

"You can't do this to me." My voice cracks, and I clear my throat. Tears burn my eyes, and my lungs clench, the sadness so thick it's harder to breathe in than the musky incense.

"Don't cry, please," he says softly, his face scrunching in a grimace as if my anguish causes his own. "Let's talk about it."

He opens his arms, the snug zone beckoning. The idea of his comfort, of his help, tempts me, and my foot shuffles forward an inch. The chime sounds again from his phone, and I freeze. It's enough to jostle my senses.

"No. You have to stop using. If we see each other, you'll want to keep protecting me. I'm the problem. It's me." *Did I accidentally quote Taylor Swift?* Yes. But her heartache is real too.

"You wanted me to use black magic when you were trapped in it. In fact, you begged, and I freed you." His frustration sharpens the edge of his words, filing them to weapons. "I don't regret it. All I want to do is keep you safe. And someone is after you again, hunting you down."

"That's never going to change. I'm the necromancer. Did you know there's only one every three generations?"

"Uhh, no. You're the only one I've ever met. Ever heard of."

"Because I'm the only one. I will always be hunted." I really am the problem. "What are you going to do? Use black magic the rest of our lives? We have to find a better way."

"Yes! We! We found out about Rivera, together. Took him down, together. We're supposed to be a team." He faces me, his beautiful blue eyes pleading.

"A team?" Anger sharpens my words now. "You talked to my mom behind my back and secretly stole loose pieces of my hair."

"I know. I'm sorry!" he shouts, running a hand through his hair, clenching the strands.

Taking a calming breath, I measure my words. "Please tell your mom. Or Lucy. I don't know how to help you with this. What I do know is that I make it worse. And I love you too much to do that."

Another ding on Zach's cell, and this time he snatches it off the counter, his thumbs tapping the screen with force.

"You've gotta be kidding me. I see what's going on now." His chest heaves, and he squeezes his phone until his knuckles turn white. "I'm such an idiot."

"What's wrong?"

"Tell me the real reason you want to breakup, CeCe."

"I don't want to break up. That's not what I said." Panic spikes my heart rate. *How did the conversation get here?*

"I know what's really happening. Don't deny it, I have pictures." Turning around, he slams his hands against the counter, his loud *uhhh* echoing in the otherwise quiet shop. He's never yelled at me before, not in anger.

"Calm down. Please. What pictures are you talking about?" This isn't the Zach I know and love. This is a version tainted by his addiction

"You'd rather forget about me and spend time with Luc." He spits out the last word like a bad taste in his mouth.

"What?"

To prove his point, he grabs his phone, swiping the screen to show me. An image of me and Luc pops up, a freeze frame with me staring up at him, my finger on his chest. His tongue juts out, licking the corner of his lip. Portia stands just out of the frame, waiting to hear Luc's answer to my demanding question, *are you the Rougarou?* But to anyone looking at the photo— *like Zach*— it appears to be something entirely different.

"Where did you get this?" My interaction with Luc happened *maybe* ten minutes ago. The turnaround from the front of the theater to lighting up Zach's phone seems suspiciously fast.

"It doesn't matter."

"It does, because someone is stirring up trouble. How could you even believe I'd betray you like that?" I grab the phone from his hand. He lets me, not putting up a fight. With a few screen swipes, I realize someone texted Zach the photo. One of his best friends. Portia's ex-boyfriend. "Devin?"

He reaches for the phone, yanking it back, stuffing it in his pocket. "He's looking out for me. When he sees my girl-friend with someone else, he sends the proof."

Except the "proof" blatantly misrepresents the situa-tion. "I know it sounds cliché, but that snapshot isn't what it looks like. At all."

"Then tell me what happened." His tone softens, and his eyes plead, shifting from dark navy to cerulean blue. Glimmers of *my* Zach, the loving boyfriend with a gentle nature, overrides the shadows brought on by black magic.

"Portia went out with Luc, and I joined as a tag-along." We stand close enough that if either of us lifted a hand, we would touch. But we both stay still, holding our unspoken truce. "He said I'd been marked by the Rougarou, which is a whole other thing, and he took me to this witch doctor, Baba Geaux—"

"No, CeCe. No, no, no, no! Stay away from him, and from all the mystics at Jackson Square." He jams his hands in his pockets, his movements unsettled.

"You know him?"

"Remember I told you that when I escaped the black magic crowd, they made it clear I was a traitor?" He waits for my response, and I nod. "That's the crowd. The mystics of Jackson Square. Especially Baba Geaux. They all use deep black magic and manipulate the natural balance of things. So, yeah. Don't get anywhere near them."

"I'll stay away." I felt Baba Geaux start a spell, the slick power swirling around me, and I have zero desire to go back. "But I still don't understand how Devin got that picture. Is he following Portia? Maybe he's not over her."

"He's definitely not over her, but that's not it." Zach closes his eyes, tipping his head back. His butt rests against the counter and he curls his fingers around the edge. "I haven't had the chance to tell you."

"Tell me...?" There cannot be any more revelations. My breaking-news meter maxed out at least an hour ago.

With a resigned sigh, he meets my gaze. "Devin got the picture from his new girlfriend. Julie Jolley."

Devin, a guy who has misleading snapshots of the whole picture. A corner of my secret identity, a few pixels of my magic, and just enough of the truth to be dangerous.

That guy is Julie Jolley's new boyfriend.

Of course.

CHAPTER THIRTEEN

BLACK WREN VOODOO: THE BRACELET

Breathe in, breathe out. I take a moment to ground myself. First the incense, then the choking sadness, followed by Zach's jealousy, and now the idea of Devin and Julie dating. I might never inhale easily again.

Zach leans against the counter, gripping the edge and biting his lip, waiting for my reaction. The toes of his red Nikes tap the gray tiled floor. "I'm sorry I yelled at you. Are you okay?"

"Do you trust Devin with our secrets? Will he tell Julie?" Not everyone is aware of magic or understands what happens in the shadows of New Orleans. Even less know about me. But every day that number seems to grow, now adding Luc, The Hijackers, Baba Geaux, and Simone to the list. I miss the days when three people knew about my necromancy: me, my dad, and Portia.

"Devin won't say anything. He may act like an idiot, but he's solid." Zach releases the counter, standing up straight.

"He *is* an idiot," I agree, and Zach smiles.

It starts small, his lips tipping up, which makes me return the smile. Then his deepens, exposing his dimpled perfection, and my pulse races. *What impressive face dents you have!* My fingertips tingle, wanting to reach out and weave in his hair, to pull his mouth to mine. How long has it been since we've kissed? A thousand years? A million?

Ugh. I really like kissing him.

"Zach," I sigh, wanting nothing more than to cuddle up. But between his oily touch and his mood flip-flopping like a soap opera plot line, I keep my distance. "Please talk to your mom. Or Aunt Lucy. Let them help you get better."

"I hate this." The smile vanishes from his mouth, and he slides to the ground, elbows on his knees, hands covering his head. "You're right. It's in me again, and all I want is to chase the feeling."

Though I'm relieved he admitted it, a punch of guilt jabs hard. A painful blow twisting at the reminder that this is my fault. He spoke the truth when he said I begged him to use black magic. Rivera had created a nearly unbreakable supernatural connection between us, and I pleaded with Zach to save me.

Which he did.

"I'm so sorry," I whisper, a hard ball of regret bowling my insides. "But it's gonna be okay. You've conquered it before, and you'll do it again."

He nods, staring at the floor, his shoulders slumped. "I love you, CeCe. But I do need some space. When you're near me, I get confused. This...need to protect you consumes me." He lifts his face, meeting my gaze, and his expression changes. Eyes narrowing. Jaw tightening. "I can do it with the right spells."

"No more black magic. We'll find another way." My heart breaks watching the war he fights with himself. I want to go back in time, just a few days, when we sat on my couch and snuggled, that calm moment before this storm of chaos drenched us.

"It's just that black magic is so much more potent. More powerful. Without it, we're going into battle with water guns, and the other side has tanks." His voice grows louder, and he taps his toes, his legs getting jittery. "We have no chance without matching their firepower."

I recognize his building frustration and speak calmly. "We're not in a magical shootout, and the only battle you need to worry about is your own. You can beat this."

He stares at me. I stare at him. Silence stretches like skinny jeans, the uncomfortable, wriggling kind. Music filters from outside, barely audible in the store, a jazzy trumpet going for the high note. A building accompaniment to our weighted standoff.

Dropping his gaze, he pulls the phone from his pocket. The breath releases from my lungs in a relieved sigh.

"Hey Aunt Lucy," he says into his cell, rubbing the back of his neck with his free hand. "I need help."

I give him space, browsing the shelves while he initiates the difficult conversation with his aunt. She walked him through his recovery the last time he fell into black magic, and it can't be easy for him to ask again.

Incense burns in a stoneware voodoo doll, smoke seeping from the eyes. It's cute, but the strong scent gives me a headache, sandalwood overpowering everything else. I pull my shirt over my nose as I look through the baskets next to the burner. Herbs for different remedies, blessed crystals to enhance the wearer's desires. Stones are sorted in small bins, each segment stuck with a miniature sign announcing the type and the properties it boosts. Things like, *Jade: for balance,* or *Citrine: for luck.*

I do a double take at the unique, reddish-orange stones filling a bin. I've seen those exact stones before on a bracelet, but not in person. From the dreamscape. On the wrist of the woman who said, "she's here," while I tried to escape the moon's spotlight.

Angling close, and pulling the shirt from off my nose, I read the sign. *Red carnelian: for ambition.*

Ambition?

Scooping a handful, I roll them in my hand, the cool rocks heating from my touch. The variegated color shifts in the light, the specks and stripes of each stone different. There's a milkiness to it, more translucent than transparent, and I rub my thumb over the smooth surface.

I get lost in the colors, studying each one, unaware Zach hung up the phone until his voice sounds behind me.

"Red carnelian is a bold energy stone."

"What does that mean?" I turn, resisting the urge to tell him about the braceleted Hijacker. No need to stir up more trouble.

He takes a fiery rock from my hand, his fingers lingering against my palm. "It has a stronger natural power than most, meant to boost confidence and motivation." He points to the miniature sign. "Ambition."

"Could your mom make a piece of jewelry out of these? Like a necklace or a bracelet?" I close my fist, holding them tight. It might be my imagination, but I feel a slight hum emanating from my grip.

"Of course she can. Do you want her to put something together for you?" He holds the stone up, the light catching like glowing embers.

"Maybe?" I drop my rocks back into the basket, wondering if I want to twin with one of the Hijackers, reverse friendship bracelet style. Wrathful wrist décor? "How did it go with Aunt Lucy?"

A low groan leaves his mouth. "That was rough, but she's on her way here."

"You're lucky to have her."

"Yeah." His eyes close briefly, scrunching at the corners, and he takes two steps back. "This is hard to say, but I can't see you for a few days. At least until I get this under control."

As much as I want to wrap him in a hug, my arms stay put. "I know."

"I want to talk to you, though. Every day. Promise me that we will." His eyes take me in, from head to toe, an almost painful examination. "I need to know that you're safe. With the person trying to track you down and what happened in the morgue...you know how to build a stronger protective circle, right? Use graveyard soil with the salt."

"I know." Emotion tightens my throat, clenching in an agonizing grip, and I clear it. The truth is, I do love Zach. Watching him struggle rips a piece of my heart away, leaving a hollow, desolate space where only he fits. "And we'll talk every day. I promise."

"Last time was bad." He gives a small shudder. "Luckily, it won't be as hard this time since I'm not in as deep. But I need to be ready for music rehearsal next week."

"Forget the play and focus on your recovery."

"No, I need something to look forward to."

I want to sweep his concerns away. To walk away from *Voodoo Bayou* and live in our ZeCe bubble. "Just...take it one day at a time."

"I will." He reaches out, the red carnelian in his palm. "Take this. It's always a good time for bold energy."

"Thank you." My fingers lightly graze his skin as I pick up the stone, our magic humming at the touch. "I'll call you tonight. I want to hear how it goes with Aunt Lucy."

He nods, and with nothing else to do but longingly stare at him, I head for the door.

I leave Black Wren Voodoo heavy-hearted. Space is the right thing, I know it. Zach knows it. But my chest aches. An actual, physical pain that leaves me wanting to curl in my bed, headphones in and music blaring to avoid anything outside the four corners of my mattress.

With no desire to browse the various shops or sit in the simmering soup bowl of direct sunlight, I head to Le Petit. Since I'm a glutton for punishment, on the short walk, I pull out my phone. *MM(19)* here we go.

An immediate, *I'm sorry, the person you are trying to reach has a voicemail box that has not been set up yet...* answers, and I jam the red button to disconnect.

My emotions dance at the surface like an annoying mosquito skimming a stagnant pond. Anger, frustration, and hurt all stopping points on the path. Plus, the Julie Jolley problem.

Ugh!

Since we met in sixth grade, her life goal has been to tease, belittle, and bully me. In the beginning, I thought she wanted to be friends; she invited me to her birthday party. But after pin the insult on CeCe, followed by a game of "salon," which ended with me holding a handful of my hacked hair, I was disabused of the friendship notion. She's actually the reason my hair is pink now. When I got home, sobbing over my "new style," Mawmaw took my hand and told me to choose a color, any shade I wanted. Then she drove me to a real salon where I got a trendy haircut, dyed pink. Mawmaw made it not just okay, but amazing. Julie's hair practically turned green with jealousy when I showed up at school the next day.

Thus the rivalry rose from the scattered strands of my severed hair.

Julie Jolley absolutely cannot learn my secrets.

The loud, squeaky door of Le Petit Theater creaks as I pull it. Blinking my eyes, I walk through the foyer, opening the second set of doors leading into the auditorium. A few cast members sit in chairs set up on the stage. All of them hold scripts, and the show director talks with a loud voice, her hands flying to enunciate her words.

A guy with thick, Clark Kent glasses stands from the front row and meets me halfway down the aisle. "This is a closed rehearsal. You need to leave."

"She's with us." Aubree Bloom, the drummer for *Voodoo Bayou*, manifests next to Clark Kent, a wide smile on her face.

The man raises his eyebrows, looking me over. "You're in the band?"

"We said she's with us." A head pops up from behind Aubree. Lovelie Delva, the double bass player. "So, yeah, in the band."

"It's true," I confirm. "Guitarist."

The man nods, and Aubree turns, leading me to where she and Lovelie were sitting. The two could not be more different. Aubree's wavy blond hair, pink cargo pants, and Barbie-esque quality to Lovelie's Bantu knots, ripped jeans, and rock star vibe. I end up between them, Barbie on my left and rock star on my right.

Both wear light jackets (a glittery bomber vs. camou-flage denim), and it only takes thirty seconds to understand why. The air conditioning blasts, the temperature set some-where near arctic. After walking around outside, sweating buckets, the polar ice cap chills me in no time, and I wrap my arms around myself.

Aubree nudges me with her shoulder. "Are you here to watch Beau? That's what we came for."

Beau. Luc's character in *Voodoo Bayou. Do they know anything about him? Have any inkling of his potential werewolf tendencies?* "No, I came with Portia. She plays Kate."

"That's right. Your best friend," Lovelie says.

My initial surprise fades as I remember passing her a note when we met, writing that, "my best friend" would share the stage with Luc.

"Mercy me! Could you imagine landing the role as his co-star? I'd melt into a gooey puddle." Aubree sinks lower into her chair, emitting a dreamy sigh.

Melting sounds pretty good at this point, considering the goosebumps covering my flesh. Maybe I should have stayed out in the soup bowl of direct sunlight.

"Does he have a girlfriend?" Lovelie asks, never taking her eyes from the stage. But since Aubree turns to me with an expectant look, I assume she means for me to answer.

"I don't really know him." Truth. But also omitted truth. How do I say my best friend *might* be dating him in the near future if no major supernatural red flags get in the way? "Y'all came just to watch him?"

"You've noticed how hot he is, haven't you? Even Satan sweats looking at him." Aubree twists a section of hair around her fingers, winding it in a spiral.

I grunt, a non-committal sound that could be interpreted as an agreement. Or disagreement. Or an impersonation of my dad, the king of grunting.

"You're with Zach, the piano player, right?" Lovelie pulls at the loose threads fringing the open knees of her pants.

"Oh yeah, he's hot too." Aubree fans her face, and I wonder if her brain only thinks in terms of attractive guys.

"He's my boyfriend," I confirm.

"Lucky." Aubree turns back to the stage, and something peeks from her jacket sleeve, something I might not have noticed if I hadn't just been holding a cluster of them in my hands. Unique, fiery orange beads circle her wrist, the dim theater lighting unable to hide the bright color.

Aubree Bloom wears a red carnelian bracelet.

I slip my hand in my pocket, rubbing the smooth surface of the rock Zach gave to me, wondering why Aubree has a seemingly identical bracelet to one of The Hijackers.

Coincidence? The way my day is going, I'd bet all the beignets in the world the answer is no.

CHAPTER FOURTEEN

PORTIA'S CAR: THE CONVERSATION

The show must go on. And so must show practice, even through the new and curious revelation about Aubree Bloom's jewelry choices. I steal furtive glances at her, wondering about her bracelet, where she got it, if she always wears it, if she spends her evenings joining with others to chant around a fire. *Maybe I should ask?* About the bracelet, not the chanting.

But what do I really know about her? Nothing aside from her penchant for pink and a talent for drumming. And the fact that she could maybe, possibly be one of The Hijackers.

Dad's voice whispers in my head, *you're jumping to conclusions*. He'd tell me that assuming her guilt over one piece of circumstantial evidence invites missteps and mistakes. Especially since shops all over the French Quarter sell crystals and stones. Zach even said his mom could make a piece from the red carnelian.

So, WWDDD, What Would Detective Dad Do?

Establish what I know. Gather more evidence.

Closing my eyes, I picture the dreamscape. The Hijackers gathered around a fire, their wooden masks concealing their faces. I took stock of each one, searched for hints about identity. *She's here,* a female voice announced, the one who wore the glowing red carnelian.

I pause that moment in my brain, search the recesses of my memory for what I saw. Female, age unknown. Hair color...blond? The fire front lit everyone, the masks alive in the dancing flames, leaving everything else in shadow. Her build resembled Aubree's, I think, with a petite frame and slender fingers. Her voice, maybe a deeper timbre than Aubree's, though she only uttered two syllables.

Basically, I know nothing.

Which leads to gathering more evidence.

If she chanted with The Hijackers to find me, she probably has magic. If she has magic, she can't hide it if I touch her, skin-to-skin.

Cue Operation Initiate-Physical-Contact-with-Aubree. Or Operation IPCwA.

The plan might prove challenging. With her hair down, long-sleeved bomber jacket, and cargo pants (come on, it's *summer*), I strategize how to accomplish skin-to-skin contact. A fake stumble where I grab onto her forehead to avoid a fall seems unrealistic. Maybe just a handshake.

Practice passes in a blur. Once Luc starts reading lines, my seatmates go silent, aside from a few hushed comments about his (fill in the blank): looks, voice, shoulders — which I almost mention are named Thor and God of Thunder, but decide to keep that between me, myself, and I.

Portia shines on stage. Even without blocking, only clutching a script and reading her part, the words flow in a beautiful swirl of expression. Somehow, she makes Kate step right off the page. A true embodiment of the character, brought to life.

"The wind's gone still," Kate/Portia murmurs. "Like the whole bayou's holding its breath, waiting for whatever comes next."

Yeah, me too, Bayou.

But I'm not here to obsess over Portia's stellar performance skills.

Here goes Operation IPCwA. "Aubree, I love your bracelet," I whisper. "Where'd you get it?"

"It's one of a kind. My dad got it for me. Cute, right?" Her jacket sleeve slips a couple of inches to show off the red carnelian.

I swallow down my nerves, and take her hand, pulling it towards me, pretending to get a closer look. "Super cute."

No vibration at all. Not even a hum. Aubree Bloom doesn't have magic. *Huh.* I expected that to go differently.

The possibility of black magic stirs in my brain. No one is born with black magic, it's corrupted, and something learned. Practiced. Hence, no inherent vibration. If someone has no natural magic, there's no hum of power that subtly changes to an oily residue. Like what I felt in Zach. Instead, you feel nothing.

Could she be using? Or maybe I just want Aubree to be guilty since she declared Zach as "hot."

The bracelet rattles as she pulls back, and the hue shifts to a paler orange under house lights. *Is it even the same one I saw in the dreamscape?* The stones might be rounder than I remember. More evenly cut. Or maybe the firelight and shadows skewed their shape and color.

Maybe I know less than nothing. The director excuses everyone with, "Six days to be memorized. Get out of here and get working."

We get up from our seats, and I watch Portia and Luc make their way to me.

"Hey girl, how'd I do?" Portia glows from the effect of being in her element. The stage is her natural habitat, where she flourishes in the spotlight and forages for applause.

"You are incredible." I throw my arms around her, squeezing with every ounce of *you-are-capable-and-beautiful-and-talented-and-the best-of-besties* I can harness.

She laughs. "All I did was read from the script while sitting in a chair."

"And even the chair was entertained."

During our ten second conversation, Lovelie and Aubree maneuvered closer to Luc. He tucks his hands in his pockets, all charming grin and dreamy eyes, and my bandmates eat it up. Several people pass by us, other cast members heading out, and we scoot to the edge of the aisle in a single file stretch with me in the back, unable to see much around my taller bestie, and Luc as the bookend on the other side. I rise on my tippy toes and lean to listen in.

"Let's grab some food and chat." Aubree scoots extra close to Luc as another person passes by. "With all the time we'll be in rehearsals together, we might as well get to know each other."

"I could eat," Lovelie pipes in.

"Maybe another time, honey. 'Scuse me." Luc moves around them to collect Portia, grabbing her hand. "You ready?"

"Yeah, we should head out," Portia says, barely acknowledging Lovelie and Aubree. "Wait! My script!"

Portia pulls Luc along, back to the stage, and I wonder, *what would their ship name be?* Lortia? Puc? No good options there. Pretty much a lateral move from her previous Porvin.

"Are you coming to all the practices? Or just waiting for music rehearsal next week?" Aubree takes off her jacket, preparing for the heat wave outside the door.

"Um, I'm not sure." It takes actual effort to keep my gaze off her bracelet. There's something about it that makes my eyes want to stare. *One of a kind.*

"Then maybe we'll see you around." Aubree waves, the red stones glinting.

Lovelie holds out her hand to me. So I reach to shake, why not? Apparently we're extra civilized.

She brushes off my bumbling gesture and scoffs. "What are we, politicians up for reelection? Here."

Between her fingers is a folded piece of paper. A note. I take it.

"Thanks?"

"Bye." With that, she and Aubree make their way out, leaving me to wonder WWDDD next?

"Were you going for the role of awkward girl approaching the cool kids?" Portia giggles. "If so, well done."

"Ugh. Let's just go."

So, no magic for Aubree. A red herring on the bracelet. A wasted hour where I sat in the theater and cast her as the villain.

I unfold the note from Lovelie and read.

FYI. Aubree is super jealous of you.

"Of course, Aubree's jealous." Portia looks over my shoulder. "Who wouldn't be? You're adorable. Your boyfriend is adorable. And you have an amazing best friend."

"All true. But why would Lovelie tell me this? Don't you think it's weird?"

"Of all the things that happened today, on a scale of one to weird, this barely hits a two." She nudges me forward and gets us moving.

I laugh. "You're right."

The three of us head to the car and Portia explains we're giving Luc a ride home since he's staying with a cousin in the French Quarter. The sweltering outdoors relieves my freezing body from the ice box theater, but in no time the temperature shift makes me long for air conditioning.

I pull Portia's keys from my bag and toss them to her as her red Fiat comes into view. It seems to shrink the closer we get, and I watch Luc's gaze bounce on the nearby cars, looking hopeful at the other, much larger vehicles, but somehow knowing the tiny tin can belongs to Portia. At the telltale click of locks disengaging and flashing taillights, he winces.

Tall boys + micro machine = uncomfortable drive.

He folds himself into the Fiat, his height and shoulders too much body for the small space. His head hits the roof as he adjusts; his shoulder bumps the window.

"Do you want the front seat?" I ask him.

"It's fine," he says, his knees closer to his chin than the floor.

Portia bites her lip to keep from laughing. "I should have warned you I have a small car."

"I noticed," he mutters as he wrestles with the seatbelt, stretching it to capacity before clipping it in.

He gives Portia his address, and she starts the car. Warm air blasts from the vents, not quite cold yet, and it circulates the heat.

"So..." I clear my throat, jumping into the conversation

we left hanging. Back to Detective Dad's next steps of gathering information. "Tell me about the Rougarou."

Instead of dragging his feet or pretending he forgot about it, he takes the dive with me. "I wasn't completely honest when I said I was huntin' the Rougarou. What I'm really huntin' is the Hijacker." He rests his forearms on his knees, his body leaning forward. "The curse stays with a bloodline, and it passes to a different member of the family twice a year. We call it the Rougarou lottery."

"But someone outside the family stole it." I prompt him. "Stole it from *your* family. Right?" I shift in my seat, sitting sideways to keep my eyes on him.

He pauses for a few seconds before speaking. "Yes. And I need to recover it as soon as I can." A deep sigh heaves from his lungs and he sits back, his head grazing the roof of the car. "The curse has followed my family for generations. We grow up learnin' what to do when it's our phase."

The leather steering wheel squeaks under Portia's tightened grip, but she stays quiet otherwise.

"And when it's your phase?" I ask.

"The goal is to stay invisible." His forehead scrunches and his eyes narrow. "I don't prey on kids and kill people."

"That's not what I meant." I backtrack, hoping to gain Luc's cooperation, needing to be on the same side. "What I want to understand is how it works."

"The curse strikes twice a year, first, on the summer solstice when wildlife and weather are at their wildest."

"Hurricane season." Portia glances at him through the rearview mirror.

"Exactly." His eyes darken, and for a moment, I see him. Not the charming guy he tries to pass as, but the animal behind the mask. "The second time is the winter solstice, the longest night of the year, and the longest moon presence."

"How do you know which family member draws the Rougarou lottery and phases?" I ask.

"I have one siblin', my sister Zula Mae. And there are aunts, uncles, and cousins galore. Any one of us can trigger the curse." He attempts to run his hand over his hair but hits the roof instead. "It's all about violence."

"What do you mean?" I ask. The car feels smaller with him in it, not just because of his size, but the way he occupies it.

"Any act of violence triggers the curse, whether you bump into someone, swat a bug, or even violence against yourself, like squeezin' a pimple." He smirks and I get the impression the pimple thing happened to him. "After the solstice, the first family member to commit an act of aggression becomes the Rougarou for one hundred and one days."

"Seriously? That's...well, not the weirdest thing I've ever heard, because my best friend is a necromancer. But still. Maybe a five." She flips her turn signal and the *click, click, click* echoes in the car. "You live in the bayou, right? So, what about fishing?"

He chuckles. "The fish gets stabbed by a sharp hook. So, off limits until after the Rougarou lottery."

"Basically—" I hold up my hand, getting back on topic. "Twice a year you, or one of your family members, becomes the Rougarou for one hundred and one days. But you don't kill anyone, you try to stay invisible, and most people don't know you really exist."

"Correct," he says.

I shake my head. "Then why is the stolen curse such a bad thing? Your family can be free."

Sadness radiates from his whole being, the weight of the world carried on Thor and God of Thunder. "I wish it worked that way. But it doesn't, and time isn't on my side."

"If hunting the Hijacker is such a big deal, why did you try out for *Voodoo Bayou?*" A note of hurt enters Portia's tone. Winning the lead role means everything to her, hours and hours of preparation poured into her audition and now learning the script.

"The Hijacker is connected to Le Petit. I need a reason to be there," he says. "Whoever it is, that's where they've been shiftin'."

Aubree Bloom.

The name pops in my head, and I picture her in all her glittery glory, from her blond hair down to the red carnelian bracelet. But if it's her, that means...

Black magic.

Could Aubree be the Rougarou? It's one thing to think of her as a Hijacker, chanting in the middle of the night to find me. But for bubbly Aubree to change into a giant werewolf and murder people in cold blood seems ludicrous.

"How do you know that's where they shift from?" I ask.

He rubs his chest, where the tattoo inks his skin. "The Loa, La Siréne, helped me. But even her powers are limited."

"The Loa don't help out of the goodness of their hearts." While my knowledge of them is limited, magic always has a cost. Universal truth.

"No. We made a bargain. I petitioned her, and she answered," Luc says. "She gave me the gift of sight and song. Music is her passion and, because of her sigil on my skin, it was easy to land the lead in *Voodoo Bayou.* Got me access to the theater."

"That's cheating. I worked hard to play Kate." Portia keeps her voice soft, her eyes on the road.

"What's your part of the bargain?" I ask.

"This curse thief, the Hijacker, has been superchargin' the moon. It's affectin' her realm. The tides are off, the waters are angry."

A supercharged moon. My blue fingers in the morgue. The blasting cold. The crush of excessive power. "I've felt it."

"I have to stop the Hijacker from blowin' up the natural order of things by gettin' the curse back. Hopefully that puts the moon to rights." His eyes dart to look out the window, his gaze lost.

"And if it doesn't fix it?" Portia chews on her bottom lip. The sense of foreboding fills the car, making it hard to sit still.

He turns back to us. "Failure's not an option."

We all know this is a risky bargain at best. But maybe I have a clue for Luc. A possible lead with Aubree and the bracelet she wears. Which would mean talking about the dreamscape and The Hijackers. Telling him the things I saw in the morgue with Mary Mosley. And does he know about the magical plane? That might require an explanation as well.

"This is the house?" Portia points to a Creole cottage just ahead.

"It is." Luc leans forward, inch by incremental inch, until his head hovers between Portia and me. The dark intensity returns, seeping into his gaze and posture. "Do you want to see why my family can never be free of the curse?"

"What do you mean?" My question comes out in a whisper.

"Come inside and see for yourselves."

CHAPTER FIFTEEN

LUC'S HOUSE: THE SISTER

Portia's red Fiat idles on the street a few yards away from the white Creole cottage that belongs to Luc's cousin. Green trim and shutters stand out against the bright exterior, and two dormer windows protrude from the roof. Several pedestrians shuffle by, the French Quarter always bustling.

"You want me to follow you inside?" I clarify. Because going into an almost stranger's house, especially a guy who moonlights as a werewolf, seems stupid.

"Yes." After his forthcoming info dump on the drive over, the weighted *come and see* feels ominous.

A healthy hesitation stalls me. Dad would chew steel and spit nails knowing I went into the house of a guy I just met, let alone the admitted Rougarou. But I need information, and sometimes collecting it comes with a little risk.

I turn to Portia and put my hand on her arm. "Stay here and—"

"No way, Amigo. If you're going, I'm going." She cuts me off before I get to the *if I don't come out in five minutes* bit.

"But we don't know what's in there," I whisper.

Luc laughs, the building tension broken by his amusement. "I save ritualistic killin's for the second visit."

"I save peeking through cabinets and drawers until the third." Portia opens her door and steps out, rejecting any further protests, but she bends to stick her head back in. "That's a lie. I'll definitely snoop if I have the chance."

"Good to know," he says, as we get out of the car.

Rather than enter from the street, Luc unlocks a side gate and leads us to a courtyard. Tan bricks pave the ground on a path to the back of the house where lush plants line the walkway. Caladium in different shades, lemon grass, and flowering passion vines crowd raised beds, and trees provide shade overhead. Water trickles from a tiered fountain, and a cozy bistro table with two chairs sits in the open space for a comfortable haven.

I take it all in, everything from the location (super desirable) to the private courtyard, (fancy, fancy) and I know the beaucoup bucks it must be worth. "This is your cousin's place?"

"Technically, it belongs to Uncle Jay, but he prefers livin' in the bayou." He pauses with his hand on the doorknob and his lips tighten. "Listen, my family wouldn't want me to show you what's goin' on."

I wait for him to say more, but the only sounds are his heavy breaths and the gurgling of the fountain.

"Your mysterious vibe can be super sexy, but right now it's not cool." Portia juts a hip, her shirt shifting to show a gap of skin. "I've got chauffeur duty tonight for Peter's baseball practice, so if you've got something to show us, let's make it quick."

"That's your brother, right?" Luc waits for her *mmm hmm*, and then asks. "How many siblin's you got?"

"Five. Peter, Presley, Piper, Penelope, who we call Penny, and baby Pace, who's actually four but will always be the baby."

"A handful." A deep line creases between his brows as he nods. "Then you understand family."

"I do." Her voice turns soft. Solemn.

"And you would do whatever it takes to protect them." Luc holds Portia's gaze. Not the dreamy lustful stares they often share but a real connection. An understanding of the responsibility they carry.

"I would."

The conversation holds a weighted tone lost on me. While I love my dad and would do anything for him, we only have each other, and a healthy avoidance on the topic of Mom. These deeply tangled roots, stretching from siblings to cousins, to aunts and uncles, tread new ground. An undeniable force keeping them planted together. Like a story in a book, or pictures on a page, it's something I see but haven't really experienced.

A pang of melancholy opens in my chest, and I blink back an unexpected sting in my eyes. Longing for those tangled roots swells inside me, a nostalgic panorama of unlived moments.

"I'm runnin' out of time, but I think y'all might be able to help." Luc slowly nudges the door open. "Just keep quiet. Loud noises bother her."

"Who?" I ask.

"My sister."

Darkness greets us as we enter, all the lights off, all the shutters closed, but I see the faint outline of cabinets, counters, and a table. Tall ceilings stretch overhead, and the open concept makes the space feel huge. But the whole place smells like sick, musty and thick. I unconsciously hold my breath until my lungs protest and then practice the art of quiet gasping to hide the fact that I fight for oxygen.

A soft glow emanates from the front of the house and my eyes adjust, focusing on that beacon. As we make our way toward the dim light, we walk past a wall with two huge, ornate frames. The thick, gold metalwork glints faintly, and I strain to make out the pictures inside.

Both paintings depict the same setting, a long wooden dock stretching across a shimmering lake surrounded by cypress trees. But in the first, a woman stands on the wooden planks, the sun shining down. She lifts her chin, as if enjoying the warmth bathing her face. In the second, the sun has changed to a moon, and a trail of light glints on the water. The woman is now a howling wolf, her muzzle tipped toward the sky.

Such an odd choice of décor. The pictures practically scream, "A werewolf lives here."

"Does your cousin ever have people over?" I ask.

"Verily's too busy with work to entertain."

"Your cousin's name is Verily?" Portia touches the frame of the second picture, the werewolf painting, running her finger along the golden edge.

"Yeah. You'll like her. She's got spunk, just like you." He stops and straightens his shoulders, taking a breath for fortitude. "My sister's name is Zula. I told you that she's sick."

Portia frowns and puts a hand on his arm. "That's tough."

"It is." He licks the corner of his lip. "Once a solstice, and only once, there's an opportunity. A sort of backdoor out of the curse. Let's say someone's travelin' or busy. A family member can take the curse from them and finish out the hundred and one days."

"How do they take it?" The more I learn about the Rougarou, the more complex it seems.

"Violence, of course." He offers a sad chuckle. "Usually it's a solid punch, right to the kisser. But not Zula."

He rubs the back of his neck, and tips his head, staring at the ceiling. "The person who stole the curse knew she was phasin'. It's like they were watchin' and waitin' for the moment. As soon as she changed, they attacked. Barely old enough to phase, and this is what happened to her."

"What did happen?" I ask, trying to follow his story, but not understanding.

"I don't exactly know. Me and my cousin Verily were there. Zula Mae fully phased, the Rougarou took over, and then this. We didn't know what was goin' on until it was too late. An invisible person with an invisible blade stabbed her. How do we fight against that? How is it even possible?"

Black magic. The answer comes to me in a flood, everything I know and experienced pouring through my mind.

"Zula was *stabbed?*" Portia gasps, covering her mouth. "That poor girl."

Luc stares at the framed picture. The non-werewolf print. "This is why my family can never be free. The curse can only be stolen while the person is in the Rougarou form. And if a person is injured while changed, they can only heal in the Rougarou form. Understand what I'm sayin'?"

Unfortunately, yes, I do. "Zula needs to transform into the Rougarou to heal."

"Things like this" —he pulls the cure from Baba Geaux out of his pocket— "are temporary fixes and only ease the pain for a short time. I have until the autumn equinox to find the thief and get the curse back to Zula. If she lasts that long." He whispers the last words under his breath.

"If the curse can only be taken once a solstice, how do we get it back to Zula?" I ask.

He leans against the wall, like he needs the extra support "That's the catch. Only the original person to phase can reclaim it. And only in the same way it was taken."

Portia tugs on her earring. "Zula has to stab the Rougarou?"

"Yes."

A weak cough comes from the other room, and Luc straightens. "C'mon."

All the windows are shuttered, and a floor lamp softly glows. But I see a girl, presumably Luc's sister, laying on the couch with a heavy blanket tucked around her. A pillow supports her head and pieces of her black, curly hair wetly cling to her cheeks.

Luc steps closer, grimacing as he puts the back of his hand to her forehead. Dropping his chin, he blows out a deep breath and stares at the floor before visibly gathering his composure.

"Hey Zula Mae, I'm back." The gentle tone of his voice matches his touch. "I brought some friends with me, they're here to help."

A gut-wrenching moan comes from Zula, the pain so apparent I flinch at the sound.

"I know it hurts. I'm sorry." He plucks the sticking strands from her cheeks, brushing them from her face.

We all hover in front of the gray leather sofa, looking down at his sister. It feels intrusive, watching her in agony, unable to do anything but stare.

He folds down Zula's blanket and a horrible odor

escapes, a rotting ammonia-like scent that I associate with the dead.

Zula has on purple polka-dot pajamas, the bottom few buttons of the shirt undone, similar to how Portia wears her top. But this one exposes a bandaged area on Zula's stomach, just below the ribcage.

Luc and Portia lock gazes, and that loaded family understanding passes between them.

"Did you get it?" Zula shifts, raising up only an inch before she falls back to her pillow.

"I did. Baba Geaux promised this one should last a few days at least." Luc crouches next to her and peels off a gauzy pad, throwing it in the nearby garbage can. A two-inch long gash puckers her skin. It seeps with infection, a thick, yellow puss oozing from the site. The whole area swells, an angry skin volcano ready to burst.

"Oh, you poor thing." Portia drops to her knees, nudging me back as she takes Zula's hand.

Standing outside the circle of care, I observe from a few feet away, which might as well be a few miles. I don't know how Portia does it, stepping in and asserting herself. They don't even know each other, and Portia dabs Zula's brow, murmuring soft reassurances while Luc puts the new cure over her wound.

"Who are you?" The question wheezes from Zula, each word a pained breath.

"I'm Portia, Luc's future girlfriend."

"You're"—she pauses to cough, and groans at the effort—"from the future?"

"Nah." She laughs. "I just know where things are headed." She dabs Zula's brow. "So, how old are you?"

"Thirteen." Her closed eyes scrunch in pain, and sweat glistens on her upper lip.

"My sister's thirteen too. Presley is super dramatic and always getting in trouble. Last week she turned up all the radios in all the cars, so when we left, our ears got blasted."

The tiniest smile lights Zula's expression. Luc's lip edges up as he watches the exchange. It's such a tender moment, shared between the three of them, that I feel like a worthless NPC in a video game. Maybe that's why I indelicately insert myself into the conversation.

"I know how it can happen. The invisible person with the invisible knife."

"What? Just a second..." Luc holds up a finger and puts a new gauze pad over Zula's wound, then pulls up the blanket. "Let's talk in the kitchen."

"We're gonna help you. Okay Zula?" Portia softly tousles her hair.

He takes us to the room where we entered from the courtyard and flips a switch. The under-cabinet lighting gives off a soft, yellow glow. Dark granite countertops complement the pale wood of the cabinets, and a wide, bronze range hood stretches all the way to the tall ceiling. A stone arch leads to a recessed space with a glass door reading, *pantry*. I can't even find the fridge, probably hidden behind one of the massive wood panels.

Everything poshly proclaims *money, money, money*. "What does your uncle do?" I ask.

"Fishin', mostly."

Portia and I sit at the dining table, waiting as Luc washes his hands. I lift my eyebrow at her, an unspoken, *are you okay?* Not only did she admit to feeling excluded because of her lack of magic but finding out your crush doubles as a werewolf kind of sucks. She responds with a shrug, a *what can you do* expression on her face, proving once again that my bestie is too good for this world.

Luc pulls out a chair, swinging it around so he straddles the back, and folds his arms on the top. He nods at me, my signal to start.

"A couple of months ago, there was a murderer who killed from the comfort of his casting room."

"He used voodoo dolls to kill people and steal their organs," Portia says

"Voodoo dolls?" Luc tips his head. "Zula was stabbed."

"Right, but it could be any weapon infused with black magic. Voodoo dolls or a knife. Or a ham sandwich." It's been hours since Café Du Monde, and I'm starving. I'm also jumping too far ahead into the explanation, and I start at the beginning. "Do you know about the magical plane?"

"I'm not sure," he says.

And so begins my simplistic explanation of the space that has no simple explanation. "The physical plane is the base level, what you see, smell, taste. All the major senses, right? But beyond that, there's another plane; somewhere you can't access with your physical body. It's where magic exists. And some spells can connect these two planes. Still with me?"

"Like with the Voodoo Loa?" Luc asks.

I don't know about that, and I tell him, "I don't know about that."

His voice goes soft, a serious tone underlying his words. "La Siréne took me while I slept to work out the terms of our arrangement. My body never left my bed, but I was there. In her underwater kingdom."

"Yes. That sounds like the magical plane." I pause to gather my scattered thoughts. "When these two planes cross, they can interact with each other. Especially with black magic."

"Black magic." Luc taps his lips, his eyes narrowed in thought. "Like what I saw in your boyfriend?"

"It's not the same thing at all," Portia jumps to Zach's defense. "He used it to save CeCe's life a couple of months ago. It just takes time for it to run its course."

"If you say so." He needs no sarcastic eye-roll to convey his skepticism.

Hearing the words from Portia, the explanation sounds ridiculous. A wave of regret hits me, *how could I have been so stupid not to see it?* I hate to address it here, in front of Luc, but Portia deserves the truth. Both as Zach's defender and as my best friend. "There's something you should know. Something I just found out." Without warning or permission, tears well up, blurring my vision. "Zach started using again."

"What?" she whispers. Her chair screeches on the floor as she scoots closer to me, and she rubs my back in small, soothing circles. "I'm so sorry. Are we mad at him? Do we hate him?" She interrupts her own questions with a gasp. "That's why you had a fight. It was about black magic."

I jerk my head up and down, my voice still held ransom by my emotions.

"I saw the darkness in him. Is he one of these Hijackers?" While his face remains calm, a tangible anger hides behind the mask.

"No," Portia and I say at the same time.

"He would never hurt anyone," I clear my throat and swipe away any evidence of tears. "Zach used black magic to protect me from the Hijackers and *they're* the ones who stole the Rougarou curse."

He nods. "How do we find them?" A hush passes over him, the depths of his eyes swallowing the little light in the room. The hairs on the back of my neck stand at attention, and I remind myself I'm not his target.

"You said they have access to Le Petit Theater?" I wait for his confirmation and continue. "There might be a connection with Aubree Bloom. The drummer for *Voodoo Bayou.*"

"The flirty blond?" Portia lifts a doubtful eyebrow.

My phone vibrates, startling me, and I tear my gaze away from her. But I realize it's not just my phone. All three of us check the buzzing notification.

> Public Safety Alert: The mayor of New Orleans has issued a mandatory curfew from 9 pm to 6 am for all Districts north of the Mississippi. Violations may result in arrest.

I tip my head back and stare at the ceiling. This cannot be good.

CHAPTER FIFTEEN POINT FIVE

LETTERS FROM ZACH

CeCe,

Seeing you was hard. Amazing and hard. I love you, and desperately want to be the person you think I am. The perfect boyfriend. The good guy. But what if, deep down, I'm not strong enough? What if black magic makes me that guy? The one who can be your rock. The one who can protect you.

Please, please understand I'm trying to beat this. And I will. After you're safe. Later, when there aren't so many...obstacles. All this danger. It makes me crazy thinking about it, everything inside me screams, and I'm trapped here with Lucy telling me to "take a lap" and so I pace around and around the circle in the casting room when all I need is to gather a few things and perform the protection spell. But she's always watching, and I can't get away. And I keep hearing Constance's voice warning me that you're in danger. What if something happens to you while I'm stuck here?

If you ever read this, I know you'll be pissed that I took more of your hair. But the loose strands were right there as I tucked them behind your ear. I also scoured the floor after you left, crawling around to see if I could find more. If you were here, and not pissed, you'd probably laugh and tease me about some tourist from Poughkeepsie getting an unexpected dose of magic.

AHHH! My heart hurts. It's not just you I miss. I miss us. Like together, we're the person I can't live without.

I love you,
Zach

CHAPTER SIXTEEN

MY HOUSE: THE SILENCE

Portia dropped me off in a hurry, hustling to get her brother, Peter to baseball. I'm also in a hurry, hustling to my room to call Zach.

Hopefully things went well with Lucy, he owes me an update. And if he has a spare decade, I'll tell him about my day.

Even though Dad's not home, I close my door as I debate FaceTime or audio. After a quick glance in the mirror, *hello sun-baked CeCe,* I go with audio.

"Hey beautiful girlfriend," he says. Happy fireworks spark in my chest, the earlier tension melted by the sound of his voice.

"Hey cute boyfriend."

We both start talking at the same time and I laugh. "Sorry. You go first."

"CeCe...I love you." A heaviness weighs down the declaration, the sorrow intense. "I really do. But once we hang up, I can't talk to you for a while."

"Zach." Hours ago, I told him we needed some distance. Not speaking is a whole other level. "You said we'd call each other every day."

"I know, but Lucy told me no phone. No visits. No contact." He shuffles around, and I imagine him running his fingers through his hair. "I'm gonna kick it. This time for good."

"Yes, you will. I believe in you." Pausing to get control of my clenched vocal cords, I swallow my sadness. There'll be plenty of time for that later. "I'll be here. Ready for the ZeCe reunion tour."

A soft chuckle. "Do you still love me? I need to hear you say it."

"I do love you." A physical ache caves in my chest. "You are the only leading man for me."

A huge, relieved sigh echoes on his end. "Aunt Lucy wants to chat for a minute. I'll put her on."

The phone rumbles; then Aunt Lucy. "Hi sweetie. Thanks for encouraging Zach to reach out. How are you doing?"

"I'm..." My usual sarcasm fails me, my well of humor empty. "I'm really sad."

"Yeah, me too," she says. "The situation is rough, but we'll get through it."

"I know."

She lightly clucks her tongue, like she's thinking through her next words. "So...Zach has some work to do. While using black magic, he didn't even realize the sacrifice he offered. While his life magic is strong and untouched, he fed the spells pieces of his voodoo. The imbalance has done damage. I'm not sure how much."

"No." My stomach rolls. I feel sick. "Can he get it back?"

"I don't know. But now he needs to isolate. He has to build a new magical plane, one that isn't corrupted."

Easier said than done. Creating a space of peace and protection, where your magic thrives requires time and focus. I understand it better now more than ever. "You'll be there with him, though. To help him through it?"

"Yes, I promise," she says. "Don't be a stranger. Come see me at Black Wren."

"I will. There are a million things I need to learn about." Voodoo, Life magic, Rougarou curses, carnelian bracelets, just to name a few.

"The casting room is open for you. Anytime."

"Thanks, Lucy." I hang up the phone and immediately burst into tears, allowing myself a good cry before taking a Rougarou mark removal bath.

Where I also cry.

FROM THE JOURNAL OF CECE LEBLANC:

Day one without Zach: This morning I crossed paths with Dad. His crazy schedule has him up early, and home late with barely a passing hello between. The FBI mandated the curfew. Just like he predicted, they stepped in, and now he works with two feds, Agent Broussard and Agent Woods.

I plied him with questions, trying to keep my foot in the investigation door. A door that got slammed in my face because Dad said, "This one's too dangerous, baby girl."

Ugh. Ten years of being the Watson to his Sherlock, and he shut me out for a little danger and a smidgen of trauma.

Portia's hectic schedule kept her busy, between family and play practice, she couldn't stop by. So, I utilized public transport and went to Black Wren, read at least four thousand books, and practiced for over an hour in the casting room.

Reminders of Zach were everywhere, and it was almost too painful to stay. The look on his face when I walked away yesterday haunts me. A hopeless stare, his whole body shrinking into itself. The only comfort I have is knowing Aunt Lucy is getting him the help he needs.

I miss him so much.

Attempting to step onto the magical plane: fail.

LETTERS FROM ZACH

CeCe,

Lucy won't back off. It's nag, nag, nag non-stop. I never should have called her. It was a big mistake. Every time I try to gather things to cast a protection spell, she asks what I'm doing. GIVE ME SOME SPACE, LUCY! Nag, nag, nag.

She basically kidnapped me, and I'm kept in a room in her house. Prison would give me more freedom. Between Lucy and Mom, I'm never alone.

I gotta get outta here.

The only comfort I have is knowing Mom saw you today at Black Wren. She said you look good. At least one of us is okay.

I worked on my new magical plane. Trying to build it felt like playing the piano while missing half my fingers. I didn't realize how much of my magic I'd sacrificed. The harmony of my voodoo is absent. I reached for the familiar notes and ended up with a bunch of dissonant chords.

Thinking of you keeps me going, though. Needing to create a quiet corner where no one can nag or kidnap or hunt us down. Just you and me together.

I miss you,

Zach

FROM THE JOURNAL OF CECE LEBLANC:

Day two without Zach: Something I learned today: whenever I use magic, I plug into the moon, not drawing energy from it, but acting as an amp and adding fuel. In necromancy, the moon token helps catch the excess, keeping balance and preventing lunar discord. Hypothetically, without the token, an overflow of power could boost the moon, affecting the tide, the amount of daylight, even gravity.

Heavy stuff.

Every magic, whatever the source, utilizes some sort of safety net to ensure universal equilibrium. All except the dreaded black magic, which uses sacrifice and pollutes the natural ebb and flow.

For the first time, after reading about the importance of balance, I felt a kinship to my mom, catching a glimpse of her why. One tiny piece of understanding into a person who continues to elude me.

I reached for my phone, wanting to call Zach, an instinct as natural as breathing. Then the pang hit. The perpetual pit in my stomach reminding me that I can't. The hours drag on and on as I worry about him. The pain of being without him constantly stabs in my heart.

Attempting to step onto the magical plane: fail.

LETTERS FROM ZACH

CeCe,

Guess what I'm doing?

Patching up the wall I punched a hole through last night. Not my proudest moment. I lost it. Everyone was on me, telling me what I should do, what I shouldn't. No room to breathe. No space to be. I kept shouting, "Let me live my life!" But if I'm honest, I don't even know what that looks like anymore. I used to think it was about us, the ZeCe team. But you abandoned me when I needed you most. Maybe I deserve it.

Maybe it's for the best.

Lucy had to draw the black magic out of me. Again. For the third time in two days. I did the same thing when you were flooded with black magic. Holding onto you while my life magic crowded out the darkness. If you don't remember, it HURTS. Like molten lava poured over your skin. Like your soul is peeled raw and stretched. That pain…it's almost unbearable.

Yesterday, building my magical plane felt like I was missing my fingers. Today it feels like I'm missing my arms. Lucy tried to reassure me that it's okay. Told me healing isn't a straight line. Whatever that means.

Anyway, wall's patched. My hand is sore. Heart's sorer. I'll keep trying.

Zach

FROM THE JOURNAL OF CECE LEBLANC:

Day three without Zach: I asked Portia to visit. I'm beginning to forget what interaction with my friends looks like. She laughed and told me she's watching Zula while Luc goes hunting.

Ah, Luc, the crush, the co-star, the cursed.

Another trip to Black Wren, and I placed a tippy toe in the reflective pool of my magical plane. Then, the clouds began to blacken, and I think I heard a voice. How is that even possible? It's my plane.

Lucy was there and I asked about Zach. My vocal cords nearly seized at the mention of his name. It's not just missing him but knowing the battle he fights without me by his side to help. When I started word-vomiting these thoughts to Lucy, she pulled me into a hug and emphasized how much he needs the space to heal. I maybe cried.

I definitely cried.

Attempting to step onto the magical plane: almost.

LETTERS FROM ZACH

CeCe,

I sat in front of the patched wall for a while, just staring, looking at the dry spackle that I'll paint over later today. It reminds me that damage doesn't have to be permanent. You can fix things if you're willing to put in the work.

Lucy and Mom have been quiet. I think they're giving me space to want this for myself. That's how it has to be, right? Not staying clean because someone's watching. Staying clean because I don't want to carry this poison around anymore. The black magic still carries a dull hum under my skin, but softer. Cleaner.

I thought about you. Ha! As if I ever stop. Have you been working on your magical plane? Pulling yourself there? My new plane is taking shape, building in staccato drumbeats, but I sense the harmonies. Feel the echoes of song at my fingertips. And every inch of it is stamped with you in mind.

Zach

FROM THE JOURNAL OF CECE LEBLANC:

Day four without Zach: I started a new series on Netflix, a weird show with mermaids who solve underwater mysteries. Considering it research on La Sirène possibly treads the thin line of ehhh. It involved a fish cartel who kill their victims with helium. Spoiler alert, the Coalition of Mer-People caught the king pin.

~~Is helium dangerous to La Sirène?~~

I need to leave the house.

Still no word from Zach. Not even a text.

HOW LONG WILL THIS TAKE? Yeah, I know it's only been four days, but in summer break time, that's like a decade. A long, lonely decade where I watch stupid shows on Netflix and miss my boyfriend.

Last night I dreamed about kissing him again. His lips on mine, no black magic between us. I woke up to a house so quiet, my breathing echoed against the walls.

Is he okay?

Attempting to step onto the magical plane: Called my cicadas. Multiple times. Silent.

LETTERS FROM ZACH

CeCe,

I did something today that probably doesn't seem like a big deal, but it was a huge step for me. Remember that bit of your hair I'd been holding onto for the protection spell? I flushed it. Gone. Just like that. My hands shook, my whole body shook, and for a second, I wondered if I'd made a terrible mistake.

But you're right. We'll find a way through this without black magic. The tourist in Poughkeepsie will continue forward, magic free.

I wish I could hear you laugh.

More improvements on my magical plane today.

It's slow, the kind of slow that tests my patience and my pride. But it's there. Things that came easily before now take all my effort. I used to create entire landscapes without even blinking. Now I break into a sweat trying to coax a blade or two of grass from the ground. It's frustrating. Humbling. And I understand better what Lucy means that healing isn't a straight line. It doesn't always look like growth. Sometimes it looks like struggle.

You're worth the struggle. We're worth it.

After this letter, I won't write anymore. I'm gonna put them away and wait until I feel ready to give them to you. Which isn't yet. Maybe never. But all my energy needs to focus on healing.

Zach

FROM THE JOURNAL OF CECE LEBLANC:

Day five without Zach: Portia is coming over tonight, a full hour before curfew. Finally. And she'll be sleeping over. I'm saved!

The *knock knock* propels me from my seat, and I throw open the front door. "Hey bestest best friend in the whole wide world. How was work?"

She laughs. "Long day?"

I sigh. "The longest."

"Sorry, girl. I had a long day too. I found the cutest top, a shirt with a boatneck and oversized sleeves. But I didn't hide it in the back, and someone else stole it right from under my nose." Working at *Swapped,* a trendy clothes consignment shop, affords her the ability to dress the way she does and continue in her fashionista lifestyle. "I almost cried when I rang it up at the register."

"The one that got away." I lead us into the kitchen and rummage through the pantry.

"I'll forever dream of puffed sleeves in a polyester blend." She catches the bag of Zapps Voodoo-Heat Potato Chips I toss and rips them open. "Luc came in to see me. He said it was to drop off my script that I accidentally-on-purpose left at his house, but I know the truth. He can't live without me."

"I can't live without you either, so I don't blame him."

Even knowing about the Rougarou, she still gets giddy when talking about Luc. Which is a lot. They've seen each other every day this week, outside of play practice too, and I'm not sure how to feel about it. On the one hand, she really likes him, and he seems to like her, win/win. But on the other hand, and by his own admission, he'll do anything to save his sister, and I worry the whole situation will end up hurting Portia.

"CeCe." She takes a deep breath, and I peek from the pantry to look at her. "Any word from Zach?"

I blink my eyes, keeping them closed a second longer than needed. "No."

A pinch forms between her eyebrows, there and gone just as quickly before she fills the role I need most.

A distraction.

"Then let's gorge on junk food and relax," she says.

With my arms full of snacks, I walk to my bedroom, Portia on my heels.

"What's with all the books?" She surveys my small

kingdom, which now contains stacks of tomes I borrowed from Aunt Lucy.

"Just a little light reading to pass the time." Dodging through the mess that is currently my room, I spread the snacks on my desk. "You want peanuts, licorice, or more chips?"

"Licorice." She swipes a red, chewy vine as she reads the titles on the book spines. "*Mystic Harmony, Voodoo Unveiled, Spirits of the Bayou.* Wait a second. *La Sirene: Queen of the Sea.* Have you read this one?"

"Not yet." Honestly, I picked it up on a whim. It's thin, more like a comic book, and filled with illustrations. I looked through the pictures, though. Very well done.

She sits on my bed and thumbs through, the pages whispering as she turns them. "Did you know La Siréne is an actual mermaid? That's crazy!"

Yeah, I watched the mermaid show on Netflix because of that. But do I admit it? Nope. "That is crazy."

I pick up a bag of Ragin' Cajun Peanuts and put a handful in my mouth. The only thing that tickles my taste-buds at night is the burning fires of pepper and cayenne. Or any of the spicy spices.

With the supercharged moon still a problem, every evening I feel the effects. This arctic blast feels different than necro-shivers. That cold emanates from inside, starting in my core, and traveling outward. This current wintry wonderland seeps into my bones, like an icy blanket draped over my shoulders.

The heat touches my tongue fast and quick. Then gone. I toss another handful into my mouth.

Portia gasps, not a little gasp, a shut-the-front-door-Gap's-canceling-their-summer-sale kind of gasp.

"What?" I sent my peanuts flying and now kneel on the floor to retrieve them.

"Luc..." she whispers his name and points a trembling finger in the book.

"Okay, okay. Something about Luc." I sit next to her on the bed.

"Seven years." She takes my hand in both of hers. "What was he thinking?"

"I need a little more information." Holding hands, easy. Interpreting the cause of her distress, improbable.

She stares into my eyes, her beautiful brown orbs glistening with a sheen of moisture. "Luc said he made a bargain with La Siréne, she marked him with her sigil."

"Yeah, he told us that."

"He didn't tell us what happens if he fails his end of the bargain." Dropping my hand, she stands to look out my window. Even though the blinds are closed. And it's night. "Seven years. He has to live with La Siréne in her underwater kingdom for seven years. He'll be an old man before he gets out."

I'd hardly call twenty-five an old man, but so much life happens in a span that long. "Then we have to make sure he doesn't fail."

She stays by the window, and we lapse into quiet, both lost in thought. Her buzzing phone breaks her away from her aimless stare.

"It's Luc." She swipes to answer. "Seven years? What were you thinking?"

I can't hear his end of the conversation, but I watch Portia soften, she nods her head. "For Zula, I know. But I don't even like fish."

As they talk, I flip through *La Siréne: Queen of the Sea* and check out the beautiful illustrations in cool shades.

Blues, greens, and a turquoise that reminds me of my sky oasis. I find the part that caused Portia such distress:

If the seeker fails to complete their end of the arrangement, they forfeit their life for seven years to serve La Siréne in her underwater kingdom.

Failure's not an option.

"CeCe, Luc has a new development." Portia sits next to me and puts the phone on speaker. "We're here."

"Hi ladies," Luc drawls in his syrupy voice. "I hate to jump right in, but the Rougarou killed again."

"Another murder? How do you know?" My dad, the detective coordinating with the feds on the case, hasn't said anything. And Luc got the inside scoop?

"My cousin Verily told me," he says. "Happened last night. From what I understand, it's another busker."

One of the mystics of Jackson Square. Baba Geaux told me they were being targeted. "You're sure it's the Rougarou who did it?"

He blows out a breath. "Positive. The condition of the body...you get the idea."

"Yeah." A chill travels down my spine, and I try not to think about Mary Mosley in the morgue. But an image of her scratched face and missing ear pop in my head anyway.

"Is Zula okay?" Of course, Portia remembers to ask about Luc's sister. "It's gotta be hard to hear about everything going on."

"She doesn't know. We haven't told her anythin' about the murders." The usual Luc charisma is missing, and he sounds tired. "CeCe, I need your help."

It's the first time he's used my actual name, no *honey* or other endearment. And for some reason, that triggers my desire to help, like we're finally in this together. "What can I do?"

"Can you do your necromancy thing and see their last moments? It might give us the advantage we really need."

"It doesn't work like that," Portia says. "She has to be in the room with the person, which she does in the morgue, and her dad's cut her from the investigation."

"I'll do it." Before I think of the logistics or the consequences, I put it out there. "I can take the entry card from my dad, but we'll need to act quickly before the body gets moved."

"You cannot be serious. You know I like a little mischief, but come on. There's curfew. And...and...the morgue." Portia steps in as the voice of reason, a role that fits her like an out-of-date trend. "There's your dad. What are you going to do? Ask him to pretty please let you borrow his access to a government building?"

"Seven years, Portia. We have to help," I say. "I'll borrow it. Without permission."

"Some people call that stealing." She tosses back.

"Listen, if you can't, it's okay." Luc sounds resigned, all his charm shriveled and dead.

"For Zula, it's worth the risk." I look at Portia as I say it.

She chews on her lip before giving me a nod. "Fine, I'm in. But if it all goes downhill, I get to say I told you so."

I hope I'm not making a huge mistake. "Luc, can you pick us up? 2:00 a.m., take the back roads, drive with your lights off, and for the love of gumbo, if you get caught, just cooperate. The police have been sending people home unless you give them a reason to suspect something."

"Alrighty, then. I'll be there at 2:00." His voice drops, a dark excitement lurking. "Let's go huntin'."

CHAPTER SEVENTEEN

THE MORGUE: THE BREAK-IN

At 1:50 a.m., my phone vibrates on the nightstand, not enough to wake Dad, but enough to jar me from my half-slumber. I silence it and nudge Portia awake. My nerves are on edge, my body trembling. The state of constant cold contributes to my shakiness, but the added dose of anxiety doesn't help.

I've never snuck out before.

First, because Dad's a cop and I'm not stupid. Second, there's never been a reason to. Until now.

Standing outside his door, I listen for any signs of consciousness. A light snoring comes from the other side, such a faint noise I strain to hear it. But it's there, so I grip the cool doorknob, twisting it open.

A creature of habit, Dad always keeps his stuff in the same place. Gun in the safe, phone on the nightstand, keys and entry card on the edge of his dresser. I tiptoe the few steps to the tall bureau, guided by the faint light from the window. Holding my breath, I slide the card to the edge of the dresser and pinch it between my finger and thumb, borrowing his card without permission.

In no time, I slip from his room, Dad still soundly sleeping.

Portia waits for me back in my room. She lifts her eyebrows, and I nod, holding up the card.

After layering a black jacket over my black shirt and black pants (the official color for sneaking out), I grab my magic bag and dig through my purse to get the house key. Gotta lock up after myself. I pull it out, and it catches on something. The tarot card Simone gave me. Except, instead of a pink-haired girl and a large moon, something else catches my eye. Numbers written in glow-in-the-dark paint. A phone number, to be exact, invisible to the daylight. *Her message is there. Read it.*

All this time, I held a message, *a phone number,* from my mom, and I left it stuffed in my purse. An urge to text or call hits me, so strong I almost give in. But I clench my fists, and set it on my desk, not even daring to show Portia and risk blabbing my emotions.

We move to the front room and look out the window, waiting for Luc to pull up.

Too many thoughts muddle my brain, the questions I want to ask my mom, the tarot reading from Simone — so much going on there, not to mention the Death card she drew for Portia. *It doesn't mean what you think it means.*

Ugh!

A scream builds in my throat. But all this pent-up stress needs to disappear. It'll only keep me distracted and on edge. With curfew in place, and the excess moon power, careful focus could be the difference between getting information and getting caught, and I refuse to waste more energy on my mom.

I'll call the number later, and if it's not my mom, I'll track Simone down and ask her to connect us.

Stay calm, stay focused. Breathe.

A dark-colored Bronco pulls up to the curb, and I deactivate the house alarm. We walk out the door, and I lock up behind us, officially sneaking out for the first time in my life. I briefly consider leaving a note, *breaking into the morgue. Be back before sunrise,* but figure if Dad wakes up, he will un-alive me whether I tell him where I went or not.

Portia sits in the passenger seat, and I hop in the back. Closing the car door might as well be death metal pumped through Bose speakers. But we drive away from my house. And then my street. And the world continues to turn.

"Where am I headed?" Luc asks in a whisper.

"Sorry." I shake my head and give him directions.

Other than that, we stay quiet, driving below the speed limit, and taking backroads. Luc keeps the headlights off as we sneak through town, hoping we avoid all of Dad's friends of the NOPD. If I get arrested for being caught after curfew, Dad will double un-alive me.

Despite my cold shivers from the super charged moon, nervous sweat dampens the back of my neck and my armpits. I clutch my phone, positive Dad will call, and I mentally run my excuses like lines in a play.

CeCe: I actually did it for you, to help solve this case. We don't want anyone else to die, right?

To which he would probably respond:

Dad: You've broken my trust, and my heart. I have to disown you. Kick you out to live in the shady crawl spaces of Bourbon Street. Good luck becoming an unhoused street-performing orphan.

My nerves might be getting to me.

Luc and Portia hold hands over the console. His thumb

slowly rubs her knuckle in a more-tender-than-just-friends way. More signs of their growing relationship, all happening while I've been away from Portia. It hurts a little, watching from the sidelines, missing out on this huge part of my bestie's life. Completely left out as her status changes from *single* to *it's complicated.*

I wonder if this is how Portia feels with magic.

The city passes by in an eerie silence. No traffic, no people, and something I never thought I'd say, no music. I'm used to living in a haunted city, but New Orleans as a *physical* ghost town totally creeps me out. Gas lanterns flicker, their shadows trembling on the sidewalk. Pieces of crumbled paper and loose trash blow down the deserted street like tumbleweeds in a sleepy western town.

"So weird." Portia stares out the window, clearly on the same page as me.

"Yeah," I whisper.

Soon enough, we crawl into the parking lot, the tall, stone building hiding us from the street. The tension leaves my shoulders, and I let out a breath. That drive was stressful. For a few breaths, a sense of safety calms me. Tucked in the car, a little sanctuary suspending us from reality. Then Luc opens his door. Portia follows.

Welcome back, Nerves.

I lead the way to the building, and try to tap Dad's access card, but my erratic movement confuses the sensor. The red *entry denied* light glares at me. My arm shakes like a jackhammer hangs from my wrist, and I can't entirely blame the cold. Good ol' fashioned fear makes me unsteady.

Portia puts her hand over mine. "We don't have to do this. It's okay if you're not ready to start our life of petty crime."

A part laugh, part scoff blows through my nostrils. "We're breaking into a government building. Not so sure that's petty."

"We're not robbing a bank or mixing polka dots and plaids." She gives an exaggerated shudder. "And we're not breaking in either. We have an access card."

"That's stolen," I remind her.

"Borrowed without permission." She throws my earlier words back at me.

Luc dips his head, joining our whispered conversation. "Listen, if you want to head home, return that little card from where you took it, it's okay. We'll figure things out another way."

As my mind usually does, it wanders to Zach. How he risked everything to keep me safe. I think of Luc's sister, hurt and miserable, with a festering wound that will kill her unless we find the Rougarou. Unless she *stabs* the Rougarou.

I can't sit back and do nothing.

"Let's do it." I steady my hand, pressing the card on the panel, and the light turns green. "For Zula."

"For Zula," Luc says.

We head down the stairs, and I explain to them the steps of necromancy. A quick overview from the moment I light the candle to when I release the spirit, emphasizing the need to stay in the circle. By the time I finish, I bring out the access card again to open the door into the morgue.

The smell comes first, a stench of death that never quite gets covered up, no matter how many chemicals are used. It hits like a punch to the nostrils, the pungent rot suffocating. Portia coughs and covers her nose, but Luc shows no reaction, his face impassive.

Then comes the cold. It usually chills me to my skeleton, but tonight it seems less frostbite-y. Maybe since a bitter chill has followed me for days already.

Luc looks around, his eyes falling on the wall where all the gliding tables hide behind thick, metal doors. "How do you know where the victim is?"

"A little research." I pluck through the stack of files on the counter, looking for the newest resident by the dates listed on the top. "Here we are."

"So, this is where you necromance." Portia runs her fingers along the fridge wall.

"Yep." I glance over the information, pausing at the name of the victim. Everything goes still inside me, and a rock lodges in my throat. My fingers grip the file folder until I crinkle the edges. "No, no, no. It can't be her."

"Who?" Luc asks.

"CeCe, what's wrong?" A note of concern pinches her words.

"Hold on." In a daze, I walk to the fridge wall, tingles of dread spiking over my skin like frozen rain. My heartbeat: double time. My stomach: swooping.

Opening one of the doors, I pull the table. Whenever I come with Dad, the victim hides away in a body bag, and he limits what I see. But with this body, bare feet roll out first, and a white, plastic sheet covers everything else.

"I'm, uhhh, gonna stand over here." Portia, the person who cleans up her siblings' vomit, and didn't even blink at Zula's infected wound, retreats from the table, her skin ashy.

I nod, my attention on the body. An identity tag hangs from the big toe, and I check it to verify I have the right person.

Stay calm, stay focused.

The cold amps up, my jacket useless as I move to the

head of the table. Luc hovers over my shoulder, his breath a warm puff of air that glances off the top of my hair. I reach for the plastic sheet, and it crinkles, the echo loud in the enclosed space.

Dirty blonde hair, dark lashes, and little green jewels trailing like tears down her cheek bones. Her eyes may be closed, but I know their color. I've seen them before.

"It's the fortune teller," I tell Portia. "Simone Cotuna."

"She said there was a connection between us." Portia's voice comes out in a chokehold. "I should have let her read tarot for me."

"I liked her. She was always kind when Baba Geaux was bein' difficult. Definitely didn't deserve this." Deep lines etch Luc's forehead, and he tucks his hands in his pockets, taking a step back. "You'll see her memories, right? Of her last moments."

"Yes." No visible wounds scar her face, which means most of the damage must hide below the plastic cover.

"Then let's find who did this. I'm tired of the Hijackers destroyin' things that matter." He turns away to stand next to Portia, putting his arm around her shoulders.

I take a deep breath, the chill heavy in the air, and move to the middle of the room. I'm ready to get started.

CHAPTER EIGHTEEN

THE MEMORY: THE TRAP

The hum of the air conditioner kicks on, a steady thrum. I sit on the hard, tile floor, and dig into my magic bag. Portia and Luc watch from their spot in front of the door.

I take out the supplies and light the candle. Then I mix the graveyard soil and water, making a paste. Dad's seen the ritual dozens of times, but Portia and Luc never have, so I dialogue a little through the process.

"The soil has to be from a graveyard because it's ground hallowed for the dead." With the paste in my palm, I walk to Simone, wiping it on her eyelids. "And I put it here to connect our vision."

Having Luc and Portia with me, and explaining my steps, eliminates the raging anxiety from last time. No blinking away the pit of dread or struggling through the looming memory of Rivera.

"Next I pour a circle." The canister hisses as I dump the

salt, and I continue. "The protective ring keeps unwanted magic out."

"But what about Rivera? He broke through." Portia keeps her eyes on my pouring and avoids Simone's body.

"Because he connected to me with a spell." I pick up my pouch of graveyard soil again and sprinkle it over the salt. "But I'll use this to fortify the protection, just in case. You two should stand inside the circle."

They both step carefully over the poured barrier.

"This is complicated." Luc chuckles, shaking his head. "With the Rougarou curse, we just phase and run around the bayou. No spells, or salt, or candles."

"Or moon tokens." I tip the candle, dripping the hot wax in my palm. "We're lucky we can do this tonight. A couple more days and we'd have a new moon, which means no moon token. Which means no necromancy."

"You can't talk to the dead when it's a new moon?" Portia asks.

"Nope." Technically, my necromancy book says the ritual "isn't recommended" in that circumstance, and I've never tried. Dealing with death involves more than instructions on a board game box. So, maybe I could. But why risk it?

I form a small crescent and then decide to make another. Can't be too careful.

"That little wax token holds the person's body down so they can't move?" Portia leans over my shoulder, watching me work.

"Yes." My no-nonsense approach puts her at ease, allowing her curiosity to replace the initial uncertainty.

"Why doesn't the person just...I don't know, brush it off?" Her gaze lands on the table.

"They may look like simple pieces of wax, but these little things"— I hold up the two tokens— "are filled with magic. Once I add blood."

I pull out my penknife and, out of habit, run my finger over the engraved words. *Death is good for the soul.* Mawmaw made me promise I'd never raise her, and her words on my knife, always help me feel close to her.

Poking my pinky, I paint a dab of red on each token.

"Is that even sanitary?" Portia asks, and I laugh, glad she always manages to lighten my mood.

"I dug it out of a dumpster. There's only a little rust, but I'm sure it's fine." I clean the blade and put it back in my bag. "Now I snag a hair from the victim."

Luc takes everything in, his face curious. "What if they're bald?"

"You don't want to know." Since I told Portia the story about plucking a hair from a never-to-be-discussed region, she knows exactly what happens. And her current giggling fit tells me she remembers.

Shudder.

Carefully stepping over the salt, I approach Simone. With her thick, dark eyebrows, the dirty blond hair surprises me. The purple veil always covered her head, and I imagined her differently underneath the fabric. I mutter an apology as I yank out a strand.

In all my times talking to the dead, I've never spoken to someone I knew. A surge of sadness punches me in the chest, and I bite my lip, allowing the melancholy some space. I didn't spend much time with Simone, but Luc's right. She was always kind. Now, no more conversations. No more tarot readings.

Death.

She'd pulled the tarot card with the black-hooded figure, and I thought it was directed at Portia. *It doesn't mean what you think it means.* Suddenly, I wonder if she drew it for herself. Did she know this was coming?

Back in the circle, I sit in front of the flickering candle and burn Simone's hair.

"No way," Luc whispers as the flame turns blue.

"Simone Cotuna, show me your killer, and you can rest."

Wind blows, the file folders shuffling along the counter, but not the shrieking wail of last time. Portia startles as a few papers flutter to the ground, and she spins to look behind her. Luc takes her hand, staying surprisingly steady.

"I feel the moon." He tips his head back and sniffs the air.

"It's strong." A surge of power floods me, but this time I'm ready for it.

Closing my eyes, I let the magic build, the iciness moving from the fingers of my right hand, all the way through to the fingers of my left hand. "Simone Cotuna, show me your killer."

The memory overtakes my vision, and I hover above, watching. Trees surround her, tall oaks dripping with Spanish moss. Crickets chirp and frogs croak, the proper sounds of a New Orleans night. The ground, strewn with stumps, sticks, and patches of green, has a wide, salt circle poured. Multiple lanterns dot the area to provide light, and a few wooden benches sit in the middle. A group of six gathers there. I recognize a few faces. Simone. Baba Geaux.

My mom.

I fight to stay focused on Simone, to see what happened that left her lying on the metal slab, but my gaze keeps wandering. For the first time in ten years, I see the face of my mother. Smooth skin, high cheekbones, eyes a little too wide-set to be conventional.

Just like mine.

Her dark, brown hair, cut in a blunt bob, hits her chin. It swishes as she slowly checks the salt perimeter. Knowing she runs a weird underground magical mafia, I imagined her in a showy get-up, maybe something like the purple dress and veil Simone wears. Instead, she has on jeans and a navy tee.

Everyone seems to be working on something. Baba Geaux mixes herbs with a mortar and pestle. A middle-aged man next to him thumbs through a large book. Simone sits on the ground, a tarot spread in front of her. The cards lay out in some kind of cross shape, the images too small to make out clearly. I pull myself in to see, and her head whips up.

At first, I think she somehow feels my presence, but then a twig snaps, the loud noise echoing. My mom holds up a finger, moving to the center of the circle. All eyes focus on the direction of the sound. The clearing has gone silent, all the croaks and chirps of night critters hushed.

A woman with two long braids stands, and she tugs at them nervously. "Did they find us?"

"Yes." If my mom worries about whatever approaches, she shows no visible concern. Her face remains passive, even as the tussle of undergrowth comes closer.

Simone rises from the ground, her head tipped, eyes scrunched. Her feet step lightly, making no noise as she moves to the edge of the circle. I want to tell her to stop. To retreat, because I know how this ends.

A loud growl rumbles from the shadow of trees. And

then I hear the chanting. The rhythmic whispers slink around me. Through me. Trying to draw my attention away from the memory. It lulls like a boat drifting on calm waves, urging me to relax and let go. But I stay focused on Simone.

A towering silhouette emerges into the clearing. Its breath huffs, deep snarls rattling in its chest, and the long snout sniffs the air. Clawed feet dig into the ground, the strong legs ready to pounce.

The Rougarou has arrived.

"Now!" My mom yells, and a heavy cargo net drops from the trees, landing on the beast. The Magical Mafia expected this. They set a trap.

Chaos erupts after that. Two people jump down from their perches in the oaks, slamming silver stakes into the ground to hold the net down, and then dive into the protective circle. The middle-aged man shouts out a spell, his finger following along in the book he holds. Baba Geaux hurls his mixture of herbs onto the wolf, muttering his own words. Everyone has a job, organized pandemonium to catch the hulking creature.

The Rougarou struggles, thrashing under the constraints, its angry growls thundering. Spittle drips from its nipping muzzle, and the sharp claws slash. The twisted ropes glow, infused with some kind of magic, and they hold.

In all the commotion, I forgot to watch Simone, and I turn back to her. She stands at the edge of the circle, holding a hand up like a stop sign, her body barely inside. The expression on her face remains neutral, her eyes closed, no reaction to the chomping and snarling happening a foot in front of her.

She reaches into her robe, retrieving a tarot deck. Without looking, she shuffles her thumb along the edge, drawing out one card. From my angle, I can't see, but her face pales, and she shakes her head.

"It doesn't work," we yell, me from the morgue and her as she turns her back on the Rougarou. "We have to run."

Up to this point, I've felt nothing from Simone, but now fear pounds in our chests, a shot of adrenaline saying, *go!*

The ropes snap, loud popping noises like gunshots, and the net slumps to the ground. The Rougarou stretches to its full height, tipping its head back with a murderous howl. Saliva glistens in the lantern light, covering its maw and chest.

The Rougarou leaps, crossing the circle and tackling Simone. The tarot deck flies from her hand and scatters, creating a halo of cards around her. Baba Geaux screams, but another man holds him back, tackling him to the ground.

"We can't risk losing you too. Get out of here!" Despite her warning, my mom sits in the middle of the clearing as everyone scrambles to run. As the Rougarou rips a chunk from Simone's shoulder and she shrieks.

Does my mom even care? Simone digs her fingers into the dirt, dragging herself away from the attack, but she's no match for the strength and speed of the Rougarou. It presses into her, the front paws using enough force that something inside her cracks. Red stains leech from where sharp talons gouge into her back.

I listen to the swirling conversations of the retreating magical mafia, things like, *did someone break the circle?* And the braided-hair lady crying and muttering, "I told her a protective circle might not stop it. The Rougarou is a curse, not magic."

My mom ignores it all, pulling a penknife from her pocket and cutting her pinky. The action so similar to what

I do, that it feels like a strange déjà vu. With the fresh cut dripping blood, she draws shapes on the ground.

"Show me who you are, Rougarou," she says, slamming down her hand.

An immediate silence follows, like someone pressed mute. The sudden change disorients me, one of my senses ripped away. My mom's mouth moves, but no sound comes out. Simone's eyes go from wide, to slack, to empty, and the thumps of her heart slow. Stop. I suddenly wish Dad was here, draping his suit jacket around me.

Like with Mary Mosley's memory, I stay in this vision, unable to come back to myself in the morgue. The Rougarou rises, kicking Simone aside, and lifts its snout to the sky. The wet nose twitches, searching back and forth. This giant beast just ran off six magic users after crushing Simone with its massive paws, and now it moves towards me. Fear hits like a flash bomb, blinding me to everything but the white flare of terror. I try to draw away, but stay frozen above, unable to do anything except watch as the Rougarou comes closer, inches away. My spirit body thrashes, fighting to return to Portia and Luc.

I'm trapped. Completely stuck on the spiritual plane in this nightmare.

My mom spreads her arms, maybe shouting? It's hard to tell while living in a silent movie. Blood runs from her pinky to her wrist, in a bright red trail, nearly glowing in the moonlight. Her forehead creases, and her eyes narrow.

Even though I experienced it before, I'm shocked and disgusted as the slimy muzzle brushes my cheek, down my jaw. Crimson scraps of dripping flesh dangle from sharp teeth. The slimy tongue paints a saliva streak along my throat. Unwilling to meet the amber eyes of the wolf, I avert my gaze and catch a movement in my peripheral vision.

My mom shakes her head, her hair bouncing with the frantic motion. She lifts her hand high in the air, holding it there for a few seconds before slamming it on the ground. The world of sound comes rushing back, a blaring blast after the noiselessness. Huffing breaths by my ear. A moist lapping at my neck. And the chanting. The loud, melodic chanting of sound magic.

"A retrospect spell. CeCe, it's a trap!" Scrambling for her bag, she flings it over her shoulder. "Get out. Get out now!"

How does she know I'm here? And what's a retrospect spell? Between the wet slurping, the rhythmic monk song, and my mom's words, my world spins in a bewildered fog. But the confusion turns to frustration as, rather than help me, she walks away. Not the first time in my life to see that view. Especially when things get hard.

The chanting grows louder, the voices right in my ears, distracting me from anything other than the steady hum. The moon blazes bright above, all its light gathering into a spotlight, which shines directly on me.

That can't be good.

It's time to get my act together and get back to the morgue. With me physically there, sitting on the cold floor, I just need to focus long enough to reunite body and spirit. Which should be easy. Yet, I can't even bring an image of the morgue to mind. Something blocks my thoughts, holding me here.

It's a trap, get out. It's a trap, get out. I think the words, but in the same tone and rhythm as the hypnotic cadence. In fact, the chanting takes over my thoughts, the unfamiliar language drowning out everything else.

The Rougarou steps away, putting space between me and its disgusting snout. My short-lived relief morphs into terror as I see what waits behind the beast. A man. More specifically, the old man from the dreamscape. The head Hijacker in charge.

"Finally." He lifts his chin, staring directly where I float above. "I've waited a long time to meet you, granddaughter."

CHAPTER NINETEEN

THE MORGUE: THE ESCAPE

*G*randdaughter. I stare at the old man, looking for something, anything, that connects us. Face shape, nose, eyebrows. But all I see is a madman. Suddenly, my world swirls, not just figuratively, but a literal kaleidoscope spinning until I find myself in the dreamscape. Giant oaks circle the clearing where a fire burns and Hijackers chant. My feet touch the ground, my spirit shifting from hovering above to standing upright. The disorienting change adds a layer of confusion. I can't focus on anything; can't even figure out how I got here. Like falling into the middle of a nightmare, nothing makes sense, and everything seems dangerous.

The other Hijackers wear the same masks as last time, hiding behind the wooden faces. They all sit cross-legged on the ground, hands resting on their thighs. The chanting fills my brain, blocking all other thoughts.

The old man, my *grandfather*, approaches. The firelight reflects on his face, casting sinister shadows, changing his expression with each dance of the flame. I hear the crunch of sand under his shoes, the rustling of his clothes.

Is he physically here?

He wears a suit and tie, all in black, and a black button-up shirt. An outfit more suitable for a fancy event, not a fireside kidnapping. His white hair is cut short, his beard neatly trimmed. An air of authority flows off him, from his rigid stance to the superior smugness in his smile.

"Constance has hidden you long enough. It's time to join your family."

Family. That word jars me from the stupor, bringing to mind Portia, Luc, and Zula. Watching them huddled together in a weighted awareness. I think of Dad, the only true family I have. My safe place who's always been my comfort and support. Who sat by my bed every night, waiting until I fell asleep because thoughts of Rivera haunted me. Not this man, claiming a role as my grandfather, telling me to join the ranks. No.

I want to shout my denial, maybe add in a classic, *not in this lifetime*, but I stand frozen in the moon spotlight, unable to do anything.

He reaches into his pocket and pulls out a knife, flicking the blade open. The white handle's pearly finish shimmers iridescent in the light. The silver, razor-thin edge is sharpened to stabby perfection. Fear pounds inside me. I instinctively try to curl my hand into a fist, to cover the scar where Rivera sliced my palm open.

But the old man doesn't point the knife at me. He turns it toward himself and knicks his pinky, just like I do when I use magic. Just like I watched my mom do. Blood dribbles from the cut, and he lifts his hand, a trail of crimson dripping.

His lips move, muttering quiet words, and then he says,

"to see," and swipes his seeping pinky across my forehead. Impossibly, I feel the warm, wet, sensation, and my stomach turns, disgusted to be wearing the old man's blood.

CeCe! I hear Portia's voice, a faraway call. *CeCe, what's going on? I'm freaking out here.*

A jolt shakes my body, not my spirit, my physical body. The palpable motion helps me tune out Grandpa Hijacker and the continued hypnotic chant, sifting through the static to hear my bestie. She sounds distressed. Spooked. *But why?*

Concentrating on Portia, I picture her. Curly black hair. Bright, happy smile that always hits like rays of sunshine through the clouds. But what was she wearing tonight? What were we doing? If I can just remember, I know it'll drag me from the fog.

CeCe! Another bump rattles me and for a second, I feel my physical body. The smell hits first, an astringent scent of formaldehyde stinging my nose. Then the discomfort of sitting cross-legged with the cold, hard floor beneath me.

The morgue!

Grandpa Hijacker lifts his pinky again, ready to paint me with more DNA juice, and clarity kicks in like a S.W.A.T. team breach. I remember Simone and her murder. The stress of sneaking out with Dad's access card. I picture the space where Luc and Portia wait for me. Simone waits too, confined by my moon token, ready to be freed from this vision and put to rest.

But the Hijackers hold my spirit captive. In a state of magical sleep paralysis, I hear and see all that happens while otherwise frozen. Panic grips me in its sharp talons, shredding any semblance of calm.

Digging through my mental MacGyver bag of escape, I

try to figure a way out of this. Physical abilities? Nil on this magical plane. Clarity and focus? Shot. My necromancy? A solid maybe.

The moon pulses like a welcoming beacon, and I plug into it. Grab onto the power and take it in. The force fills me, stretches me. I'm a size or five too small to contain it all, and I strain near to bursting. Since the moment Zach cut my link to Rivera, I somehow lost the added boost of my sound magic. But the hum of my cicadas doesn't compare to the incredible rush of moon energy.

It gives me the needed injection to break free from the stupor. Like waking from a deep sleep, I drag myself from the Hijackers and escape their hold.

I come to my physical body in the morgue. A coughing fit catches me as I open my eyes, frozen air gusting into my lungs. Portia sits to my left, vigorously shaking my shoulder. Luc crouches to my right, talking in a low, urgent voice. But a loud clanging drowns out everything he says, and I look toward the sound.

Simone thrashes on the table, her body wildly flopping. The banging reverberates off the walls and fills the small room. Arms and legs fly like puppet limbs attached to strings that lift and release, lift and release. The frantic movement shifts her close to the edge, offsetting the balance and making the metal door bash repeatedly.

"You're awake!" Portia shouts her relief. "What's going on? Why is she doing that? How do we stop it?" Her questions hit rapid fire as she points to the convulsing Simone.

And then Luc's quieter drawl breaks through the noise. "What did you do to the moon?"

"I don't know," I say as an answer to everything. Because somehow, between the vision and the dreamscape, I lost my connection with Simone. No more communication with her spirit. No more tug from my chest like a rope tying us together. The flame of my candle glows a warm orange instead of blue, and the two tokens I made lay discarded on the floor, now useless pieces of wax.

Cold shivers through my body, my blue fingers unable to grip my jacket to wrap it around me. And I feel the moon. The powerful moon pulsing like a living thing. The indomitable force pulls me, like high tide coming in, dragging me under water. My ears nearly burst with the pressure as my head squeezes tighter and tighter.

"I need to release Simone's spirit." Hunching my shoulders, and slapping my hands over my ears, I try to minimize the strain. If I can just recall how to finish the ritual. Which should be easy. But with the relentless brain squash, I barely remember what color my hair is.

Focus.

Step by step, I run through the process. Come back from the vision, say the words, blow out the candle. That's it.

Folding my hands in my lap, I speak through gritted teeth. "Simone Cotuna, you can—" my voice breaks off at a shattering crash. Portia shrieks and shuffles backwards. Even Luc jumps up from his crouch.

They both stand behind me, staring at Simone, who now slumps on the floor. The clanging on metal is replaced by thumping against tile. She fell in an unnatural position, one leg sprawled behind her, dirty blond hair thrown forward over her face. The plastic sheet somehow wound more tightly making a body burrito from shoulder to knee.

I look back at the candle. "Simone Cotuna, you can rest now. It's over." Leaning close to the flickering orange flame, I blow it out and wait for her body to settle.

And keep waiting.

Watch as she wriggles her knees under her, sliding her

wrapped torso forward, a weird corpse caterpillar inching along. The plastic sheet rustles, and her face squeaks as it skids against the tile. A fleshy patchwork of gnawed skin and bone peeks from the corner of the covering, the Rougarou's bite on her shoulder a reminder of her murder.

"Is this supposed to happen? This feels like it shouldn't be happening." Portia's voice rises in volume and pitch.

No. This is *not* supposed to happen.

"Just stay in the circle." I try to keep the panic out of my words, but my heartbeat? Triple time. My stomach? The swoopiest of free-falling swoops. The pressure in my head? Squeezing like it's in a brain juicer.

Digging through my magic bag, I search for my lighter. I've been through something like this before, at Lafayette Cemetery when Rivera sent zombies after me. But that time I didn't contend with an amped up moon funneling power through my veins. Or an unpredictable werewolf.

Shush, shush. The corpse caterpillar scoots closer. Somehow Simone worked an arm free, and the sheet droops off a shoulder. Her stiff fingers claw to get a grip, flecks of dirt and blood speckling the white tile.

Focus!

"Where is it?" I mutter, swiping my hands on my pants before dumping the contents of my bag on the floor.

How can I be so cold and so sweaty at the same time?

"Luc, are you okay?" Portia asks, and I look up at him.

His fists clench, a sheen of moisture glistens on his forehead and upper lip. Unsteady breaths huff from his flared nostrils.

"The moon's tellin' me to run. To hunt."

"Do not leave this circle!" I find my lighter, *finally,* and get the candle burning again. My hands shake so hard it's a miracle the flame catches hold.

I grab the pouch of graveyard soil, dumping a small pile of dirt on the floor. Though tempted to hurry things along, I wait for the wax to melt, needing the moon token to catch the excess power. The vibration of magic buzzes in the air and rattles my teeth. Cold descends, filling every breath. .

Portia walks behind me to stand in front of Luc. Usually, I pour the salt circle with two people in mind, just Dad and me. But three's a crowd. Literally. Adding another person tests our space. Especially with everyone moving around, shuffling from side to side.

"It's okay, sweetie." She puts her hands on his shoulders and kneads the muscles. "Relax and look at me. Focus on my eyes."

I trust Portia to handle Luc and his werewolfy tendencies while I watch Simone. She's worked herself to within a couple of feet from us, and the plastic crinkles with each awkward accordion slide. A sharp sting of chemicals wafts off her, the pungent scent of the dead. This close, I see her torn shoulder, and a sharp piece of bone protrudes from the jagged wound. A flap of flesh jiggles, the loose skin barely hanging on by a thread.

Panic attempts to force me from fight to flight, but I remember the zombies from the graveyard, pressing against the protective circle, unable to get by. Their skeletal fingers scratched and clawed, and though I felt the vibration through my bones, the barrier held.

I pour wax into my palm, blowing on the paraffin to cool it faster as I mold the token. With that formed, and ready to catch the magical runoff, I start a new ritual— not to speak to the dead— to connect and guide.

Opening my pen knife for the second time, I nick my pinky, squeezing the reopened cut to dribble a few drops of red onto the pile of dirt. I pinch a portion of the mixture between my fingers, feeding it to the candle, and the flame turns blue. A breeze kicks up, blasting the file folders off the counter behind us.

"The moon in my palm, my blood in the flame, the graveyard soil grounding the magic." I murmur the words directly from my book as easily as if I'd read them.

Power tingles along my spine, my skin charged like static electricity. I close my eyes, stretching my metaphorical necromantic fingers to connect with the dead, and their spirits reach back, those within these walls answering the call. The deceased hate disruption to their state of rest, and my head fills with noise. Anger, sadness, and frustration all clash, banging cymbals making it hard to sift through the chaos.

While Simone's spirit remains elusive, her physical body draws closer, the rustling sheet and formaldehyde stench nearly on top of me. *Shush, shush.* And then I find a spirit that feels different than the others. Still restless and troubled, yes, but this one carries a confused denial. *I'm not dead,* it screams. *Help me. Save me.* With that comes a consuming need to attach to the living.

"CeCe. She's going to touch me." Portia's voice rises, her exclamation a panicked squeak. At some point, she spun around to face the crawling Simone, pressing her back into Luc's chest. He wraps an arm around her, holding her tight, his eyes wide.

"Stay in—" I start to issue another reminder of the protective barrier, and suddenly I can't breathe, my oxygen held captive by the intense stab of fear. Portia's toe is outside the circle.

PORTIA'S TOE IS OUTSIDE THE CIRCLE!

Her black sneaker, smeared through salt, breaks the

continuous line. Which breaks the barrier. Which means no protection.

And Simone reaches her dirt-caked, dried-blood encrusted hand toward my bestie. Touching her. Wrapping her stiff, discolored fingers around Portia's bare ankle.

"Noooo!"

I think I scream, or maybe Portia screams, and my ears ring with the sound. With panic-induced adrenaline I lunge, diving across the salt to shove Simone. I push her torso, avoiding contact with her skin, and the now still body slides a couple of inches. Not nearly far enough, even though it breaks her hold on Portia. The next room wouldn't be far enough.

"Darlin', what's wrong? Portia!" Luc's frenzied tone sounds different to anything I've ever heard from him, his normal, charming demeanor smothered in fear.

Portia crumbles, her legs giving out. Luc holds her limp body, catching her under the arms and keeping her upright. Her complexion already turns a shade of grayish. Purple bruises darken under her eyes.

I rise to my feet, brushing the hair from her face, running my fingers along her forehead and cheeks. "Please be okay, Portia. Please, please be okay." My voice chokes out in a cracked whisper.

Her skin: cold and lifeless. Her breathing: barely there and shallow.

She looks like the dead.

But more than what I physically see and touch, it's what I feel. Or rather, what I don't feel. No more traces of Simone's restless spirit. The cyclone of distress vanished, and the voices of the other dead hush.

I experienced this once before, a long time ago with Dad.

Luc lifts Portia in his arms, holding her close. Her head lolls against his shoulder, rolling to fall back, and he adjusts to support her neck. "What happened to her?"

It physically pains me to breathe, every inhale infused with razor blades. "She's haunted."

This can't be real. It doesn't feel like my mouth speaking. The words float from some horrific dream, surrounding me in a crescendo of terror. My throat aches as I swallow the building scream clawing to get out.

And running through my mind is one line. One horrible line from my necromancy guide. The narrator in my head keeps reiterating it, over and over, an incessant rewind and repeat. Rewind and repeat.

Sometimes the haunted lose their battle for control over the dead and never wake, crossing the threshold from "haunted" to "possessed."

CHAPTER TWENTY

MY HOUSE: THE MAGIC TOUCH

Somehow, I end up in the backseat of Luc's car with Portia's head resting in my lap. I don't remember leaving the morgue. Barely remember stopping Luc from rushing to the hospital. No one there can help.

Everything is a blur. A horrible canon event of before the touch and the current reality.

The necro-shivers amp up, and I cling to Portia, fighting to keep her on the seat with me. Luc blasts the heat without my asking. The flood of warmth pouring from the vents alleviates the earthquake-level shaking.

I run my trembling fingers over Portia's curls, brushing the dark strands away from her face. Her eyes stay closed, her body motionless. No amount of prodding, pushing, or begging elicits a response. Wanting her to wake up, desperately wishing I possessed the gift of time travel, doesn't change the circumstances. Portia is haunted.

Why didn't I notice the broken circle sooner?

Tears stream down my cheeks, and I press my fists into

my eyes, the guilt consuming. Overwhelming. I want to call Zach and tell him what happened. Ask him for help. Missing him, knowing his struggle, adds to this horrible remorseful abyss.

Zach's addiction: my fault. Portia's haunting: my fault. Even the stupid Hijackers tracking me down comes back to: my fault.

"I should've protected her." He looks at me through the rearview mirror, and I meet his anguished eyes.

"No. This is my fault," I whisper.

Still careful of curfew, we drive at an excruciatingly slow pace. Traveling on the backroads with the headlights off leaves us in a darkness only broken up by the soft glow radiating from the dashboard, highlighting the frustrated slash of his brows.

"What does it mean to be haunted?" Luc's question punches me in the gut. Just hearing that word twists the guilt deeper.

"Necromancy disturbs a person's spirit and they're no longer at rest." I smooth out the collar of Portia's black jacket, knowing scrunched fabric bothers her. Keeping my attention on her, rather than Luc's gaze, helps me focus. "Something happens when I share a vision with the dead. I force their spirits and bodies to reunite, but they aren't harmonious anymore. It confuses them."

My chest clenches, the pound of my heart painful, and I force the explanation out. "They search for a living anchor. They become spirit parasites."

He slows the car, watchful as he turns a corner. "And their touch haunts a person."

"Yes."

"Everythin' in your world is so complicated." He rubs his palm along his jaw, probably massaging the tension from clenching it. "How're we gonna break Portia out of it?"

I shake my head before he finishes his question. Free her like she's in some kind of physical jailhouse? Escaping Alcatraz would be easier than the current prison of her mind. "We can't. Portia's the only one who can fight this battle. She has to exorcise Simone's spirit."

His deep sigh lays heavy in the car, his worry thick. "Do you know anyone who's been haunted before?"

"My dad. About four years ago." I turn to the window, watching the deserted streets of New Orleans pass. "He never used to stand in the circle with me, and I never insisted. All it took was a misplaced moon token on a murder victim. Didn't even notice until it was too late."

"Your dad's okay though, right?"

"Yeah. But after he was touched, I waited in the morgue for almost three hours. I couldn't carry him out, and I couldn't ask anyone for help." I feel like that young girl again. Weak and powerless. "He finally came to, enough that I guided him outside. I got a cab, and the driver just figured Dad was drunk. Once I got him home, we waited. It took a full 48 hours before he fought off the haunting and came back to himself."

Two full days where Dad stumbled around the house with a deranged mind. Hours upon hours of me alternating between hiding from his destructive rages, forcing him to eat, and begging Dad to please gain control.

"With her personality, that ol' fortune teller doesn't stand a chance," Luc says with a determined nod.

I don't have the heart to tell him that sometimes the haunted never remember who they are.

But not Portia. She'll remember. She has to.

He glances at me over his shoulder. "You got marked

again. I felt the exact moment it happened. Moon pourin' through the room like we could drink it, and then the Rougarou was there. But not where I could see it."

I groan and lean my head back. Luc's right: everything in my life IS complicated. "I watched it kill Simone. It was horrible. And then it came at me."

"We'll need to visit Baba Geaux and get another cure. Otherwise, you might end up with the Rougarou on your doorstep."

"Isn't that what we want? Just let it find me, and then maybe you can catch it, or kill it, or whatever you need to do."

"CeCe." His voice is soft but sharp. "I don't want anyone else gettin' hurt. First Zula, then Simone, and now Portia. Everyone around me is fallin' like flies."

My short-lived outburst shifts back to the remorse abyss. "I know. You're right."

We stay quiet after that, and I clutch Portia's cold hand, rubbing where her pulse gently thrums. My soul hurts seeing her like this. As the most vibrant and vivacious person I know, her unconscious form destroys me. Fighting another bout of tears, I hold my breath until spots dot my vision. Pain rips my chest open. Claws my insides. Everything about life dulls without my best friend to add her sparkle.

What happens now?

I drag myself from the guilt long enough to think about the next step. Portia can't go home until she wakes up, not in her condition, and I can't leave her with Luc. Which means she stays at my house, where my light-sleeping, police officer Dad lives.

In Happy Fantasy Land, we get Portia in quietly enough that Dad stays asleep. She wakes up in the morning like nothing happened, and Dad remains oblivious to my growing list of crimes. But in Dreaded Reality-ville, I left my mark all over the morgue, the mess and magic unquestionably pointing to *CeCe broke in and necromanced here*. Plus, my best friend unconscious in supernatural sleep screams suspicious. And Dad is not a fool.

Ugh. I have to tell him.

No matter how the lines run through my mind, the words never sound any better, the undeniable facts condemning. I stole Dad's access card, snuck out to the morgue, and my best friend is haunted.

I may never leave the house again. Grounded for eternity. Forever an inmate at Casa LeBlanc. Something I'd happily accept if it meant bringing Portia back. Surrendering my freedom for her healing would be a small price to pay, and I wish it worked that way.

The car slows as Luc pulls in front of the familiar periwinkle wood siding and white porch rails. Home sweet home. He turns off the engine and I wait for him to lift Portia from my lap before I step out. Sounds of the night surround us, the jug-o-rum of a bullfrog, the hum of cicadas. And even though they're not *my* cicadas, the familiar buzz steadies me, a comforting song in the chaotic darkness.

"You want me to carry her inside?" His soft voice barely rises above the froggy croaks.

She's got five inches on me, and even dragging my backpack around wears me out. "If I could do it I would."

"Right. I'll follow you."

We walk to the house, and something feels wrong. Because of curfew, the streets are empty, and no one could see us anyway, with the porch covering us overhead. It takes a few seconds to realize a soft glow emanates from the front window. I stop Luc, putting a hand on his arm.

"I didn't turn on any lights." Choosing instead to stumble in the dark and minimize the chances of getting caught.

"What?" he asks.

Dreaded Reality-ville waits just inside. "My dad—"

The door swings open and Dad looms before us, backlit from the lamp which casts his face in shadow. He changed from his pajamas, dressed and ready to go out and find me. Even though I can't see his eyes, I know the moment they land on my unconscious bestie. His soft gasp hits me like a sledgehammer, cracking open my tear ducts.

"I'm sorry, Dad. I'm so sorry." With my jacket sleeve, I swipe at my running nose, ducking into my elbow to cover my sobs.

"What happened to Portia?" He steps aside, and the instruction is clear: *get in here and get explaining.* "What happened to *you?* You're shaking and your lips are blue."

They are?

We cross the threshold and the definitive click of the door seals us in. Everything about Dad, from his posture to his expression, gives off worry and frustration. Anger and hurt.

"We went to the morgue." My gut churns with guilt, and I tuck my chin to my chest, unable to meet his gaze. "Portia was touched...she's haunted."

Dad pinches his eyes closed and rubs his forehead. I don't know what else to say, and I stand there swiping the steady stream of tears. The emotion engulfs me, and I just want to go back in time and stop Simone from touching my best friend. I want Portia to wake up, to laugh and nervously babble excuses to try and get us out of trouble.

Without her, the uncomfortable silence stretches, only broken up by my snuffling sadness.

Dad tips his head to study the unexpected visitor. "Who are you?"

"Luc Etienne, sir. I'm datin' Portia."

"He knew there was a new victim. That's why we went to the morgue." Not sure why I blurt that information. Or why I attempt to shift the blame away from me. But there it is, in the open and un-take-back-able.

The weight of Dad's stare changes from studious to suspicious. Eyes narrowed. Brows lowered. A cutting directness that only comes from owning a badge. With the power of his piercing gaze, he causes the unflappable Luc to flap.

"Uhh...my cousin, Verily Broussard, told me. You work with her." He rolls Thor and God of Thunder, adjusting Portia in his hold.

"Agent Broussard?" He waits for Luc's confirming nod. "Your cousin is one of the FBI agents working this case?"

"Yes, sir."

Wait, what? The cousin Luc lives with in the expensive Creole cottage in the French Quarter works for the FBI? My tear trails run dry as I wrap this new information around my mind. No wonder he had an "inside track" on the newest victim.

After a million years, Dad asks me, "Did you leave any trace?"

In our morgue visits, we live by a rule, just like the boy scouts, we leave no trace behind. Salt gets swept, fingerprints wiped, everything cleaned to *we were never here*. I think about how I left things. File folders strewn about. The broken circle. An open fridge with no body. Simone crumpled on the floor.

"It's a mess." That phrase describes everything. The morgue, the situation. My life.

Dad sighs and goes back to rubbing his forehead.

Luc clears his throat. "Can I lay Portia down somewhere?" At this point of holding her, his arms must be ready to fall off. Admittedly, Luc's strained muscles rank low on my priority list.

"Let's put her in my room," I say, but Dad cuts off the very suggestion of moving by lifting his hand.

"This is what we're going to do." Dad covers his face, his hands slowly sliding down his cheeks. "CeCe, you stay here with Portia. I'll drop Luc off at his house, and then get the morgue cleaned. Tomorrow, when it's not curfew" —he gives a little *ahem*— "Gina and I will drop off Luc's car after breakfast. Got it?"

"Got it," I say, even though I hate dragging Dad's "sort of" girlfriend into this. Hopefully involving her in car drop-off doesn't add any more fuel to her *Clairvoyant CeCe* fire.

Nudging Luc forward, I get him moving. "You can put her on my bed."

I flip a switch as we walk down the hall and flinch at the sudden infusion of light. The glow of the lamp matched my mood, dim and gloomy, and I blink a few times against the sudden brightness of the overhead fixture. I catch sight of myself in the hanging mirror, and my reflection shocks me. Puffy eyes and extra pale skin. Pink flyaways escaped from my ponytail to tangle around my face. Blue lips, just like dad said, legitimate blue, like I lost circulation to my face.

I duck my head and keep going.

Enough light emanates from the hall that I leave it off in my room. A trace of vanilla candle lingers in the air, but other than that, the rest of the area gives "slob" vibes. Some dirty clothes hang over the hamper to pile on the floor and books cover every surface. My guitar case, where the beautiful VanHellSing rests, lays in the middle of the room, and I step around it to clear the week of studying from my bed.

"Sorry," I mutter, tossing books and papers onto my desk. "Careful of the salt."

Dad stands in the doorway, a vigilant guard, everything about him on high alert. A watchful stillness, like at any moment he might pounce.

Luc steps over the poured circle, edging past me to lay Portia down. Her limbs flop onto the mattress and her dark hair fans across my pillow "Take care of her, okay?"

"She's my family," I tell him.

He nods. Enough said.

"Luc." Dad folds his arms, his patience at its end. "Let's go."

"I'll be back tomorrow. Call me if anythin' changes."

I listen to their footsteps move down the hall, some quiet murmurs and shuffling around. The front door opens and closes, and I'm alone with Portia. My heart hurts, my stomach clenches. Even though I received a temporary stay of punishment from Dad, I know he'll be back to lay down the law. But I can't dredge up an ounce of worry for that with a haunted best friend.

My shivers settle to stinging. Standing next to the bed, I watch the steady rise and fall of her chest. Her eyelids glitter in the low light, her sneak out special including sparkly shadow. Where she got that from, I have no idea. *Only Portia.* The black jacket bunches around her and I try to straighten it out. Then I work on her shoes, pulling off her classic Nikes.

"Please wake up." I sit next to her, taking her hand. A vibration dances along my skin.

A MAGICAL vibration. *What the what?*

That was definitely not there on the ride home. I held her hand, brushed hair from her face. *So, what changed?*

I grab her wrist, clocking her steady pulse, and gauging the buzz of power. Slight, but there. Both the pulse and the magic.

It feels like voodoo.

Closing my eyes, I ride the sensation, brushing my fingers along her hand, moving to her other hand. The gentle flow passes over me, a wave of steam, warm and ungraspable. It mingles with my power, a familiar vibe, though not quite the instant 'zing' connection to Zach's.

Why does Portia suddenly have magic?

I don't have the answers, but I know who might.

Time to find out if that phone number belongs to my mom.

CHAPTER TWENTY-ONE

MY ROOM: THE LIAR, REPRISE

I pick up the tarot card Simone gave me and stare at it. In the low light of my bedroom, I see two distinct layers. The picture of the girl with pink hair and the words "The moon" in thick, bold ink. And then the glow-in-the-dark phone number. The one that maybe belongs to my mom.

Rubbing my thumb over the slightly raised paint, I turn the digits over in my mind, memorizing them. A few hours ago, the thought of calling might have caused nerves or anxiety. But looking at Portia, I only feel determination.

I reach for my cell.

The home screen lights up to a selfie of Zach and me. He hams it up with a huge smile, and I pucker my lips, my green eyes laughing. Ugh. I miss him so much. Especially now that I sit in my room, the weight of being alone overwhelming. No Zach. No Portia. Dad gone. And at 4:00 a.m., the list of people I could reach out to is limited.

Entering the number, I double check to make sure I got it right before hitting the call button.

"CeCe, you got my message." A note of satisfaction resonates in her voice, the voice I heard tonight as I watched Simone die. The same voice that lives in my earliest memories.

Mom.

She sounds wide awake, not a trace of sleep to her words. "It's late. What happened?"

Suddenly, my vocal cords reject me. A rapid beat flutters in my chest, not like happy butterflies, but angry bees, buzzing and stinging. My tongue darts out to lick my lips, and I try to gain control over the rampant resentment.

I always assumed talking to my mom would appease the young girl inside me craving a maternal, nurturing figure. Wrong. It feeds the hurt of loneliness and the rage of abandonment.

Pacing the length of the salt circle, I walk back and forth, back and forth. We listen to each other breathe, neither of us making the effort to speak. Until my eyes pass over Portia, and I tuck away all the annoyance for later.

"I need your help." I pull out my desk chair and sit.

"That much is obvious." No surprise on her end. Calm, emotionless Mom, unaffected by our first verbal conversation in a decade.

"Is there a way to undo a haunting?" I imitate her cool demeanor. "Black magic isn't an option."

"Black magic is always an option. You need to accept that it's a useful tool. Stop being afraid of it, and face the inevitable. I've got a spell that would pull someone from the haunting by morning." She laughs. "Who was touched anyway? Your father again? How is Cooper doing?"

Again? She knows about Dad being haunted? I spent

two days in total misery, and she tosses it out there, all *ha ha ha.* It kicks the beehive in my chest, stirring up the swarm.

"We're not going to talk about Dad." The words shoot from my mouth like poison darts, and I count to three in my head. My anger won't get answers. "I need to know how to cure my best friend."

"Was it Simone that touched...what's her name? Portia? Please tell me it was Simone," she says.

"You sound excited at the prospect."

"My dear." Even though the word is an endearment, the way she says it sounds condescending. "Simone has voodoo. If it was Simone that haunted your friend, there's a good chance we can save her."

A desperate hope blooms. "Yes. It was Simone."

"That's good. That's very good," she mumbles excitedly. "Is there an echo of magic in your friend?"

"Yes!" I roll my chair from the desk to the bed and take Portia's hand, the steady hum still flowing between us. "Why is that?"

"Magic is a living thing, an extension of the spirit," she says. "It can live on, attach to someone. It works the same way a haunting does."

Like Jeff Goldblum says (ish), *Magic finds a way.* "So, it'll fade in a couple of days?"

"Perhaps. If she wakes up."

If. I hate that word. "You said we could save her. How?"

She tsks. "I can answer you, but I need something in return. A trade."

Seriously? The bees flare, loud and stinging. Taking a breath, I calm my racing heart. "What do you want?"

"I want..." She pauses, and for a brief second, I wonder if I get the gift of dramatic flair from her. "Lunch."

"Lunch?" That was unexpected.

"Yes, lunch. You and me. After the Rougarou situation is taken care of."

Just like a "favor" from Baba Geaux isn't something simple like borrowing a cup of sugar, I know "lunch" with my mom means something more. No idea what, but I can't refuse. Not with Portia's life on the line. "Deal."

She offers a noncommittal hmm. "Open the necromancy guide I gave you. There's a section on moon tokens."

Just as I begin to control the burning rage, she takes credit for someone else. "Mawmaw gave me that book."

"And where do you think your Mawmaw got hold of a book on magic?" She places a heavy emphasis on the *magic.* "No, that was all me. Had to steal it from the family even."

The necromancy guide I live by, came from my mom? Not once, in all the years I read it, did I wonder where Mawmaw found it. When she handed it to me, she said something basic, like *this will help you.* And I took it without question, figuring she found it on a random shelf at Dauphine Street's Used Books.

My mom plows forward, unaffected by my shock. "They would have wanted me to bring you in. The family, I mean, but I hid you. For a long time. You've really had me scrambling to protect you."

An image of the dreamscape comes to mind, the plane within a plane. The grove of oaks and Spanish moss camouflaging me from the chanting Hijackers.

I think that was her.

But none of this saves Portia, and I open my desk drawer, pulling out the necromancy guide. "Moon tokens. I'm there."

Listening to her talk, I clear a space to set the book down.

"Read the part about a supermoon event. Because even though it's not a current phenomenon, this artificially loaded moon applies."

My finger skims along the page. "So…a bigger token is needed. At least twice the size to catch the runoff of energy."

"Yes, dear," she says. "More moon power means a bigger token."

"While this is fascinating," it really is. I never thought about adjusting the size, just adding an extra. "What does this have to do with Portia?"

"Isn't it obvious? You need to use your necromancy."

If I lived in a movie, this is the moment thunder would roar. A booming accompaniment to her pronouncement. Maybe a flash of lightning, flickering across the motionless Portia on the bed.

Mom speaks over my surprised silence. "The retrospect spell may be a complication."

Right before she walked away in Simone's memory, I heard her mention it. "What do you mean?"

"The family's been killing. Laying traps and hoping you'd use necromancy to travel through the dead's memory so they can capture you on the magical plane."

A punch of guilt settles in my gut. All this killing to trap me. Simone dead because my family chases my magic.

She keeps talking, oblivious to the knockout jab to my solar plexus. "It's so intricate, planting a supernatural stop-watch in a certain place and time, waiting to see if you'll show. You'll have to avoid jumping into Simone's memory where the trap is laid." Her palpable excitement trembles on the line. It reminds me of when Zach and I researched dark spells, and an eager fizz danced along his skin. "The magical plane doesn't work like the physical plane. Time and space are relative. With the right spell, you can cross any boundary. The possibilities are limitless."

"How do I help Portia?" The crux of the whole conversation. My reason for calling in the first place.

"You need to use life magic. You have it. Did you know that?" she asks.

Of course I know. I learned about it earlier in the day. "I've never used it before."

"I'm going to tell you what to do. Pay close attention."

"Okay." I don't have time to worry if I should trust her, if she's really set on helping me, or if she hides some ulterior motive that benefits her and her mystical syndicate. This is about Portia. Grabbing a loose scrap of paper, I take notes.

"Pour a salt barrier, and inside draw a sunburst on the floor, a big circle with five rays pointing out. The very top of the sun should look like it's missing a line. In that space, write Simone's name. Inside the sun, write Portia's name."

I sketch a sample of what she describes on my paper. "Do I need last names, or...?"

"No," she chuckles. "First names are fine. You'll also need to write their names on separate pieces of paper. Do you have a purple candle?"

"Yes."

She describes the rest of the ritual, and I write it all down, every detail. My confidence builds—I can do this. I can bring Portia back—until she gets to the end. "Once everything is set up, go to your magical plane. Perform it from there and you should be safe from the retrospect spell and from the effect of the loaded moon.

Just like that, all my confidence sinks. Forget swimming, Portia and I are doomed to drown.

"I haven't actually gotten onto my magical plane yet."

Mom laughs, a tittering like tinkling bells. "You'll be fine."

"Sure. I'll just figure it out." I grit my teeth, irked that she shrugs off my concern.

Pulling the phone away, my finger hovers over the red button. A furious tear slips free, and I erase it before it can fall. Weeks of trying to connect, all the unanswered calls, and it comes down to this: My mom is laughing at me.

But she also knows this world of mysticism better than me.

I picture her like I saw in Simone's memory. Bobbed brown hair. Eyes the same shape as mine, though not the same color. The way she took control of the situation, both efficient and capable. That's the person I need answers from.

Bringing the phone back to my ear, I ask, "If I follow this ritual, it'll wake up Portia?"

"Yes. I wouldn't lie to you." Right. My mom, the liar, would never lie.

"I have two more questions. Since you wouldn't lie to me." I use her words, arming myself against her. "Where did you get the heart? The one you gave to Rivera?"

I've wondered, not to mention Dad and the NOPD at large are curious. After low-key accusing my mom of murder, I want to put this question to bed.

"Some lowly cousin the family sent after me. He got too close, and we had to take care of him."

"We?"

"The mystics, dear. Those keeping the magic in harmony," she says.

So yeah. Murder. Maybe self-defense? Maybe not? Maybe mom? Maybe Baba Geaux? I asked hoping to get an answer. Now I just have more questions.

She clears her throat. "What else do you want to know?"

Right. My breathing slows, and I aim for casual, even though my adrenaline hovers somewhere between sugar rush and brain freeze. "Why didn't you answer any of my calls or texts?'

"What number did you use? This one?"

"No. The one you texted me from. After..." I trail off. She knows when we texted.

"Dear, that was my burner phone. Got rid of it soon after our chat." A flurry of noise comes from her end. Yelling and a loud crash. I hear the words *move now.*

"CeCe, I have to go." She sighs deeply, a long and somber sound. "You know I care about you, right? I'll be in touch for our lunch date."

And with that, she hangs up.

It takes a few seconds for me to pull the phone from my ear. A few more seconds to shake myself from the stupor my mom caused. The shock seeps away, water wringing from a towel, and an angry disappointment refills the gap. How could this woman be my mother? Everything from her patronizing tone to her assertion that *black magic is always an option* shreds the image of a nurturing mom.

You know I care about you, right?

No. I don't know that at all.

But at least I know what to do.

Standing at the bedside, I take Portia's listless hand, the buzz becoming a familiar part of her.

"Please be okay," I whisper, and gather everything in preparation for the ritual. Forget the super charged moon and the retrospect spell. The risk is worth it to save my best friend.

CHAPTER TWENTY-TWO

THE MAGICAL PLANE: THE RITUAL

Salt circle poured? Check. Both candles lit? Check. Giant moon token from green wax? Check. And now, per mom's instructions, a Sun symbol (more like a wax ball) from purple. Portia holds both tokens, one in each hand, the emblems of life and death literally at her fingertips.

I sit in the middle of the floor, staring at the sunburst I drew on the hardwood with a black marker. My finger runs over Portia's written name, circling each letter, going around and around. The stress and strain shut down my senses and all that's left is numb.

Poking my pinky with an Exacto knife, since I left my penknife in the morgue, I drop a spot of blood in the middle of the circle. Then one over Simone's name. Usually, I take comfort in my knife's inscription, *Death is good for the soul,* it helps me remember Mawmaw. But tonight, it's an ominous pronouncement.

Come back to me, Portia!

Years of friendship float through my memory. This room, with its white walls and stacks of books, holds innumerable echoes of laughter and shared secrets. I think about the first time I confessed my biggest secret to her. We were twelve, having a sleepover.

"I'm a necromancer," I whispered, nerves and a weird shame causing me to duck my head.

"Is that like a dancer?" she gasped. "You're not a stripper, are you?"

"What? No!" My laughter burst out. "Necromancer. It means I talk to the dead. I help my dad with his investigations."

"I'm so glad. For a minute there, I was worried it was something weird."

And that was that.

Now I look at her lying on my bed, her body cold and still.

Failure isn't an option.

As of yet, I haven't done more than step a toe into my magical plane. But with Portia's life hanging in the balance, I need to pull myself together and get my spirit there.

On two small pieces of paper, I write each name. I take the one reading *Simone* and hold it over the green candle, watching it burn. A breeze blows over my skin, the flame shifting to blue. The super charged moon amps up the chill, icing my insides. I lean into the recognizable magic though the cold is intensified.

For the first time ever, I prepare to pull from a different source; the sun.

I picture it, the bright glowing orb in the sky. With trembling fingers, I put Portia's name in the purple candle. The paper catches fire, the edges curling and turning to ash. The color of flame brightens, the dancing orange like heated metal, changing to golden yellow.

The spark of life magic subdues the cold in me. It starts in my heart, warming my chest and spreading. A new sensation runs through my veins, the fire pumping through my body. It soon overtakes the cold as the intense streak of lava burns a path, the ice not just melting, but boiling.

My fingers turn blue, the moon struggling against the sun. My body battles itself, hot then cold then hot then cold. The temperature tug-of-war tortures me in the unbearable extremes.

I fall over, my whole body shaking. The pain blisters my bones, and I clutch my arms around myself, trying to hold it together. My leg twitches, kicking without my permission, and I worry about the integrity of the salt circle. Have I smeared it? Despite pushing my desk away to give myself maximum space, I didn't account for convulsing in the fetal position.

Get to the magical plane. I hear the words, maybe think the words, I don't know. But I pinch my eyes closed and fight to see my oasis. After countless attempts, bringing the clouds, sky, and reflective pool to mind isn't too hard. My spirit stays firmly rooted, the physical pain a huge distraction.

Remember Portia. This is for Portia.

The echoes of memory come alive, the history of our friendship peeling from the walls, uprooting from the floor. The sounds of our laughter, the weight of our tears, the whispers of our secrets reverberate across all the planes.

It consumes me. Freezing sharpness. Torrid heat. And then...

A ripple. My toe steps into the reflective pool, followed by another ripple. Both of my feet plant in the thin layer of water. The pain vanishes. I feel free. Unlike visiting Zach's plane or being spirit kidnapped, this one belongs to me.

The difference is here, in the way it embraces me, an excited homecoming now that I made it.

Portia hovers ahead, floating in the turquoise atmosphere. Her spirit is beautiful; bright and happy, such an inner light that emanates warmth and hope.

No wonder she's my bestie.

The emblems in her hands glow, the same colors as the candle flames. And next to her, clinging to her ankle, is Simone's spirit. Though she wears no veil or green jewels, I recognize her. Not with physical eyes, but soul to soul.

An iridescent energy travels from Simone to Portia, and the shimmer seeps inside my friend. The living tendril of energy creeps from her ankle and up to her core, branching out like veins. Simone's essence, her magic, attaches, a radiant parasite adhering to Portia's vitality.

Two mirrors float on either side of them, one to the left of Portia, another to the right of Simone. As I step closer, I come to understand they're not mirrors at all, but memories playing out. I whip my head away from Simone's side to avoid looking, afraid I might still be tied to the retrospect trap.

The memory runs, and I watch the haunting from Portia's point of view, see Simone's body dragging closer and closer. Feel the paralyzing horror and fear. I want to pause the moment, stop the haunting from happening. But I'm not here to change the past; I'm here to wake up Portia.

Keeping my focus on her, and away from the spirit of the dead, I touch the two emblems, not with my physical hand, but with my spirit. They rise in front of me, the wax moon token and the sun symbol, the blue and yellow glowing.

Merge them together, mom told me. *Inject some life magic into the moon and she'll wake up.*

I push them and meet some resistance, the emblems like magnets polarizing against each other. Not to mention it's weird figuring out how to move things on this plane. I might as well shove two streams of water together.

No. Don't. Another voice whispers in my head. But who? And why? I need to save Portia.

A new light radiates on my plane, one I didn't create or invite. A singular presence that coalesces into the outline of a person. *What is happening?* My clouds darken, a heaviness rolling in. Inky blackness seeps into the cotton candy pink, turning it thunderous.

While the slowly materializing person doesn't feel scary or threatening, something about the being feels familiar. Did I trigger the retrospect spell? Is it Grandpa Hijacker invading my plane?

I need to wake Portia and return to my bedroom. My hold on this plane is tenuous, and this new presence makes it even more so.

Using my energy, and guiding the emblems, I force them together, blue and yellow mixing into a green glowing orb. A surge of magic bursts outward, a shockwave that earthquakes in my core. The ripple shakes me on both the magical and the physical plane. It pushes me back and my feet glide along the top of the water, carrying me several feet away.

Simone's spirit detaches from Portia's ankle, but instead of disappearing or going to rest, she drifts beside Portia, touching her cheek. A horrible dread races through me, my heart pounding erratically. Is this really going to wake Portia up? Did mom lie to me?

Of course she lied.

Anger and fear and sadness converge as I watch Simone sink into Portia, merging together. Just like the emblems.

A bigger shockwave erupts, this one pushing me out of my plane and laying me flat. Everything goes black. I fall into the nothingness.

"CeCe. CeCe," a voice calls to me. I recognize it. Portia. "Come on, please wake up."

A loud groan leaves my lungs, and I blink a few times, my lids about a million pounds each. My head aches. No, more than aches. Jackhammers. Every muscle in my body begs to be put out of misery. "What happened?"

"How far back do you want me to go? We snuck into the morgue, I was haunted, you clearly performed some sort of ritual, and when I came to, you were laid out on the floor." She helps me sit up because, yes, I really need the help. "Does that sound about right?"

"You're really awake!" I throw my arms around Portia, hugging her close. As close as I can with my body shaking. Necro-shivers...sobs...? Or maybe the aftereffects of life magic? I can't tell. "Are you okay? I was so worried. And devastated. And sick."

"Am *I* okay? No offense, but you look terrible."

"You're never allowed in the morgue again." Messy tears smear my face in the worst sort of ugly cry. And I continue to shake, an uncontrolled spasming.

"Thanks for saving me." She looks around the room, and I follow her gaze.

Candles blown out and tipped over, salt circle smudged, desk pushed against my closet, and a decorative Sharpie sunburst on the hardwood. Dad's not gonna like it. "I kind of made a mess. But worth it."

"We need to warm you up." With a herculean effort she manages to drag me over to the bed and sit me down. Pulling my blanket around me, she stays by my side, holding me.

Through my chattering teeth I ask, "Are you really okay?"

"Yes, I'm fine. I didn't mean to scare you." Her head tips, a stare-into-the-distance look entering her gaze. "It was weird. I heard everything after I passed out, but I couldn't wake up. She talked to me the whole time."

"She? You mean Simone?" *Chatter, chatter, chatter.*

"Yeah. She kept reassuring me that everything would be fine." She shrugs off this monumental information.

She holds my hand, and my fingers shake like I'm holding a Polaroid. The buzz of her newly acquired voodoo runs along my skin. I pinch my eyes closed, replaying the moment Simone's spirit fused with hers, trying to process the implications of what it all means.

"Portia. You have magic."

A slow smile creases her face. "I know."

What did my mom make me do?

CHAPTER TWENTY-THREE

Surprisingly, Dad allowed us to go to rehearsal.

He dropped Portia and me off at a stop on Canal, and we rode the trolley all the way to the station before hopping cars to end up near Jackson Square. Just a quick walk away from Le Petit Theater. I hate carrying VanHellSing on public transport, but Dad didn't want Portia to drive. Having been haunted once before, he preferred to err on the side of caution, despite Portia's assurances that she's fine, never better, 100% perfect.

After a long conversation last night—lots of words from me, convincing babbling from Portia, lots of grunts from him—he said, *you're on a short leash for this one.* I know he also called Verily Broussard to check out Luc. Not sure what she said, but enough to convince Dad we need to be at Le Petit Theater. On a short leash.

It also helped that he cleaned the morgue to pristine, that Portia woke up from the haunting, and that we managed to avoid any interactions with law enforcement. A consequence-light plot twist I didn't see coming. Plus, I gained a wealth of information to share. About the family, the magic, and Mom.

Mom.

Dad's reaction to my interaction with her was strange. The deeper I delved into the phone call with her, the whiter his knuckles turned. He stared out the dark, front window, lost in thought, the silence heavy enough even Portia couldn't break it. While he normally stays straight-faced and impossible to read, I glimpsed the sadness straining at the edges of his down-turned lips. The remorse pinched at the corners of his eyes.

He finally said, *Will you give me her number? I need to speak with her.* Then he issued the new and shiny Unbendable Laws of LeBlanc for whenever I leave the house.

The rules: Check in by text every two hours. Report where I am and where I'm going. No doing anything illegal, no sneaking out, and no withholding any information. All Unbendable Laws of LeBlanc are subject to change based on Dad's whims. Basically, if he says come home immediately, I better figure out teleportation.

But for now, I head to Le Petit Theater, lugging my guitar case. Portia and I pass a singer with a big, portable amp who performs at the entrance to The Square. His rendition of "Walking on Sunshine" blasts, and several people sing along. The lyrics feel particularly appropriate since the sun scorches the sidewalk, turning it into a griddle.

As we get to psychic row, in front of the St. Louis Cathedral, Portia slows down and looks over the vendors. The normally crowded area is bare bones today, very few card readers and fortune tellers offering services. Baba Geaux's spot remains empty. No cheap umbrella and chintzy sign to announce the "world famous witch doctor," and I never thought I'd miss the sound of his animated *hoo hoo*.

I wonder where he is and what he's doing.

Scrutinizing the others, I search to see if I recognize anyone. After Simone's memory, where I hovered in the clearing with the mystics, I expect to spot a familiar face or two. But the buskers calling out to read palms or peer into crystal balls all bear a distinctly theatrical flair, much more storytelling than fortune telling.

Incense burns from a nearby table, the musky perfume mixing with the floral scent from the gardens. Music plays like a personal soundtrack, accompanying our every step. Or at least my every step. I realize Portia stopped in front of a table, speaking to one of the psychics.

"You have more than one set. Please. I'll pay you." Portia folds her hands together, pleading with a man who wears a sparkly fedora.

I put my hand on her arm. The hum of magic still pulses beneath my fingers, unchanged in the two minutes since I last checked. "Portia."

"Hmm?" She turns to me, and though I can't explain it, something feels off. Maybe a slightly less sarcastic smile. Or the gentleness in her gaze as she looks me over.

"Are you okay?"

Blinking the haze from her eyes, she laughs. "How many times are you going to ask that today? I'm good."

"Fifty bucks." Fedora guy's accent hails more New Jersey than New Orleans. Very authentic to The Square <cue eye-roll>. "Take it or move along."

Portia sighs and shakes her head. "Those cards aren't even originals. Hardly worth the paper they're printed on."

"Then get outta here." He adjusts his hat to swipe his sweaty forehead and waves us off. Portia huffs, walking away at a fast clip. With my much shorter strides, I jog to keep up.

"Why were you wanting to buy tarot cards from that guy?" I speak through increasingly strained breaths. I'm a drama geek and a necromancer, not a runner.

"I don't know. He had two sets, and the cards looked like fun. Thought I'd give them a try."

"Portia, stop." I tug at the back of her shirt, slowing her down.

She straightens the yellow peplum, the most Portia-like action so far today. "Don't ask if I'm okay again."

"Obviously I'm gonna ask!" I start ticking off the reasons on my fingers. "Last night you were haunted. I feel magic on your skin, and you have a sudden interest in tarot cards. It freaks me out, to be honest."

"CeCe. My girl. Listen." She takes me by the shoulders and leans in close. "I. Am. Good. I promise."

My hesitant nod says what my mouth doesn't, that I ain't buying what she's selling with the *I'm good*. "Right. But you're on a short leash."

She laughs. "Yes, Detective LeBlanc."

Between my bestie's new magic and stress about Zach, my anxiety hovers in the raging zone. I don't understand what's going on with Portia. I miss my boyfriend. Not just spending time with him but talking to him. Sharing worries, carrying a burden together. The week without him hurts my soul, this longing to see him more intense than waiting for the next season of a favorite show on Netflix.

I really do love him.

As if my thoughts conjured him, there he stands. The terracotta-colored stucco of the theater serves as his background, the sun his spotlight. The green tee he wears hugs him in all the right ways, and he tucks his hands into the pockets of his cargo shorts. Longish brown hair tickles his eyelashes, the locks begging for a pair of scissors. But only because the strands partially block the beautiful ocean orbs inviting me to swim in their azure depths.

Before I even think it through, I drop VanHellSing and rush to him, throwing myself into his embrace. Literally throwing. He falls back two steps, stumbling to gain his balance and capturing me in a tight hug. The world narrows to him, to us, and our magic melds like two perfect flavor combinations. Better than sausage and gravy. More heavenly than peanut butter and chocolate. A perfection that even outshines beignets and powdered sugar.

I forgot how it feels to touch without the heavy taint of oily power. Just the pure simplicity of Zach and CeCe. The ZeCe Reunion tour.

"You're here," I whisper.

"Aunt Lucy gave me the all-clear this morning. But I'm off magic again, and it seems like the worst time for that."

I shake my head against his shoulder. "No, it's okay. Everything's okay now."

Pulling back from the embrace, he holds my face in his hands. "Ohh, I've missed you."

Without giving me the chance to reply, he dips his head, his breath whispering over my lips. The kiss starts soft, the barest brush of connection. I crave more, need to feel more, and I fist my hands in his shirt, pressing closer.

Relief sparks inside me, bursting like a million SOS flares signaling rescue. Dependable, knowledgeable, beautiful Zach gives me the soothing reassurance that I'm not alone in this anymore. Tears fill my eyes, not the sad kind, but the emotional release of finally floating into a safe harbor.

"Get a room!" a male voice yells. A familiar male voice.

I slowly pull away from Zach to see Portia's useless ex-boyfriend Devin. My focus had been so wholly on my kissy face reunion that I didn't even notice him there.

He wears board shorts with hot pink flamingos, black flipflops, a gold fleur-de-lis on a chain, and a pair of mirrored sunglasses.

"Where's your shirt?" I ask.

"Shirtless summer!" He pounds his chest, caveman style, and the necklace bounces from pec to pec. I can't imagine why Portia broke up with him.

For her part, she ignores the display of primate posturing, and gazes down the busy street. The lack of attention bothers him, his body language betraying every thought. From his awkward side-stepping closer, to the puffing of his chest, to the dismayed slant of his brow.

I glance at Zach to gauge his reaction to Devin, and other than a subtle smirk, his attention stays on me. Taking my hand, he curls it into his own, his fingers squeezing tight. Looks like I'm not the only one who missed being together.

Finally, Devin clears his throat and rocks back on his heels. "Hey, Portia."

She sighs so long the rest of summer flashes before my eyes. "Hey, Devin."

"How've you been?" He shuffles another step.

"What do you want?"

"Just making conversation, no need to be prickly. It's shirtless summer, babe!" He flexes, emphasizing the *less* part of *shirt*.

"How's your new girlfriend?" Despite his sudden appearance with Zach, and his continued interest in Portia, I check on his attachment to my nemesis, Julie Jolley.

"Yeah, we broke up. She's crazy. But get this." He rubs

his hands together, and a jolt of delight electrifies his words. "She doesn't know we broke up so now I'm totally a spy."

Following his logic resembles listening to a song in another language. Words are being used, but the meaning is out of reach.

"She doesn't know you broke up?" I scrunch my eyes, as if squinting will clear up what he says.

Zach puts my brain out of its misery. "Devin decided to keep an eye on Julie for us. Apparently, she's a little obsessed with you."

"I'm talking stalker levels," Devin says.

"I did catch her following me the other day." Where she splashed me with holy water and accused me of being evil. *Ouch.* Still hurts.

"More like following you every day," Devin says.

"Seriously?" How have I not noticed her more?

"Yeah. I'm actually meeting her in a few minutes." He glances at his phone. "But I got you. I'll throw her off the track, and she won't learn your secret."

"Thanks." My opinion of Devin has greatly improved during this short conversation. Sure, he acts ridiculous, and I question his deep-thinking skills, but Zach spoke the truth. Devin is solid.

"Luc!" Portia moves from her spot leaning against the building to greet her approaching co-star.

His easy swagger radiates confidence. In his usual shorts and tank top, this one a slightly lighter shade of black, he doesn't need to go without a shirt to show off. Thor and God of Thunder do that all on their own.

"Darlin'. You're a sight for sore eyes." Luc opens his arms to hug her, and as soon as they touch, his eyes widen.

Surprise tenses his muscles, and his breath quickens. "Somethin' interestin' happened since I saw you last night."

The gift of sight from La Siréne. What does he see in Portia?

"Last night?" Devin inflates his chest, straightening to his full height.

Luc lifts an eyebrow, his head turning slowly to take in the rest of us. "Nice to see you again, CeCe. Hey, Zach. And... friend."

"'Sup, man?" Devin gives a head nod, his sun-bleached hair falling into his eyes at the motion, and he brushes it away in the perfect boy-next-door swoop.

Portia sighs again, this one only half the summer long. "That's Devin. He's living the shirtless summer life."

"Cool." Luc shrugs, reaching one hand behind his neck to fist his shirt, and pulling it over his head. The sigil of La Siréne inks his impressive chest, followed by an equally impressive six pack.

Four, five, six. Yep. I count to make sure. Just to be accurate.

Luc wears shirtless summer a lot better, and Portia's drooling awareness speaks to that. Poor Devin. Not well played if he hoped to win her back.

"I got here just in time." Aubree Bloom practically runs to join our group, her bubbly giggle chasing after.

"Hi, Aubree." My greeting breezes by as she ogles the guys.

She walks up to Zach, bold as you please, and strokes his bicep. "You gonna join in, cutie? I'm sure you have something to offer."

I pluck off her hand. "He does."

Between couch snuggles and summer swimming, I

know what hides under his tee. Aubree Bloom doesn't need to.

"I'm refraining," Zach says.

"Pity." She bites her lip and moves on to Devin. "Hey handsome. Who are you?"

The abundance of hormone stew simmering in front of the theater could feed every tourist in the French Quarter. Aubree adds to the already crowded sidewalk cast including the shirtless summer ex, the werewolf, the suddenly voodoo'd best friend, the freshly rehabbed boyfriend, and me.

It sounds like a character list for a Taylor Swift Halloween special.

A sharp elbow jab to my side jars an *oof* out of me. Rubbing my ribs, I turn to my bestie, who, for some reason, chose violence. She attempts to engage in silent conversation with an exaggerated eyebrow lift and an enthusiastic chin jut. But my interpretation skills let me down because I've got nothing.

What, I mouth, ignoring the Aubree show, where she attempts to engage all three guys in thrilling conversation, like asking if they could bench press a small mammal. Luc puts his tank top back on, and even Devin looks longingly at everyone's shirts. All the while she gawks and giggles.

It seems deliberate, an act to make everyone uncomfortable. Either that or she has no people skills.

"We should head in." Zach takes a step closer to the entrance.

"Yeah, good luck today. I gotta go meet my uhh...Julie." Devin makes a quick turn to leave down St Peter Street.

Portia continues to give me eyebrow, and I grab her by the pointy and dangerous elbow. "You go ahead. We'll be right behind you."

"Ooh, I have the best escorts." Aubree inserts herself right between the two guys.

Zach scrunches his forehead, his confusion real, but I wave him inside. "Seriously, right behind you."

Once the sidewalk clears, Portia drags me away from the door to a semi-quiet spot across the street. Let's be real, it's the French Quarter. Quiet doesn't exist. Drumming echoes through the air, an ensemble of repurposed buckets playing a peppy rhythm. Further down the sidewalk, a pumping bass blasts from an open door of a shop.

She glances back and forth, then leans in. "Aubree is one of the Hijackers."

Whatever I expected her to say pales in comparison to what she actually said. My heart thumpity thumps and my breath whooshes out. "How do you know?"

She shakes her head. "Just trust me."

"Portia, I trust you more than anyone in the world." I look into her deep, brown eyes, so familiar and yet something different shines in their depths. "But please tell me. How do you know?"

She chews on her bottom lip. Taps her fingers on her leg. Then her voice drops to barely audible. "Simone told me."

"What?" My shout gets a sideways glance from a couple strolling nearby. A pit opens in my stomach. I never should have believed mom.

"Okay, so, she still talks to me. Don't make it into a thing." She abandons the effort to stay quiet, her voice rising with mine. "Let's focus on the fact that someone in the *Voodoo Bayou* quintet is after you."

A breeze picks up, normally a welcome reprieve from the heat, but the wind whispering on my skin and the leaves skittering down the sidewalk add an ominous touch. "Are you sure? I mean, is Simone sure about Aubree?"

"Positive."

I glance over my shoulder, staring at the doors where Aubree entered. Everything inside me freezes. I'm talking Elsa level *Let it Go* traveling a path through my veins and icing my core. "She doesn't have magic. I touched her skin. Which means..."

"Black magic," Portia and I both say at the same time.

CHAPTER TWENTY-FOUR

LE PETIT THEATER: THE REHEARSAL

After Portia's *totally normal* revelation about hearing voices, I expect a stressful rehearsal. Add to that my confirmed suspicions of Hijacker Aubree and her carnelian bracelet, and I shudder at the thought of spending an entire hour and a half sitting next to her. But Chance, the music director, keeps us busy, and I don't have time to think about anything other than my instrument. Our quintet plays in the orchestra pit, and the actors work above us on the stage. With no microphones hooked up, we can all practice in the theater and avoid getting in each other's way.

I pluck at VanHellSing's strings, loving the vibration under my fingertips. The music, a jazz noir with a gothic twist, haunts the pit in a dark, mysterious sound. The four other musicians merge their playing with mine, Aubree on the drums, Lovelie on the double bass, saxophone guy, whose name I still haven't learned, and Zach on piano.

From the corner of my eye, I watch him. His body rolls

with the rhythm, his hair falling across his forehead. Every so often he flicks his chin to clear the strands from his gaze, and it's really sexy. Like an Easter Egg in a movie, a special treat on display for anyone who looks for it.

And yeah. I keep looking.

The final note of the intermission sequence rings out in a flourish and Chance slashes his hands through the air to cut us off.

"Take five." He turns and walks away, and we all gawk at his retreat, instruments still at the ready.

I gently lay VanHellSing in her case and join Zach at the piano. He shuffles through his music, setting out the next pages. Sliding on the bench next to him, I put my head on his shoulder.

"I've been watching you. Totally fangirling."

He laughs and runs a hand through his hair. "Am I gonna find pictures of myself on the Internet?"

"No way." I pull my phone from my pocket and wriggle it in front of him. "These unsolicited photos are all mine."

"Well, you should know that I'm a fanboy. My girl knows how to make a guitar look good," he says, but I only half-listen. A bunch of text messages fill my phone, all from Portia.

PORTIA: Did you tell Z?

PORTIA: I told Luc about BB.

PORTIA: BB is code for Aubree.

PORTIA: 4 Bubblegum Barbie.

PORTIA: We R making a plan.

I tip my phone so Zach can see it, and he reads Portia's ramblings over my shoulder. "Tell me what?"

I blow out a breath, puffing my cheeks. "So. Many. Things. I could fill a novel with everything we need to talk about."

"Hey y'all." Aubree pops her head next to mine.

I screech, bobbling my cell, bouncing it in my hands a few times before it lands with a cacophonous slam against the piano keys.

"Aubree! Hi!" My tone hovers in the shrieking range. "What's up? How are you? Nice drumming, by the way. Very on beat."

The word vomit pours out, my lack of control appalling. Aubree's smile slowly droops, shifting from cheery greeting to confused cringe. All the while my mind spins, *did she see the texts? Does she suspect we know about her?*

"Staying on beat is kind of the point." She moves next to Zach and nudges his shoulder. "But you! Watching you play is hot. Makes me thirsty."

Ew. Apparently Aubree wants to join my fangirl club. *Application denied!* Only one person gets the right to say flirty things and bat eyelashes at the sexy pianist. And, spoiler alert, it's NOT Aubree.

"Thanks?" Zach states it as a question, and his gaze catches on Aubree's wrist. By his fixed stare, I know he recognizes the stones, realizes I asked about them at Black Wren. "Nice bracelet. Is that carnelian?"

"Oh...yeah." She tucks her hands behind her back.

"Chance is brutal." Lovelie joins our group, shaking out her arms. "My fingers are going to blister."

"He's brilliant. Not everyone can direct with such intense focus." Saxophone guy wanders over as well, and *what is this?* The interrupt CeCe parade?

Meanwhile, my phone vibrates in my hand, probably another text from Portia, and I quietly die inside, wanting to check, but unable to with Aubree standing so close.

"Of course he's brilliant. All evil geniuses are." Lovelie pulls at the fringe on her shirt. It's an orange crop top with long, beaded strips that hang all the way to mid-thigh. Somehow, she manages to lug the double bass around and play it without catching the dangles.

"I'm with Lovelie. Chance is positively savage." Aubree's bubbly voice contradicts the harsh put-down.

"Have any of y'all worked with him before?" Sax guy asks. "I did last summer on Music Man."

My phone vibrates again, and I clutch it in my hand. As sax guy starts sharing his detailed history of playing in an orchestra, I slip off the piano bench.

"I'll be back in a few. Gotta use the restroom." And check my texts without a certain Bubblegum Barbie hovering over my shoulder.

"Oh, me too." Aubree dodges around the Interrupt CeCe Parade to follow on my heels.

"Okay," I say, hoping my smile looks sincere while my internal narrator lovingly prepares a multiple-choice test.

Aubree is going to the bathroom with CeCe because:

   A. *She saw the texts on CeCe's phone and wants to wrestle it away to read them all in greater detail.*

   B. *She's on an information gathering mission for Grandpa Hijacker.*

   C. *She plans to kidnap CeCe, hold her for ransom, and solicit enough revenue to start a carnelian bracelet business.*

   D. *She needs to use the bathroom.*

We climb the stairs out of the pit, me in front and Aubree behind. The temperature changes above ground, the air conditioning given space to breathe. My immediate relief from the sweaty depths of the pit shifts to the miserable chill of an over-cooled room.

Welcome to summer in New Orleans, where you never regulate your body thermometer.

Portia and Luc stand on the stage, running a scene. She looks so good, like this is her natural habitat, and even without a spotlight blazing down, she shines.

Aubree moves to my side, close enough our arms brush. "How long have you and Zach been dating?"

Ah. The answer is B. Information gathering.

"A couple of months," I tell her.

"Really?" She sounds genuinely surprised. "I would have guessed longer. You seem closer than that."

Experiencing trauma together builds a relationship in triple speed.

Of course, I don't tell her that.

"Yep, we are close," I say. With Aubree right here, all friendly-like, I decide to turn the tables. Gather some information of my own. "So, what do you do when you're not playing drums for *Voodoo Bayou*?"

"Oh, I'm boring. I just do...regular stuff."

Regular stuff. Right. Like spend her evenings chanting with The Hijackers to spirit kidnap me.

"What school do you go to?" Come to think of it, I don't know how old she is. Has she graduated? Going into senior year? "What grade are you in?"

"I'm homeschooled," she says, ignoring the second half of my question.

"That's cool." Appear interested. Just a chummy

conversation among bandmates. "Do you live far from here?"

Her bracelet rattles as she rubs the stones. "Not too far. How about you?"

"Not too far." Trying to lever information from her is harder than opening a stuck oyster shell. Turning the edges, finding a spot to slip the knife, and pry, pry, pry.

I pull the heavy bathroom door open, and we go into separate stalls, where I finally—FINALLY— check my texts. They're from a new group message, Zach, me, Portia, and an unknown number I presume is Luc. I take a moment to update the contact: *Woofy.* He'd hate it, but it brings me joy.

> 4 ZULA; PORTIA: Starting this group chat. Gang's all here.

> 4 ZULA; PORTIA: We have a plan. Luc's going to ask BB out. He can B a spy 2. Don't let her leave after.

> 4 ZULA; WOOFY: I'll find out what she knows.

What? I read the texts again, wondering how Portia feels about sending her crush into enemy territory. Not to mention my circle of people has more spies than a James Bond movie. Julie stalks me. Devin watches her. Aubree, the undercover agent, attempts to covertly obtain data, and now Luc plans to join the espionage party.

> 4 ZULA; CECE: Zach can distract her with shirtless summer.

> 4 ZULA; ZACH: Pass.

I bite my lip to keep from laughing at his response.

"How did you meet Zach?" Aubree's voice echoes in the tiled room, and I startle, bobbling my phone again. Unless she possesses X-ray vision, or reads minds, she has no idea what my messages say. Her timing, though, is pretty impeccable.

Also, doesn't she understand bathroom etiquette? You don't to talk to someone while they pee.

"Uhhh...hold on." Once at the sink, and washing my hands, I finish. "We met at drama camp."

She asks me a few more questions (I keep my answers vague), I ask her a few more questions (still prying for that opening), and we walk back to the pit. Chance stands in the corner, talking on his phone. As soon as he notices us, he stabs a finger on the screen and tosses his cell in a bag on the floor.

"I said five minutes, not eight. We're here to work." He pulls sanitizer from his pocket and thoroughly murders any germs daring to occupy space on his hands.

Aubree and I both apologize, hurrying to our instruments.

The rest of rehearsal passes in a blur of scattered notes and swirling tempos. Even with the chaos of my life, I find myself getting more excited for the play. The drama geek inside me squeals, the script and music combining into what promises to be an epic production.

Chance swipes the air, cutting the quintet at the final note. I love this moment, when the echo of music hangs in the air. The briefest flash, before any talking or applause, when it floats like a spirit of the dead; not there, but lingering. The world pauses, and the melody settles, a breath of emotion heavy, and thick, and beautiful.

"Not bad. See you tomorrow." Chance gives one nod and picks up his bag to leave.

His declaration of our performance might as well be effusive praise. *Not bad.* Compliment received.

It takes me less than two minutes to pack up my guitar. Another fifteen seconds to gather my music. But Aubree already heads for the stairs. I throw my bag over my shoulder, lug VanHellSing with me, and hurry to catch up. In my rush, my foot clips a music stand, and I propel forward, grabbing onto a chair to keep from face-planting.

"Are you okay?" Zach takes VanHellSing and helps me straighten.

"Yep. Fine. Great." I'm already on the move again, my sights on where Aubree disappeared up the stairs.

Trusting Zach to follow, I fast-walk to catch her. The stage rehearsal ended, the cast cleared out, and I search the theater, looking for Aubree. For Portia.

My hustle was unnecessary because Luc stands a few feet away, talking to Aubree, no shirtless summer distraction needed to keep her around. She touches his arm, her body pressed closer than casual. I wonder where Portia is, and what she'd think about the rampant flirt going down. Then I hear what Luc says.

"Why don't we skip dinner and go straight to my house."

Whoa. It didn't take me THAT long to get up the stairs. Another gaze around the auditorium and I see Portia, hanging out by the entrance, pretending to ignore her crush propositioning Bubblegum Barbie.

"I thought you'd never ask." Aubree looks over her shoulder, directly at me, and then she does the weirdest, cringiest thing.

She licks Luc.

A long slurp on the neck, popsicle in the summertime

style. An echo of it traces along my neck where the Rougarou marked me.

Whoa.

For Luc's part, he stays motionless, seemingly unaffected by the weird show of physicality. Then again, maybe that's a regular greeting in the werewolf community.

Could Aubree be the Rougarou curse thief? Not just one of the Hijackers, but THE Hijacker?

I hope Luc knows what he's doing.

CHAPTER TWENTY-FIVE

CAFÉ DU MONDE: THE WAIT

"Waiting is the worst." Portia looks at her phone again, even though only a second has passed since she last checked. "But beignets help."

Zach, Portia, and I hide out at Café Du Monde, eating an unholy amount of the holy pastry, and talking about everything that happened over the last week. His eyes glazed over a couple of times, and when I got to the bit about Portia having magic, he touched her arm.

He shakes his head at the new, never before seen footage of Voodoo Portia. "But she wasn't born with magic. How can we feel it?"

Because I trusted an un-trustable mother who encouraged me to merge a magical fortune teller with my best friend.

We talked everything into the ground, no detail left unburied, and still, no word from Luc. Nary a phone call or text message.

What does nary mean anyway? *Mental note: google nary later.*

I glance at my phone. 5:32. *Sigh.* "I better text my dad."

ME: Still here at Du Monde. No illegal happenings. No news on Luc.

Yes, I told him about Luc going out with Aubree, who we suspect, on good authority, is a Hijacker. Possibly The Hijacker. In the spirit of the Unbendable Laws of LeBlanc, I chose not to withhold any information. Except that Portia now has magic and talks to dead people. Rather, a dead person. And that person, Simone, identified Aubree as a Hijacker.

Unnecessary details for Dad.

CHIEF DADDIO: Be home before curfew.

The squeak of a chair pulls my attention from my phone. I look up to hot pink flamingo board shorts and a shirtless torso.

"What's up, guys?" Devin swings the chair out and sits.

"Uhh, hi Devin." Portia lifts an eyebrow, tipping her head at me. This time I read her silent communication loud and clear.

Why is he here?

I shrug and ask, "Why are you here?"

He takes no offense at the bluntly worded question and scoots in, close enough his shoulder rubs Portia's. Which makes Zach scoot closer to me, and I'm not complaining.

"I convinced Julie to go home. Told her I'd watch for anything suspicious the rest of the night," Devin says.

After confronting Julie, I knew she dug her feet in, determined to figure out my secret. But this level, watching my every move, takes things beyond obsession. "Why is she so..."

The right word eludes me. Nothing quite conveys *completely fixated with something dangerous and none of her business.*

"Crazy?" Devin fills in my blank. "Look. She knows something more than a prank went down at Lafayette Cemetery. And the fact that it's you, CeCe, makes her manic. She hates the idea that you, of all people, might pull something over on her."

"How do we get her to back off?" Zach asks the question and my chest lights up. I've missed having him with me to navigate these complicated situations.

"Leave it to me. I'm the spy." Devin puts an arm on the back of Portia's chair, making no move to give her space. "So, what'd I miss?"

"Literally nothing." Portia groans and slouches lower.

Picking up my phone, I check the time again. 5:41. But on my screen, I have a notification.

> WOOFY: Come to my house. Best if you come alone.

My lips move silently as I read it again, my confusion real. "Did anyone else get a text from Luc?"

Portia leaps from her chair to grab my phone. The whole table screeches forward in her enthusiasm to snatch it from my hand.

"You could have just asked," I say.

"It's a trap." She stares at my screen, shaking her head. "It doesn't make sense. Why wouldn't he text me? Maybe Aubree took his phone and she's luring you in."

"What are you talking about?" Zach puts his arm around me, offering a supportive squeeze.

"Someone named Woofy wants her to come over. Alone." Devin has a premium spot to take in the message lighting up my cell.

"Woofy?" Zach crinkles his forehead. "You named Luc Woofy?"

"I did—"

He jumps in. "You're not going to his house alone. No way."

"Obviously. Something weird is going on, and we need to find out what." I take my phone back from Portia and get my thumbs at the ready. "How should I respond?"

"Tell *Aubree* we know it's her, and we aren't going to fall for her transparent tricks." Portia has opinions.

"This is the guy I just met? Outside the theater?" Devin twists the fleur-de-lis pendant around his neck.

I nod and continue to stare at my screen. *Could it be a trap?* Though impressive, Luc's physique would mean nothing against The Hijackers. Even one like Bubblegum Barbie. Magic beats muscle.

My mind immediately jumps to Rivera luring me to his house, using my bestie as bait. Panic surges through me, all my nerves coiled like trampoline springs.

Zach rubs my shoulder in small soothing circles. "Relax, CeCe. Ask Luc why he wants to see you alone."

"Yeah. Okay." Just ask. I can do that.

ME: Y alone?

And back to waiting. This time, my foot wriggles under the table. Zach's sneakered toe brushes my ankle. And then a gentle tap on the top of my foot. My wriggling stops. The power of ZeCe.

My phone buzzes.

WOOFY: Ur still marked. The closer to
night, the more dangerous it is.

Right. That happened.

"Luc says I'm Rougarou bait." Another itty, bitty detail I omitted in my conversations with Dad.

"Whoa. That's bad. I mean, it sounds bad." Devin twirls a piece of Portia's hair, and strangely, she lets him.

Another text comes in, and this one I read out loud.

WOOFY: Let me help U. I have a cure.

When did he have time to get a cure? Is it from Baba Geaux?

"Looks like we're going to Luc's." Portia scoots her chair back and stands. "You driving, Zach?"

"I drove." Devin also rises, pulling keys from his pocket.

"Welcome to the team," she tells him. "Luc and his family are werewolves, but someone stole the curse, and CeCe's long-lost, evil grandpa wants her magic."

Devin grins. "So, just another day being friends with Zach and CeCe."

"Hold on, hold on!" My foot resumes the wriggle. "I can't drag y'all into this mess. It's really dangerous. People are getting killed. The Rougarou" —a shudder catches and it shivers down my spine— "You don't want to see what it does."

"Sure, CeCe. We'd much rather leave you to face it on your own." Portia rolls her eyes. "Besides, the Rougarou doesn't come out until after dark. We'll be home and tucked in our beds before curfew."

"I don't know." I pinch my eyes closed, rubbing my temples.

"We're going with you." She gives me a quick pat on the back. "Where'd you park, Dev?"

"Follow me," he says.

And that's how VanHellSing and I find myself in the backseat of Devin's Suburban, making the short drive down Ursulines Avenue to the Creole Cottage where Luc is staying.

I send two texts, one to Luc (**ME:** *Headed your way now*), and one to Dad, giving him Luc's address. According to the Unbendable Laws of LeBlanc, I'm required to report my location. Plus, it's good sense to let him know, especially under the current circumstances.

Devin finds parking on the street, and we walk down the sidewalk. A smell of seafood brines the air, probably a gumbo simmering nearby, and my stomach cries. My diet of cereal and nine beignets isn't cutting it.

Zach's hand curls in mine, his magic softly buzzing against my palm. On another day, in another time, this moment would sing a dreamy rhythm of romance. But approaching the white cottage, the dormer windows reflecting the early evening rays of the sun, my apprehension grows. Fear gnaws a pit in my gut, or maybe it's my hunger. Either way.

The dark green shutters close off the front entrance, but the gate to the courtyard hangs open. I clench my fingers around the warm wrought iron.

"Should we go home?" I ask. "Last chance to abort the mission."

"We're doing this." Portia leads the way on the bricked path towards the courtyard.

Flowering crepe myrtles in blush and white cover us overhead. Caladium leaves as big as my hand brush my clothes as we crowd the walkway. It smells like flowers and earth under this canopy of trees. A short blink of paradise before whatever waits on the other side.

"Swanky." Devin turns a full circle, taking in the verdant array of plants.

The narrow walkway opens to the courtyard, and it's just as amazing seeing it the second time. The lush greenery. The trickling fountain. The relaxing sounds of gurgling water. On closer inspection, I notice the bottom tier features a carved, howling wolf. They have a theme, for sure.

"Didn't really think you'd come alone. But it was worth a try."

I startle at Luc's voice. He's semi-hidden in the shadows. He leans against the trunk of a large oak, a can of Root Beer held in one of his hands.

"There's no way we'd let CeCe fly solo." Portia steps in front of him.

"I figured." Luc nods, totally unflustered. "What's shirtless summer doin' here?"

"I'm the driver." Devin lowers his voice, a hard edge to his words.

"We shouldn't have so many people here, but it is what it is." Luc takes a drink of his Root Beer.

"What's wrong with you? You're being weird," Portia says. And I agree. Thor and God of Thunder slump, and his head hangs low. His whole demeanor radiates down-in-the-dumps, but his eyes stay sharp. Ultra watchful.

"I'm worried about Zula, but that'll have to keep." Luc crushes the can, tossing it in one of the flower beds. "Aubree's waitin' for us."

"She's still here?" I ask. Cryptic Luc disconcerts me. I share a glance with Zach, and he looks just as confused as I feel.

"She's gonna help us." He crosses the threshold into the house. "Come inside and see for yourself."

He said the same words when we came here the first time and met Zula. Seeing her, an innocent girl, trembling in painful agony because of some convoluted plot of The Hijackers, made me more determined to make it right.

I have to go in.

Portia's thoughts must be in the same space because she whispers, "For Zula?"

"For Zula," I repeat.

Like last time, very little light penetrates the inside of the house. The windows are shuttered, the overhead fixtures are off. A dim glow emanates from the room where Zula lays on the couch. Portia continues down the hall, peeking in to say hello. But Luc pivots to the right, motioning us to follow. We pass the table and chairs (where we learned about La Siréne), and through a small alcove, leading to a closed door.

"You have to understand, there are certain precautions my family takes. For safety." Luc pauses with his hand on the doorknob.

"Because you're werewolves?" Devin pushes his way to the front of our small group.

"Somethin' like that." Luc's drawl stays slow and easy even though his eyes narrow. Maybe he's annoyed that Devin knows his family has the Rougarou curse. Or maybe he just doesn't like the question. There appears to be no love lost between the two. As Portia rejoins us, both of the guys straighten, chests out, heads high, her presence reigniting the unspoken rivalry.

"She's a lot weaker than yesterday. Couldn't even lift her head," Portia says with a worried look at Luc.

"I know." He pushes the door open, we step inside, and...it's a lot to take in.

The *Room* resembles a jail cell, with a ten-foot-wide open space at the entry before the wall of bars, stretching from end to end. Inside the bars is a large cage, about the size to contain a small elephant. Inside the cage is Aubree Bloom.

"What's going on?" Zach asks.

"Help, help! This monster kidnapped me!" she screams and points at Luc.

Whelp, there goes the Unbendable Laws of LeBlanc. Pretty sure kidnapping is a crime.

"Are you out of your mind? Let her go." I walk through the open cell door and approach the cage, rattling the iron bars.

"CeCe, my hero! Rushing to the rescue." Her voice loses the chipper affectation, and her smile narrows into a sneer. Before my eyes, Aubree's demeanor changes from Bubblegum Barbie to Evil Scheming Barbie. "This was too easy. I expected it to be harder to get everyone here."

Her loud, evil cackle shrieks in my eardrums. Clutching her belly, she leans forward, her whole body rocking with amusement. "Oh, Luc. You think they'll be able to save your sister? I can't wait to watch the Rougarou kill y'all."

"I knew she was a Hijacker. I knew it!" Portia pulls me from my efforts to open the obviously locked cage door.

A loud *screech, crash* has me whirling around in time to see Luc lock the jail cell door. With Devin, Zach, Portia and me all on the wrong side.

"I'm real sorry about this. But I'll do whatever it takes to save Zula."

"Luc!" Portia shouts.

"Dude, come on." Devin puts a protective arm around Portia's shoulders, patting her to calm her simmering rage.

"Aubree might be the Rougarou." Luc takes a step back, closer to the exit. "But I have to be sure, and if it's not her, I know the real one will come after its mark."

"Don't put CeCe at risk. It doesn't have to be like this." Zach grips my hand, his pulse pumping so hard I feel it in his wrist.

"Let us out!" Portia's voice drops, the serious tone she uses with her siblings, the *you-better-do-this-or-else* threat level.

"You'll be safe in here. Don't hate me, Portia." With that, he walks away to the sound of Aubree's exaggerated howl, a loud *a-woo* worthy of any horror movie.

CHAPTER TWENTY-SIX

LUC'S HOUSE: THE UNWELCOME VISITOR

Obviously, the first thing I do is send a text to Dad.

ME: Need rescue. Luc's off the rails.
Trapped at his house.

The words hold on my screen, the send bar frozen. A red exclamation pops up, and the words "not delivered."

That can't be good.

"There's no signal in here." Aubree lays on her back, staring at the ceiling. "Look around, this is a prison."

"I can still call 9-1-1." Which I attempt without luck.

"Oh, did I forget to mention there's a magical block as well? My bad." Aubree gives me an ugly grin. "No messages or calls come in or out of this room."

"Luc!" Portia yells, following up with a combination of insults and threats, rattling the bars with gusto. Tears fill her eyes, the hurt thick. She's more than mad. The tightness of her shoulders and the trembling in her lips all exhibit the jagged stab of betrayal.

I join her at the bars, shouting for Luc to come back.

Zach and Devin both walk the perimeter, checking the walls for weakness (all concrete), and the only window to the outside is a skylight. They both try to climb the bars, no luck. And Devin even hoists himself on Zach's shoulders, but even with the extra height the opening is out of reach.

"It's no use." Aubree swings up to a sitting position, fixing her hair. "You're all gonna die."

"Shut up, Aubree." Portia lowers to the floor, resting her back against the wall.

I text Dad again, nothing, and tell everyone else to try their phones. Nothing. Devin and Zach pace, Portia and I sit. None of us know what to do.

Not knowing is the worst. What's Luc planning? What is taking so long? Every second ticks on the clock, every minute slowly stretches. An endless loop of checking the time, opening my text messages in case something slipped through the blackout coverage, then trying to distract myself and Portia with revenge plots.

We are so going to murder Luc. As soon as the door opens.

Portia yells again, her anger growing exponentially the longer we're stuck in here.

"Babe, he's not coming back." Devin puts his hand over hers, loosening her grip from the iron. "It'll be okay. He can't keep us in here forever."

"But what is he doing?" She groans and slouches, allowing Devin to put his arm around her. "It's been forever. Enough time to watch The Eras Tour and still be able to get a souvenir T-shirt."

"Nah, we've only made it to Folklore." Devin grins, and Portia smiles for the first time since Luc trapped us.

"I've missed my check-in with Dad." I lower to the floor and lean against the wall.

Zach slides down to sit next to me, our shoulders touching. "He should be here before we get to The Tortured Poets Department album."

Then it's my turn to smile.

At Café Du Monde, the seconds seemed to move in reverse as we waited. Now, I wish I could stop time. The windowless room keeps us insulated to this small space, and the skylight overhead provides only a glimpse of the outside. Colors shift into deepening purples, and I imagine the dormer windows darkening to reflect the shades of bruising. Night approaches like a group of tween girls chasing a boy band; fast and relentless.

Aubree lays on her back, dragging her carnelian bracelet along the iron bars. *Clang, clang, clang. Clang, clang, clang.* Every minute or so she howls, a quiet *a-woooo*. It annoys me, and I tap my toes on the floor, the rhythm faster and faster until I break.

"Were you in on this with Luc? And why did you lick him?" I ask.

Evil Scheming Barbie laughs. "I'm so far ahead of you it isn't even worth explaining. Everything, even that lick, I did to lay the trap. Strategic planning meets pure genius."

"You set this up?" I gesture around, emphasizing the cage trapping her. "You don't look much better off than me."

"They must have had a sale on stupid last time you shopped." She moves to a sitting position, putting her face right in between the bars. "Because you're an idiot. Fell right into Luc's trap. And he fell right into mine."

"I'd return that face to the ugly store if I were you. It's not doing you any favors," Portia shoots back.

The insult lands and Aubree gasps, running a hand over her shoulder-length, blond hair.

Zach puts his arm around me, tucking me into the snug zone. I burrow in, curling deeper into that niche between his neck and shoulder. Perfectly snuggy. Perfectly Zach. Our magic launches into symphony-level harmony, the ZeCe effect taking hold.

"I love our dates. There's something about life-threatening danger that really adds to the evening." Zach's fingers brush up and down my arm.

"Who needs movie night when we star in our own production? Zach and CeCe and the Rougarou Rumble."

"Sounds like a cartoon Portia's siblings would watch," he says.

"Yeah? You got something better?"

"Close your eyes." Zach's words whisper on my skin as he presses a kiss to my forehead.

"*Close your eyes* is a terrible title," I say, even as my lids drift shut.

"We're going on a trip." The deep timber of his voice, the feel of his arm around me, helps tune out the *clang, clang, clang,* and the soft conversation of Portia and Devin. "Somewhere far away from here."

"Far away," I mutter. "The Garden District? Metairie?"

He chuckles, and my head bobbles with the motion. "Further."

"I don't know what further looks like. I've never left Louisiana." No family vacations. No cruises, resorts, or theme parks.

"Not even Mississippi? It's like, an hour drive."

"Nope. I've barely been out of New Orleans," I tell him.

"Well, we're leaving Louisiana. Right now." He shakes off the surprise and clears his throat. "I've been working on a new magical plane. A place with no black magic."

"I thought you were off magic. Aunt Lucy said not even a little—"

"Shhh." He places a finger over my lips. "This isn't using, just setting the scene. Now, picture somewhere with mountains."

I let my lids drift shut again. "Bienvielle?"

"Not even close. We're leaving Louisiana, remember?" He brushes a hand down my hair. "These are majestic peaks, giant pyramids exploding from the ground to touch the clouds. So tall the sky seems to shrink. They surround us, everywhere we turn, reds, and oranges, and greens painting the landscape like a Bob Ross canvas."

I try to conjure the image he creates, something more than a flat vista and a horizon stretching as far as the eye can see. "Is it claustrophobic?"

"No, it's a beautiful sanctuary. The only sounds are the wind and the gurgling of distant rivers. We could shout anything, every secret or dream, and the granite walls echo back in silence. All alone in our mountain cathedral."

The way he speaks, the awe in his tone, makes me want to be there with him. Away from this jail cell, away from Luc's betrayal, and away from New Orleans. If only for a few minutes. I snug deeper into the zone, mentally and physically, ready to shut out the world and head for the isolated refuge of his new magical plane. Just the two of us, in our private paradise.

If I take out the iron bars, the hard floor, and Evil Scheming Barbie, it's the best date I've had in weeks.

A voice seeps through the haze of imagination. *To see*, it says, faint enough that I whisper, "Did you hear that?"

And Zach responds, "Hear what?"

Keeping my eyes closed, I sit up straight. My mental picture changes. Instead of mountains, my vision fills with sturdy oaks dripping with Spanish moss. Fresh, burbling streams turn into algae-covered ponds. I remember this place; it's where the Hijackers gather. Someone speaks again, and this time, I recognize the voice.

"It's time," Grandpa Hijacker says.

Aubree bursts out with a howl, this *a-wooo* loud enough to make us all jump. She tips her head back, nose tipped to the ceiling, her lips pursed in a wide *O*.

"What's your deal?" Portia's shoulders tense, and Devin grabs her hand to keep her from approaching the cage.

"Stop. She might be the Rougarou," he says.

"No. It's not her." I know that now. As surely as I know 1+1=2 or Rory and Logan belong together. Because my vision changed.

Whether from the slurping werewolf lick, or Grandpa Hijacker swiping his blood on my spirit forehead, every time I close my eyes, I see through different eyes. These ones belonging to someone shifting into a wolf. Hair sprouts from arms, seams of clothes pop and rip as the person bulks up like the hulk.

"The Rougarou's coming," I whisper.

"It's not even curfew yet." A new tension heightens Devin's tone.

Portia lightly touches her temple. Pretty sure she's doing the *talking to dead people* thing. "It doesn't have to wait for curfew. Or dark. Or anything, really."

"CeCe, are you okay?" Zach's fingers give my hand a gentle squeeze, and I realize I'm clutching his with bone-crushing intensity.

I release his hand and rub my neck, right over the mark. "It's coming here. For me. I can see it."

My eyes drift closed again, and I watch the Rougarou walk through the Le Petit theater. Just like Luc said, it transforms from there. It pushes open a door to stumble outside. Curfew fast approaches, the sun hidden beyond the horizon. Most people have cleared out of the city before true dark hits. Those that remain gasp at the creature. It ignores the few screams and the echoes of *what is that?*, unconcerned about being spotted.

It drops to all furry fours and begins to run. My heart pumps in time to the pounding of the paws on the ground, the beast running at an aggressive pace. Sound comes to me in distorted waves, a hollowed echo, like being underwater.

Gas lanterns flicker every few yards, casting a trembling halo of shadow. I try to gauge how much time we have, but my vision is limited to what the Rougarou sees. Pavement. Glimpses of store fronts. Bushes and trees. The occasional person.

Bottom line: it's moving fast, and we're not that far away.

The door where Luc walked out opens, and a loud commotion interrupts my vision. Three distinct voices blare. A female I don't know, our captor—and frequent tank top wearer—Luc, and my favorite cop from the NOPD. Dad.

Clearly the room is soundproof since we heard nothing until the door opened. They walk in, and the elation at seeing Dad melts my bones. Relief plots a course through my nervous system, the message of rescue calming all the organs down. Lungs loosen, heartbeat drops to a normal rhythm. Even intestines unclench and withdraw the threat of imminent gastrointestinal embarrassment.

He must have a similar reaction, because as soon as he spots me, he goes quiet. His shoulders relax.

The woman, in navy slacks and a white button-up shirt, bears a striking resemblance to Luc. Obviously his cousin, FBI agent Verily Broussard.

"—can't just lock people up, but he's trying to keep them safe." A note of pleading enters her tone.

Portia, Devin, Zach, and I all approach the bars, watching the ongoing argument. Aubree stays laying down, but she stops the clanging in favor of the unfolding drama.

"The cavalry has arrived," Devin says.

"Luc I'm gonna skin your hide and make shoes out of the leather." Portia stands, dusting off her shorts.

"I'll happily let you walk all over me when this is finished, darlin'." A tiny smirk lifts his lips.

"Where's the key?" Dad holds out his hand in silent demand.

"Detective, do you want another murder on your hands. Multiple murders?" Luc crosses his arms, his wide stance defiant, not an ounce of pleading. "We all wanna catch this thing. I'm just doin' somethin' about it."

Dad shakes his head. "By using my daughter as bait?"

"I wish it was me." He points to himself, his eyes wild. "More than anythin'. But she's the one who's marked. I can't keep waitin' around as Zula slowly dies."

"Let them out." Dad ignores Luc's impassioned speech and points to our cell.

"We really can't do that." Verily's lips flatten, and she gives one short shake of the head. "The only way to fix this is make sure Zula gets a strike on the wolf."

"Agent Broussard—"

"Detective," she cuts him off. "You should go in the cell with them. We don't have much time."

"Correction. We're out of time." The mark on my neck burns with cold, like dry ice presses to my skin. "It's here."

Through closed eyes, I track the Rougarou's progress as it approaches the Creole cottage's courtyard. The speedy run has slowed to a predatory stalk, the paws rolling from heel-to-toe in a deliberate procession along the paved path. Its long muzzle sniffs the air, and it moves with an eerie grace, the beast in hunting mode.

Verily shouts, *get Zula ready* and Luc's footsteps fade from the room. An argument ensues as she tries to convince my dad to get behind the bars. He refuses and tells her they need backup, which she declines. Forcefully. *It needs to be Zula.*

I tune out the raised voices and rushing chaos to focus on the beast searching for me. My pulse pounds, the beat of it pumping wildly.

It rounds the corner to the trickling fountain and slurps from the stone tier, wetting its snout. Water drips from the razored teeth sharp enough to rip flesh and snap bone. Though I know the Rougarou doesn't want to kill me, I worry for my friends sharing a cell with me. For my dad, who's ready to defend us. For Luc and Verily, who need to face the murderous beast to save Zula.

The Rougarou pauses, our vision tipping as it cocks its head. No light illuminates the courtyard, and the barely there waning crescent offers little to alleviate the cloak over the navy sky casting the yard in shadow.

But it can see in the dark.

Its nose twitches. A deep growl rumbles in its chest. It rises to two feet, a hulking form over seven feet tall, scanning the courtyard until its eyes land on something out of place. Rather, someone.

Julie Jolley sits at the bistro table, her eyes impossibly

wide. She clutches her hands together, taking shallow breaths, and doing her best impression of a statue. A frantic pulse pumps in her neck, and I see it thumping in deep red, knowing the Rougarou focuses on that exact spot.

"Oh no." I gasp, my lungs squeezing tight. "No, no, no."

"What is it, baby girl?" Dad's voice finds me through all the other noise.

"Julie Jolley is outside. With the Rougarou."

"No!" Devin's sharp denial rings like an alarm. "I told her to go home."

The burn of the mark intensifies, and I cover my neck, pressing out the hurt.

A swish of fabric, and Dad's grunt makes me open my eyes. As usual, he asks no questions or doubts what I see. Instead, he pulls his gun from the holster and checks the magazine. He's going out there to save Julie.

A part of me wants to beg him not to go. The words *please get in the cell,* tremble on my tongue.

But Dad's a superhero. The best one I know.

He nods his chin, our usual goodbye. He could add *see you later* and *I love you,* but the love is there in his eyes. It's there in everything he does.

Choking back my fear, I respond with my normal farewell. "Bye, Daddy."

CHAPTER TWENTY-SEVEN

THE VISION: THE ROUGAROU

My body trembles as Dad and Verily leave the room.

"Luc and I have tranquilizer guns. The Rougarou can't die before Zula stabs it," she reminds him.

Little, thirteen-year-old Zula, using a knife in the same way one was used on her. The feat seems impossible.

Devin paces in front of the cage, an agitated lion wanting release. "We have to help!"

"Luc, get back here, you backstabbing swamp dweller. Let us out!" Portia shouts.

Aubree resumes the clanging bracelet. My head and emotions spin as Zach guides me away from the bars, urging me to sit. Our backs press against the wall, and both Portia and Devin hover above, their incessant words like a battering ram.

Devin: *Should we call the police?*

Portia: *We can't. Remember?*

Devin: *Then what are we supposed to do?*

Portia: *Zula needs to get the curse back. Everything will be fine then.*

"Stop!" I yell, covering my ears and pinching my eyes closed. A blessed few seconds of silence follow, but then I see through the Rougarou's vision, watching as it stalks closer to the bistro table.

"What do you see?" Zach asks softly, putting his arm around me. I hear Devin and Portia settle near me as well.

"It's taunting Julie." This is a game to the beast, a drawn-out anticipation of fear and blood.

The Rougarou swings its head as the back door opens and Dad steps out, gun drawn. He walks in the opposite direction of Julie, his perimeter wide to shift the focus on him. He treats this enormous creature like any other bad guy, refusing to be intimidated by the glinting teeth or bulging strength.

"Do you talk? Or do you just growl?" Dad opens the negotiation.

I expect the Rougarou to go after him. Or maybe prowl around him like it did to Julie, but instead it launches, the powerful legs pushing off the ground to land next to the little table. Julie screams, attempting to run, but a clawed hand grabs her by the neck. Her long, brown hair catches in the grip, and it holds her head trapped at a tilt.

"It's picking Julie up." More breath escapes than words, and a sob chokes from my lips.

Three successive gunshots ring out. *Boom, boom, boom.*

"Dad shot it," I tell them. "But it's still got Julie."

The Rougarou lifts her from the chair, and she scratches at the hairy arm, yanking and tugging for breathing room. Horrible choking noises gurgle in her throat. Her impossibly wide eyes grow to bulging. Her dangling feet kick, not trying to attack, but seeking purchase, searching for something, anything, to hold onto. The toe of her sneaker squeaks over the edge of the table, brushing the wrought iron frame before falling to limply hang.

Dark streaks trickle down the collar of her shirt, and I realize it's blood from the sharp talons piercing her skin. A soft wheeze escapes. *Please,* she mouths, her bottom lip trembling and catching on the *p...p...p*.

Three more bangs echo and the Rougarou tosses Julie aside, a rag doll of flopping limbs who bounces against the trunk of the oak before landing in a pile. I can't see if she gets up, or the severity of her injuries. My vision, the Rougarou's vision, turns to focus on Dad.

"Three more shots. It threw Julie on the ground."

Verily runs out, the tranq gun at the ready. "Detective, don't kill it."

The pulse in Dad's neck stays calm, his hands steady. "Nothing's hitting it."

Two more shots, *boom, boom,* and the gun's muzzle flashes. But the Rougarou barely flinches, unaffected by the lead slugs.

Why aren't the bullets hurting it? Do only silver bullets work?

A deep, angry growl thunders from its lungs, a storm threatening. It stalks closer, moving step by slow step. Dad moves too, towards the back door where he came out, his gun at the ready.

Panic swirls, the earlier beignets crawling from my gut up my esophagus, and I swallow hard. "It's stalking Dad now. Following him to the house."

"The house? Why is he bringing it in here?"

I don't reply to Devin's question, Portia shushes him faster than I can respond. But I have an inkling of Dad's plan. Especially since Verily emphasized the need for Zula to strike with a knife.

Dad crosses the threshold into the kitchen, his eyes never leaving the Rougarou. And it tracks him, the careful stalking of a hunter. Every twitch and every breath noted. The darkened house offers no obstacle to the Rougarou's vision, and through the tall doorway, it watches him step deeper into the Creole cottage.

"I won't let you take my daughter." Dad holsters his gun and pulls out his taser. "Mark or no mark, you can't have her."

The Rougarou's eyes narrow, and I view through slitted vision. Adrenaline punches my gut, and I realize what it's going to do right before it leaps. Dad fires the taser before he ducks and rolls. The ticking barbs bounce away from the beast. The Rougarou slashes, slicing open Dad's calf. He yelps, his mouth pinched in a tight grimace.

"Get out of there, Dad. Please." I know he can't hear me; he doesn't even know I see what's happening, but I still plead with him to escape.

Zach's arm tightens on my shoulders. Fingers twine through mine, and I recognize the feel of Portia's support.

The Rougarou hovers over Dad, drool dripping from its mouth to plop on his white, button-up shirt. A wet snarl sneers from its slobbery muzzle. The dark red, thrumming pulse beats in Dad's neck, his spiking fear visible to the creature.

Tears streak my face, and I refuse to open my eyes and escape the vision, but I'm terrified to watch.

Please get away, Daddy.

A noise distracts the Rougarou, and it turns, our sight shifting to look behind us. Verily shoots a tranq dart, and steps aside as Luc propels a stumbling Zula forward, a knife in her hand. And not a little penknife like what I carry. A sharp, silver blade about six inches long.

Hair clings to her face, and her purple pajama bottoms hang loosely on her waist. Her brown eyes dart around the room, a feral animal ready to strike.

"Zula! Now!" Luc angles himself to be the first line of defense, blocking his sister from the sharp talons.

But the Rougarou's speed defies human nature, the flash of fur and muscle spinning faster than my vision can comprehend. It knocks the knife from Zula's hand. Then she and Luc both fly as it sweeps its arm, their bodies thudding against cabinet and counter. Verily pulls her service weapon and fires as it closes in on her. It slaps a taloned hand at her, and the gun clatters to the floor. Blood spurts from Verily's arm, right below the elbow, and she clutches it while diving away, swiping the gun with her other hand and firing again.

This beast is impenetrable, everything bouncing off its roughened hide, doing nothing to slow it down.

"It's in the kitchen," I say. "Everyone's hurt. They're trying to stop it."

Again, our vision spins, and it zeroes in on Dad, who lifts Zula in his arms. He limps over to Luc, dragging his seeping leg behind him.

"Get her in the cage, I'll cover you. We can't win this, not today." Dad passes Zula over. Luc takes her even though he wobbles on his feet, and a trail of blood drips from the side of his head.

A lightning bolt flashes down my neck, the mark burning an icy path where the Rougarou licked. It perks at the mention of the cage, knowing I must be there. And that's why it's here. To follow the imprint left on my skin.

The Rougarou growls and takes a step but stops to howl

in pain. I don't understand why. Its head tips back, and we stare at the ceiling. Dark wooden beams, white textured paint. A blink later, it looks at its foot where a knife handle sticks out, the same one Zula brought to the party. But it wasn't Zula that stabbed the blade into the Rougarou's skin, but her cousin Verily.

The werewolf whimpers at the wooden handle protruding from its furry paw, offering a retaliatory kick that sends Verily crashing into the wall. One of the two large, gold picture frames falls, the glass shattering over the tile.

"Agent Broussard stabbed it in the foot, and it kicked her across the room. She's not moving." I give the report, my stomach sick, my muscles exhausted from clenching tight.

A creak cuts through the silence of the room, and my eyes pop open to see the door swinging wide. Luc stumbles in with Zula in his arms, and Dad follows, his back to Luc's, his Glock in his hand.

"Daddy," I cry, standing to press my face to the bars. "You're okay."

"Keys." He snaps his fingers, and Luc struggles to pull a large, silver key from his pocket. "Back up. Move."

Dad's all business, ordering us to clear a path for him to push the cell door open, ignoring the blood dripping from his torn pants leg leaving a trail behind him. The gaping wound will probably need a million stitches, but he walked away from the werewolf fight in one piece.

An injured Luc limps into the cell clutching Zula in his arms. Her skin has turned a shade of grayish, and her limbs dangle. Hair mats to her face and the only way I know she's still alive is her pitiful moan as Luc collapses to the floor.

A primal howl echoes from the kitchen, and I blink my

eyes closed to watch as the Rougarou's meaty paws struggle to grip the knife handle before tossing it. A deep rasp rattles in its chest, and the foot seeps with a thick, blackened blood, almost like tar.

Its vision laser focuses on the small alcove leading to the cell, and it prowls toward us, huffing breaths blowing from its snout. My neck stings, a sharp bite of frigid flame, and I know it's coming for me. But with all of us behind the protection of the iron bars, the Rougarou can't hurt us, unable to do anything more than snarl and growl.

The jail door clangs shut, and immediately I see something's not right.

"Dad, you're supposed to be in here. What are you doing?" My initial confusion hemorrhages into panic, every organ in my body detonating at the sight of Dad outside the cell.

"Call 911. Tell them we have an agent down, and a civilian down. Expedite medical and backup." Dad ejects the magazine of his Glock, snapping another in its place. "I've got to help Agent Broussard and Julie."

"Daddy, no. Please come in here with us." The words pour from my heart, the desperation trembling in a rapid staccato.

"CeCe. Make. The. Call." He grunts the reminder in a harsh whisper.

"We can't. Nothing works in here," I reach my hand through the bars, trying to pull Dad closer.

Zach rattles the cell door, and it gives a frustrating jangle, the lock secure. "Please, unlock it and come in."

"I'll call emergency," he says, taking a step toward the exit.

We all fall silent as a loud, wet breathing spills into the room. Then a furry foot matted with blood slides beyond the doorway, followed by a monstrous form. Seeing through the Rougarou's vision, or watching it in a memory, is very different from experiencing the massive beast first-hand.

The red eyes glow, piercing in their intensity. The long snout snarls, sharp canine teeth protruding below the jaw, and dripping with saliva. Curved claws click together, the audible knell a warning of violence.

But worst of all, Dad stands on the wrong side of the metal bars.

CHAPTER TWENTY-EIGHT

THE CELL: THE VILLAIN

Dad edges to the corner of the room, one shoulder pressed against the wall, the other pressed to the cell. The sounds of huffing and puffing paralyzes the rest of us, the suffocating dread impossible to breathe through. My mind attempts to makes sense of what I see, the reality of the Rougarou leaving me completely unbalanced. Legs the size of oak trunks, savage claws that could slice and dice better than any chef's knife.

A pressure pushes inside my chest. My ribs squeeze so tight I wonder how I manage not to burst.

And the Rougarou stares, taking us all in, the red eyes glowing like a harbinger of death.

I know it tracks me, chasing the imprint left by its slimy tongue. Which gives me a potential course of action.

Convince it to follow me and ignore everyone else.

Glancing around our cell, Luc lays on the floor with Zula, his arm wrapped protectively around her. Devin and Portia both retreated as far as possible, their backs pressed against the cage where Aubree now stands. Her fingers curl around the bars, her lips tugged in a condescending smirk.

And Zach stays with me, holding my hand.

"Come on, Rougarou." I move across the cell, to the opposite end of the bars, the furthest away from Dad and the others as possible. "Over here."

The snout turns to follow my movement, and it keeps me in its sight. It takes a step, two, three, crossing the room in a slow, diagonal line. The more space that builds between Dad and the beast, the more space I find in my ribcage.

Zach's fingers tremble, and despite the palpable fear, he refuses to let me face the werewolf alone. His lips touch my ear, his breath a soft murmur. "Go to your magical plane. You might be able to do something."

My magical plane? How am I supposed to focus on anything other than the supernatural creature stalking in front of us.

But I reply with, "Okay," and sit on the floor.

Every time I close my eyes, the Rougarou's vision takes over, so I stare at the wooden floor to picture my magical plane. Which is so much harder. First comes the turquoise sky. More green than blue. More dark than light. A rich, vibrant aqua deep enough to swim in. The clouds roll in, pink cotton candy puffs floating like boats on smooth waters. The ground is a reflective pool that perfectly mirrors the beautiful colors, where there's no distinction between land and atmosphere, just a seamless view of limitless expanse.

Dad slides along the wall, centimeter by painful centimeter, wary of the creature that could easily tear him apart. At his current pace, he should reach the door in a century. The Rougarou progresses much faster toward me.

The long strides shake the floor, and wet huffs slobber from the mouth, the whole snout foaming. It's both disgusting and terrifying.

I need to pull myself onto the plane, into that turquoise horizon, and open the passage for my magic to thrive. Distraction abounds, one in the form of a massive monster, another in my dad, and another in Luc.

He slips the tranq gun from behind him and takes aim.

"It won't work, Luc." I keep my voice steady and low.

"Put it away. Save it for later," Portia says, and Luc tucks the gun behind him.

The Rougarou reaches the bars and presses its nose between the iron rails, snuffling to find me. Thick droplets of drool plop on the floor, and its lips snarl to expose every one of the pointed teeth. A low, menacing growl rumbles, and I fight to keep my eyes on the ground.

Portia sits on my other side, taking my hand. Immediately I feel the charge from her connection to Simone. The new supernatural source plugs me in, feeding me energy. With Zach on my right and Portia on my left, we build a complete trio of power, life, death, and voodoo in a natural harmony.

I reach out with my magic, sending my spirit to the plane. A gentle wave cascades across the reflective pool as my toe tippies on the surface. A perfect concentric circle undulating. Then a second ripple as my other foot joins.

The magical plane works differently, physical touch useless. All the senses disrupted. The intangible surrounds me, emotions thick enough to grasp, and magic visible in auras of color. I also hear something on this plane that I haven't heard in too long. A glorious humming that echoes like a summer night.

My cicadas!

Though dull and distant, I grasp onto the sound, grateful for the boost. Their music buzzes around me, through me, a healing vibration that replenishes my strength more effectively than a shot of five-hour-energy. On this plane where magic exists, I don't just feel Zach and Portia's power next to me, it breathes, a living thing. Like I could reach out and touch it. Mold it in my hands.

I can see the change in Portia, and it shocks me. Her beautiful, sunshine aura radiates, but another presence joins her. A pale, iridescent spirit I recognize as Simone, superimposed over the top. The two of them move in tandem, their energies intertwined. Simone's ethereal essence has merged with Portia's. It's both mesmerizing and unsettling, and I can't tell where one ends and the other begins.

Worst of all, the dark force of the Rougarou blows around, an ominous storm threatening my pink clouds with destruction. Where Zach's magic exudes warmth and safety, this projects a dangerous flood of chaos. Hot and cold. Windy and electric.

In the midst of the cyclone stands a tall, broad-shouldered man, The Hijacker who stabbed Zula and murdered Simone. He's impossible to identify while surrounded by the surge. *Could I somehow clear the fog?* Reaching out to touch anything near the Rougarou would be a grave mistake, probably sending me to the grave.

But a snaky cloud circles the outside. A thick, dark rope that looks tangible. Touchable. Flashes of lightning peek between the slithering cover, offering short glimpses of the person inside.

If I somehow pulled it from the man maybe I could reveal who it is. Maybe even steal the curse away from him.

If I figure out how to grab the ropey cloud.

If I don't die.

Dad would tell me the world doesn't run on ifs. Which… true. I also refuse to sit back and do nothing. So I try.

Stretching with my spirit, a tendril of magic separates like a plant shoot unfurling. To describe it would be impossible. Somewhere on the color scale of a prism, the shape an ever-changing kaleidoscope. Soft while simultaneously solid, and unearthly.

It's a piece of me. An amazing part of my power only seen on this plane.

It wriggles toward the turbulent mass. I know the Rougarou's snout snuffles and snaps a foot away from my face, but in this space, it only serves as background noise as I watch my power reach. A sprout blooming and growing closer to the dark aura. The tendril swells and splits open, and another shoot of my magic lassoes out to capture the ropey cloud, belting it right around the center.

A dark shadow touches the connection point of my magic and the curse. An electric zap shocks down my tendril, thousands of needles stabbing into me. The stinging pain both freezes and ignites in an agonizing sensory overload. My physical body spasms. My grip squeezes uncontrollably, and I worry about the fingers of my BFF and boyfriend. My vision of the magical plane blurs, the clouds and sky shivering. But I hold on. Gritting my teeth through the throbbing, I pull at the lasso, stripping the curse away.

The storm intensifies and the mass oozes black fog like spilled ink. A deafening howl splits the air, and the Rougarou jerks from my grip. The curse separates from the person for a split second, the disconnect just long enough for me to recognize the Hijacker behind the werewolf mask.

The music director from *Voodoo Bayou*, Chance.

Chance? Why? The shock of seeing his face, and the pain from whatever is protecting him, causes my power to slip, and I jar from my magical plane, losing my grip on the curse. I come back to myself like a stretched rubber band snapping into place. With a loud cry, I let go of Zach and Portia's hands to cover my head as a flash of pain stabs my brain.

Dad, who almost made it to the door, pauses in his slow creep and lifts his gun. *No,* I want to call to him, *ignore the sounds I made and leave the room.* Any warning I shout might alert the Rougarou to his presence, and I subtly wave my hand in a shooing motion. *Please get out.* His eyes stay focused on the beast as it reels from the bars, unleashing a furious roar.

The Rougarou rocks back, disoriented after our encounter in the magical plane. My energy-sapped body struggles to rise, but I need to stand up. To show Dad I'm fine and urge him out of the room.

Zach and Portia help me, taking my arms and assisting me to my feet. "I'm still here, Rougarou. Still wearing your mark."

I press my fingers over my neck since it worked last time to attract the Rougarou's attention. It shakes its snout, saliva flinging, and it grunts as it steps closer to the bars.

Focus on me. Ignore the man creeping his way to the door.

Dad gives a tiny nod and continues his silent shuffle, his feet gliding across the hardwood. A trail of blood smears the distance he walked from the front of the cage to his current location, half a foot from the doorway. His ripped pant leg is soaked and dripping. Pain reflects on his face, from the pinched grimace to the glistening sweat.

Another scoot, another couple of inches. And then he's clear. Out of the room, away from the Rougarou. The instant relief makes my legs jiggly like Jello, even though a werewolf still stands in front of me. But Dad is safe.

A jarring clang rings out as Aubree bangs her bracelet on the bars. To be honest, I forgot about her, and the loud reminder of her presence annoys me. The carnelian stones shimmer, bright, red embers on her wrist. Her smug smirk makes me wonder how I ever confused her for Bubblegum Barbie. She is all evil scheming.

Zula groans, her body twitching in time to Aubree's clanging.

"No!" Luc lifts from his injury-laden slump and stumbles to the cage. "Don't do that. You're hurting her."

"You gonna stop me, Wolf Boy?" She laughs and, though he reaches for her arm, she dodges and clangs her bracelet again, which seems to glow brighter.

"What's going on?" Devin scratches his chest, looking all of us over. "Am I the only one who's confused?"

No. No, he's not.

"You see the Rougarou, CeCe?" Aubree nods her head, and I turn to where she gazes.

In the few seconds of my distraction, I realize things with the Rougarou changed. No more confused stupor or head shaking. It stares at Evil Scheming Barbie, totally alert, and totally fierce.

"I'm the one who controls it." She plucks the bracelet, which has definitely grown brighter, the crimson stones shining. Her nostrils flare, her eyes full of such hate, I know we have a backstory I'm unaware of.

"Who are you?" I ask.

"You're an idiot. Haven't you figured it out?" She gestures around the cage as if the answers line the walls. "Grandpa's been so desperate to get you back, *cuz*. But Daddy and I have a different agenda."

She reads the confusion on my face and rolls her eyes. Then continues with the villain monologuing. "My daddy, Chance, picked up the slack when his twin sister, Constance, deserted the family. But do you think Grandpa cares about that? No. Because he hopes you, the necromancer, will come home."

Portia gasps. "Chance? As in the music director for *Voodoo Bayou?*"

"He reached out to my mom for a guitarist..." Zach's words drift off as he puts it all together. "It was a set up. He knew CeCe could play."

"She can play, she can sing, and she has all the magics." Aubree fumes, and a deep scowl creases her mouth.

"Oh, it's a jealousy thing. I get it now." Devin, bless his shirtless summer heart, sums it up nicely.

The note from Lovelie warned me about it. Aubree's definitely jealous. She and Julie Jolley could be the founding members of the I Hate CeCe Club.

Cousin Aubree: born with no magic. Desperately wants magic to serve her sinister purposes.

Me: the necromancer. Doesn't care about magic and wants a normal life.

"Grandpa's so naïve, thinking Dad and I are using the Rougarou to bring you back." She laughs. "No. We want you dead. And once you're dead, I'll get your magic."

"Magic doesn't transfer like that," Zach says. "I should know. I've tried it. My brother ended up in a wheelchair."

"You don't know anything. Dad and I set the whole stage. The last piece was a smidgen of CeCe's blood. Which she graciously provided." She pulls my penknife from her pocket.

"How did you..." *The morgue!* I left my knife there, more

concerned about Portia being haunted than cleaning up. "Aubree, let's talk about this."

"You have no idea how hard I've worked. Or what I've sacrificed." She plucks at her bracelet, shooting me a sneer. "Go kill CeCe's dad."

A cold, clammy terror seeps into every cell of my being.

"Please, no!" The words squeeze from my lungs as the Rougarou leaves the room. The same room Dad just escaped. "We can try a black magic spell to give you my power. I'll do it. I'll do anything. Just tell me what you want."

"I want you to never have been born."

Aubree ignores my pleading. My begging. My negotiations. She laughs, an evil cackle echoing in the cell, the glow of her carnelian bracelet burning in the pale light.

CHAPTER TWENTY-NINE

THE MAGICAL PLANE: THE GHOST

Chaos erupts. Portia charges the cage, yelling. Screaming. Devin reaches through the bars to try and grab Aubree, but she ignores us all, giving us her back. Luc lays next to Zula, running his hand over her wet, sweaty curls, and mumbling, *Hang in there. It's gonna be okay*.

Everything whirls around me, a galaxy forming and spinning. But I float on the outside, unattached to their gravity, living in my own atmosphere. The air presses in, heavy and hard to breathe. White noise buzzes in my head like radio static unable to find a signal. My hands shake. No, my whole body shakes. I'm in the middle of a personal earthquake, and everything inside me shudders apart.

Zach's arms catch me as I sink. My legs surrender the battle to keep me vertical. I'm exhausted from using magic, my energy sapped, and this emotional hit takes me down.

"Hey, look at me. Your dad's gonna be fine." He settles

in front of me and holds my hand. "He called the police and left to get help."

Such pretty words Zach sells. Pretty and pointless since I know Dad would never leave me locked in this cell while the Rougarou threatens us. Not just because of the cop in him, but because he's Dad.

"I wish that was true," I say.

Though I dread watching through the Rougarou's vision, I let my lids drift closed. Immediately, I see Dad. He hovers over Verily, checking her wounds, his lips moving, his whisper too soft to hear.

The Rougarou closes in, its movements light and stealthy.

"Run," I say, wishing he could hear me. "Run, Daddy!"

Something catches his attention, and his head whips up. They freeze, staring at each other, holding for a few seconds, before the Rougarou leaps. Dad lifts his gun and shoots. The beast lands on top of him, hitting his shoulders and pushing him flat on his back. Dad's head cracks, a solid whomp that elicits a pained grunt. At least Dad kept hold of his Glock, and the reverberation rings as he fires again.

Between the sounds of gunshots and growls, a wailing cry closes in. The beautiful symphony of emergency vehicles.

Apparently Dad *did* make that phone call.

Dad shoots again, placing the gun right at the Rougarou's head. It reels, howling. This time, the bullet impacted. A streak of blood stains its vision.

It knocks the weapon from Dad, which clatters a few feet away, too far to reach. The Rougarou's vicious snout strikes. Dad blocks, and it bites his arm. Blood spurts, soaking his suit jacket and painting his white shirt crimson.

Bone snaps between its sharp teeth, the sound a nauseating crunch.

A sickening wave of horror engulfs me. This can't be happening. Dad is going to die. Killed while I sit trapped behind bars watching. Unable to help.

But I'm the necromancer. If I can raise the dead, maybe I can also keep the living from un-aliving.

"Portia, help!" I hear rustling, and Portia takes my hand. With Zach holding one, and Portia the other, a soft flow of energy circulates. I grip both their hands tighter, needing the power boost. "Stay with me."

I bring my magical plane to mind. Aqua sky: check. Cherry-dipped rose gold clouds: check. My bare feet slink in the reflective pond, tiny ripples matching my movements across the thin layer of water.

With my eyes closed, I also see through the Rougarou's vision, and it projects in front of me, a life-sized production playing out. I'm an audience of one, watching a movie I have no desire to see.

The pulse in Dad's neck grows dimmer, the beats slower. A growing halo of red surrounds him, seeping across the hardwood.

Emotions threaten to overwhelm me, terror, and fury, and anguish burning a destructive path. The wildfire rages. It fuels my desperation, and I lean into it, allowing it to consume me. My pink clouds change, the billows turning smoky. Like cotton puffs dipped in ink and sopping it up. The turquoise sky lightens, brighter and brighter until the color completely ekes out, and all that's left is white.

This familiar plane I created now exists as a monochromatic sketch. A flawless porcelain expanse with ebony clouds, and right in the center, the giant movie screen showing me the attack on Dad. I keep walking, closer and closer until it's right in front of me. A thin, gossamer veil hangs across the front, and I touch it, trying to pull it aside. The curtain swishes like fabric, a moveable quality to it, but it stays an impassable blockade.

The Rougarou rises to stand over Dad, and with one taloned hand, lifts him from the floor. His feet dangle, and somewhere during the fight he lost a shoe. Blood drips from his dark sock, a leaking faucet with a steady *plop, plop, plop.*

My body quakes. A wet streak of tears stains my cheeks. The sensations call me back to my physical body, and I wrestle against the draw, battling to stay in my magical plane.

Zach's voice whispers to me, "Pull me in. Let me be there with you."

But I shake my head. He's off magic, still recovering from the addiction, so what could he really do? Not to mention I don't know how.

I see the Rougarou's intention to tear Dad's throat and feel his life drain away. My wildfire of emotion blazes hot enough to destroy everything in my path.

Everything but the gossamer veil blocking me from Dad.

Ripping at the shimmering gauze, I bang my hands against the screen. In my spirit form, touch works differently, and rather than a solid connection, the curtain shifts around me, a flowing waterfall impossible to grasp onto.

Dad's eyes drift closed, settling into resignation. There's no way out of this. No way for him to defeat the powerful beast holding him captive.

"I love you, baby girl," he whispers as if he knows I'm here.

"No!" I scream. From my physical body. From my spirit. From my soul. A piercing shriek filled with an ache that rattles the crushing reality pressing in on all sides. It echoes on every plane, the weight of anguish hanging heavily in the air.

In a fury, I reach for the curtain, and this time, I push into it. It oozes around me, covering me in slime, stretching as I step through the screen. The veil feels like gelatin, super elastic gelatin, that freezes and turns to ice the further I walk. A large crack splits the middle, spidering into hundreds of fractures, until it shatters.

I find myself standing in the kitchen. Somehow, without a spell, or a mirror, or herbs and candles, I sent my spirit through my magical plane and to the physical world.

I also stopped time. But that's to unpack for another day.

Except, I didn't. Not exactly. Things are just moving slowly. Millimeters of motion to my regular pace, like I'm the Flash, speeding around.

A blanket of heat shrouds my right side, and I turn to see a glowing light gathering. It forms into a silhouette, growing brighter and brighter and more distinct until a ghost manifests. An eerily luminescent woman. She bears a striking resemblance to my mom. A striking resemblance to me. A kindness radiates, sunshine rays wrapping me in an embrace. Her presence doesn't surprise me, almost like I expected her.

The tenderness of familiarity resonates into a keen prick of knowing. A piece of this eerie and beautiful woman lives in me, voodoo alive in the help of my ancestors. Specifically, this ghost. My mother's grandma. The last person to hold the gift of necromancy. She also holds my mom's maiden name. I feel the certainty of who she is in my bones.

Grandma Lalin.

All this time, from the moment I dipped a toe into the magical plane, she's been trying to connect with me.

Magic finds a way.

She takes my hand, her touch not quite liquid, not quite solid, and challenging to grip. And though she doesn't speak, I hear her.

Stop him.

Without pointing, gesturing, or giving any other indication, I understand what she means. Stop my dad's spirit from leaving his body.

My poor Daddy.

On the physical plane, I watched him fight until he had nothing left. In this space, with the ghost holding my hand and guiding me, I see the result of his battle — his spirit trickles upwards, the droplets the same luminescent color as the spirit next to me. An inverted puddle forms above his head, spilling upwards from his body as his life drains away.

Grandma Lalin tells me, or maybe shows me what to do. Pictures form in my mind, words sound in my ears. More than instruction; a passing of knowledge.

I allow the magic to flow through me. Drawing from Portia and Zach, I feel the buildup. My cicadas join in, a welcome chorus. Somehow, I called them, brought them here with me. I've missed them so much, craved their help and their sound.

The power rises. Tingles run through my veins, the electric current charged and ready.

"I love you too," I whisper to Dad, the emotion creating shocks of static to burst in my heart. "It's not your time yet. I still need you."

The air crackles, the delicate boundary between life and death ultra-thin. My fingers undulate through the inverted pond, and while I expect it to be icy, in the same way necromancy chills my bones, this feels neutral. Room temperature.

With the barest of taps, I send his spirit back into his body.

And then I face the Rougarou. The storm swirls, a blackened tornado raging. The ropes of clouds circle around in a twisting barrier. Chance stands perfectly still in the middle, his identity hidden behind the snakes.

On either side, a group of shadows hover, eight of them in total. So dark they emit no light; in fact, they absorb it. No speck of reflection bounces from them. I can only see them straight on, any turn of my gaze and they disappear in my peripheral vision.

They're spirits, but not like the one who holds my hand. Phantoms. They carry an ethereal malice, a *you-don't-want-to-meet-me-in-a-dark-alley* kind of vibe. They have no faces, only flat, blank, expressionless canvases. A blast of cold emits from them, like multiple AC units pumping out air.

Again, my ghost passes on knowledge.

These corrupted spirits feed on power, summoned by the Hijackers to protect the curse. And they did. Engulfing every gunshot. Standing guard as a layer of bullet proof jackets. Except for the one, point-blank blast.

I couldn't detect them before, their essence buried under layers of magic. But now, after stepping through the veil, they can't hide.

I see everything more clearly.

To remove the curse from Chance, I need to get rid of the phantoms. Which...*how?* My companion stays quiet, *thanks, Grandma Lalin!* and I decide to touch one, see what it feels like.

Reaching out, I meet heavy resistance, the air thick and

gluey. A *tick, tick, tick* passes around them like dozens of pens clicking up and down. After hearing only the song of my cicadas on this plane, the sudden noise surprises me.

Are they communicating?

My hand sucks deeper into the glue, inches away from making contact, and the curse flinches away, avoiding my touch.

The snaky cloud unwinds from Chance, stretching wide to spread in front of the Phantoms like a safety bar. The lightning and storm move with the rope, swirling around it, an individualized weather system for the dense, elongated cord.

A cavernous hole opens on the phantoms' blank faces — a gaping maw stretching wide. Each one inhales a piece of the curse in front of them, devouring it. Hiding it from me. More intent on protecting the actual curse than the one who's cursed.

And then they disappear. Poof. Gone.

Chance is left bare. Blood streaks the side of his face, and his ear dangles from the shot Dad got through. Without the Rougarou affixed to him, he looks harmless. Like the germophobe, hand sanitizing, music director.

With a dangling ear.

The temperature elevates at my side, my ghost demanding attention, and I turn to her. The ethereal glow hurts to stare at. It overwhelms my senses, an intense feeling that I stand in the presence of greatness.

Somehow, we appear in front of the bars, inside the room with the cell. I see myself, my physical self, on the floor holding hands with Zach and Portia. It's so bizarre, this snapshot of time, and me in two places at once.

But it doesn't hurt, not like when I split my spirit to trace Rivera. That left me doubled over in the most intense pain. This feels more like focused travel through the magical plane. The powerful space truly dims the effects on my body.

Take it. The two words pass over me.

Take what?

Now we stand in the cage, looking down on Aubree. The carnelian glows, waves of dark energy emanating from the stones. It's so obvious that she and her bracelet are evil, I wonder how I didn't notice sooner.

Take it.

Cupping my hands over the bracelet, I gently roll it off Aubree's wrist, and work to slide it on my own. Not my spirit, but on my physical body. It involves coordinating the physical and spiritual together, like mentally reciting the alphabet backwards while juggling and riding roller skates downhill.

Strangest thing I've done today, and that's saying something.

Immediately, the oily taint of black magic seeps on my skin. After soaking in the three magics, with Portia and Zach by my side, the zing of darkness hits like a sucker punch. A wave of dizziness tilts my world, and my grasp in this plane flounders.

Grandma Lalin prods my side. *Not yet.*

Easy for her to say. I falter, my vision spinning, the room blurring as I fight to stay.

She swipes a hand over the bars, and the cell door clicks open. It swings out, leaving a two-inch gap.

You need to go, she instructs me.

Thanks, Grandma.

The magical plane blurs, a world of static surrounding me. I focus on my physical self, propelling my spirit forward to re-enter my body. Time resumes, punching me in the core like a speeding airboat. The strain of using strong magic—communing with my dead ancestor, sending Dad's spirit back into his body, not to mention feeling out the Rougarou curse—demands a price, and my body pays it. I feel like I was overcharged as the shakes hit, hard and convulsive.

"CeCe, hang in there." Zach puts his arm around me, keeping me from tipping over.

"You're going to be fine. Just breathe." Portia speaks like she's experienced this before.

The pressure in my head demands release, a shaken bottle of Coke ready to burst. I lean into Zach, relying on his strength. But my sight narrows, caving in from the edges and threatening to take me under.

"Did anyone else notice the door's open?" Devin swings the bars wide, the hinges creaking.

And that's the last thing I hear before the walls of my vision crumble, burying my consciousness in the rubble.

CHAPTER THIRTY

THE OAK GROVE: THE RECOVERY

Snippets of conversation float into my existence. Words drifting by. Sounds splashing. I try to catch hold of anything, but a tranquil river carries me away from conscious thought, lulling me into the silent peace of oblivion.

The water laps my skin, and—opening my eyes—I realize it's not water, but leaves. I'm on land. Lying on my back in a grove of giant oaks. Soft grass pads below me, and Spanish moss hangs from the limbs above, the tendrils long enough to tickle my face. A trail of silvery moonlight glistens on the ground, and I stare at the hypnotic sparkle.

"You've been a busy girl."

I startle and look up to see a person emerging into the shimmering glow. "Mom?"

She smiles, the gentlest of expressions, the perfect photograph from my memories. "I've waited a long time to hear you call me that again."

My confused brain wants to connect the pieces I'm missing. A hint of urgency flashes through the calm. *What was I doing before this?* "I'm supposed to be somewhere else."

"Not until you're here first," she says, confusing my brain even more. "You did something tonight, something I thought was impossible."

"I don't know what you mean." Details nag at me, a flash of my magical plane. Being locked in a cell. And...Julie Jolley?

"I've kept my finger on the pulse of your magic, watched it and hidden it for years. But tonight, you broke my hold and called on a theoretical ability only the necromancer can summon. Spectral Reach." Excitement vibrates in her voice. "I'm talking unparalleled strength stretching across every plane and utilizing the magics of life, death, and voodoo. Enhanced abilities. Wisdom and knowledge passed from our ancestors. And perfectly balanced as it draws equally from every source."

More snippets of the night fill in the blanks, a beautiful, ghostly presence. The Rougarou attacking. Dad! "I have to go. Dad needs help."

"*You* need help. We don't know the effects of using Spectral Reach. Obviously, loss of consciousness. Sapped strength."

"Dad's really hurt." I stand and pull at the Spanish moss, ripping it from the trees, looking for a way out. It grows right back, closing whatever gaps I create, an endless maze of green-gray strands.

"There's nothing you can do for your father right now, and I'm worried about you."

"I'm fine. The Rougarou didn't even touch me." The oaks seem to expand, the large trunks even more massive.

The towering stature stretching up, up, up. I double my efforts, tearing at the moss.

"Stop. Listen," she says. The glow of moonlight burns brighter, the trail glaring. The silvery path illuminates beneath my feet, coming alive as it swallows my ankles to hold me still. "Tell me about what happened."

"The Rougarou nearly killed Dad, that's what happened!"

"Amplified emotions. Maybe that pushed you into the Reach." She stands next to me, and I realize—at least on this plane—we're the same height. Such a strange thing to notice. "Then what?"

"I pushed his spirit back into his body." As if the silvery moonlight acts like a truth serum, I tell her everything. The pieces all come together, my memory clearing, and I'm compelled to get it out. "And the Rougarou, I saw the curse. Saw what's protecting it."

I describe the phantoms. How they ate the curse and disappeared.

"The Rougarou is hunting you. The mark you wear still calls to it, and it'll want the bracelet back. You need to handle these corrupted spirits." She reaches to the ground and plucks a piece of the silver moonlight, stretching it like a string. Tying the thread around her index finger, she lifts my hand and connects the other end to mine.

"What is that?" The metallic line shimmers, leashing us together.

"Our link," she says. "Remember, nothing magical can get through a salt circle. Lure the Rougarou across a barrier to separate it from the phantoms."

"But I have to be in the circle too."

"No, you don't. You're weak right now, and the moon is overpowered. You can tranquilize the Rougarou and be done." She looks at me from head to foot. "Using magic would be dangerous. The scale could tip so easily. Get ready."

How? I want to ask. Before I can, she slams a hand on the ground, and the silvery light splashes, stomped water from a puddle. Absolute silence follows. The glittery string on my finger loops around, twisting tighter and tighter until I think the strand might snap. Instead, it pulses, and I feel each throb pumping in my core.

Mom nods her head, and then the oaks and moss disappear.

"She's coming around." Portia. My relief at hearing her voice almost supersedes the dread from the encounter with my mom.

Almost.

I moan, long and low. Every part of my body aches.

"Hey Sugar, open your eyes." Zach's arm around me weighs the exact right amount, the familiar touch a comfort. My head lays against his chest, and I stretch across his lap. "Drink this."

A bottle presses to my lips, and immediately I recognize the taste. The bitter recovery drink his mom makes with healing magic. Though the liquid is cold when it hits my mouth, it warms a path down my throat, and I only gag twice before swallowing it all.

It takes a few blinks to look through squinted lids, a few more blinks for my blurred vision to clear. At first, I don't recognize where we are. A room with dim lighting, the fixture overhead offering a faint glow. Wood-paneled walls in a light, ashy color. Cement floor with a circle etched into the concrete.

The casting room at Black Wren Voodoo.

"Where's my dad?" I struggle to get up, and Zach assists

me to a cross-legged position when it's clear my body's too weak to stand.

"He's at the hospital. An ambulance took him. They took Verily, and Julie too," Luc says. He's here, sitting on the floor with one knee propped up and Zula laying in front of him.

"Devin's sending updates." Portia shows me her phone, the back-and-forth texting with her ex. "We all rushed out before the police arrived, and he volunteered to stay behind. To make sure everyone got help."

"I should be with my dad." Again, I struggle to stand. Again, denied. Zach places a hand on my back to steady me from tipping.

"CeCe." His voice softens. "We had to get out. There would have been too many questions. They would've dragged our parents into it. Now we can regroup and figure out our next step."

"You're right. Still sucks." I battle the remorse of being MIA as Dad faces the hospital alone. But how would I explain...everything? "What happened to Aubree?"

"Gone." Portia spits out the word. "Slipped away in the chaos."

"Speaking of." Zach lifts my hand, avoiding contact with the carnelian bracelet I stole from Aubree's wrist. It vibrates with black magic, the greasy residue coating my skin. "How did you get this?"

"I don't really know." The stones cool at my touch as I graze my fingers over the surface. "Have you heard of Spectral Reach?"

"No." Zach shakes his head.

"Why are we sittin' around chattin' while Zula slowly dies?" Luc stands and shoves his hands in his pockets, taking a few aimless steps. "We gotta do somethin'."

Portia scoots over to Zula rubbing her back, and she responds with a pitiful whimper. "Do what? The Rougarou's gone. Not to mention it could kill us all with barely any effort."

"It was right there." Luc raises his chin to stare at the ceiling. "She had the knife in her hand, and I blew it—" His voice catches, his sadness a torrent on us all. "I let her down."

"It wasn't your fault," I say. The whole trap they set, the tranq guns and Zula hiding never would have worked. "There are these phantoms protecting the curse. I saw them."

"That's why no one could hurt it." Zach's magic sparks where we hold hands, not really excitement. But curiosity. "Phantoms."

"They stopped everything. Every bullet, every dart." Aside from the one close-range shot from Dad. "Luc, do you still have your tranq gun?"

He slips it from the back of his shorts. "I do."

"Good." I think of what Mom said, how I need to handle the corrupted spirits. "We might get another chance. It's still hunting me. If we get the Rougarou to cross a salt circle, the curse can pass through, but the phantoms can't. They'll separate and then Zula can stab it."

"We could lure it somewhere, like City Park." Zach scrunches his forehead, his brain working on a plan. "Open space, tons of trees—"

"Luc!" Portia cries out, the alarm clear.

He strides over to Zula and rolls her over. A small puddle of blood pools from where she laid on her side. Lifting her wet shirt, he checks the gauze (completely soaked) and pulls it off to expose the wound. "Oh, Zula Mae. I'm so sorry."

Without being asked, Zach exits to the shop side, saying, "Let me see what we have."

The skin volcano erupted, puss and blood seeping in a steady stream. Deep purple, almost black lines spread across her abdomen and around her back. Luc drops to the floor and cradles her in his arms. Portia stays close, offering comfort, unconcerned that her yellow peplum catches the oozing liquids.

"We'll figure things out. Just hang in there." She brushes the sweaty hair from Zula's face.

Zach carries an armful of supplies. A first-aid kit, jars of herbs, various stones, and a bottle of the recovery drink. Uncapping the lid, he pours the blue liquid over her wound. She hisses, arching her back, and pushing away from Zach.

"This is more for magic recovery, but it might ease her pain," he says.

As I watch the rush of care, herbs and gauze liberally flying, my vision blurs. The chatter and clamor wash around me in muted tones, like I observe from behind a glass wall. Zach explains something about what he places on the wound, but the muted words echo, running on top of each other.

The carnelian stones frost over, a rope of ice cubes on my wrist. Cold emanates from it and chills a path all the way up my arm. The sharp freezing turns to pain, a frigid burn that adheres to my skin. I bang the bracelet on the floor, loosening it from where it sticks. *Bang, bang, bang.*

A pressure grows in my lungs, a scream building. No. A howl.

And suddenly, I tip my head back, letting it out, the loud *a-wooo* echoing off the concrete walls.

"Uhhh, CeCe?" Zach calls my name, the words reverberating in my glass chamber. Everyone else stares. Everyone but Zula, who crumbles in pain.

"I..." Shaking my head, I pull myself from the trance. "Sorry. That was weird."

"Look." Portia points at me. "The bracelet."

The stones glow, lighting up the same way they did with Aubree. The sharp cold stings, and I bang it on the floor again, which triggers a moan from Zula. I immediately stop and instead clutch the bracelet to my chest.

"What's going on?" Zach slides to my side and pulls my hand toward him. He's careful not to touch the stones, but we both stare at the glowing carnelian between us.

I close my eyes and see Chance transforming. Hair sprouting from his arms. Sharp claws extending. And then the mark on my neck burns, poured acid eating at my skin.

No! It's too soon. "The Rougarou is coming." My voice trembles.

"How long do we have?" Luc gently lays Zula on the floor and stands. Portia adjusts Zula's pajama top, trying to make her comfortable.

"Not long. Maybe five minutes. Chance is at Le Petit." I look around the small area, imagining the gigantic beast crowding inside. I wish we were somewhere else. City Park, or any open space with places to run or hide. But we're out of time. "It's coming here."

Zach rushes from the room, and it both surprises and relieves me. No need to split my focus between luring the Rougarou into the circle and worrying about my boyfriend. It's better this way.

"Portia, you should go too. Think about your family." Adrenaline jolts through me, the fatigue and magical exhaustion burning up under the imminent threat.

"Let's pretend you didn't try to kick me out." Portia

strides over, and takes my hand, squeezing tightly. "Besties before the resties."

"This is serious. You need to leave." Fear clutches my chest at the thought of encountering the Rougarou again. "I just watched my dad almost get ripped apart, and I can't do that with you."

"It'll be fine." Somehow, she twists my arm and grabs the bracelet with her other hand, rolling it over where our hands connect, from my wrist to hers. "I need to be here. I'm controlling the Rougarou."

"Portia!"

"Don't worry. Simone and I got this." She gives herself a high five, and I want to see the humor of it.

But I'm terrified. My heart pounds in triple time. My breaths come in short bursts.

Luc pulls a switchblade from his steel-toed boot and pops it open, wrapping the handle in Zula's palm.

An invisible string pulls at my finger in the same place Mom tied a piece of moonlight. The sensation moves along my arm and through my chest, all the way to my core where it grows taut. The constriction starts small, nothing more than a slight tug. But it winches tighter and tighter, the discomfort growing.

Get ready. Mom's voice whispers in my head.

Taking a deep breath, I slowly rise, my legs wobbling like a lopsided stool. But I make it to my feet. *Quick checklist: 1 — salt, 2 — fill the circle.*

The door flies open, and Zach returns with a canister of salt, a baseball bat, a bag full of jars, and a can of mace. Of course he didn't abandon us.

I love my friends. My bestie who refuses to leave. My boyfriend who came back prepared to fight. Even though it terrifies me to have them here.

The Rougarou is coming. The silver moonlight tightens inside me, and a flush of assurance plucks at the string. *You can do this.*

Yes. We can beat the Rougarou.

I hope.

Either that or we'll all be dead.

CHAPTER THIRTY-ONE

BLACK WREN VOODOO: THE PHANTOMS

"The Rougarou's at the end of Pirates Alley." Through its vision, I see Black Wren Voodoo ahead. The now empty street looks foreign with the normal bustle shut down. Stores hide in darkness, the only light emanating from the gas lampposts flickering in a steady *whoosh* of sound. "We've got less than a minute."

We prepare as much as we possibly can. While I watch the beast's progress, Zach pours salt in the circle etched into the ground. Portia works with the bracelet to try and slow the Rougarou.

"I can't manage to stop it," she says. "It's not really about control but guiding it. I've got it confused."

And Luc waits, perched by a prone Zula, hoping to tranquilize the beast, and allow Zula to thrust in the knife.

I hear a rustle next to me, and then the brush of fabric. The smell of cinnamon and soap tells me who it is without a need to open my eyes. Zach.

He sits and reaches for my hand. "Go to your magical plane," he whispers. "I'm nervous about those phantoms."

"Why?" I hesitate, hating to lose sight of the Rougarou. Its shadow stretches across the pavement, preceding the clawed footsteps growing closer and closer.

"We don't really know what'll happen after they separate." His thumb rubs along my knuckles, soft squiggles of touch. "Bound things usually don't like to be unbound."

The Rougarou pauses in front of the voodoo shop. Its head hits the circular wooden sign hanging from the patio above by thick chains. A rough, phlegmy growl rumbles in the Rougarou's chest. Throwing its head back, it howls, the loud echo sending chills along my skin, and the mark on my neck flares.

"It's here." I open my eyes right as the front door of the shop crashes in.

Portia startles and takes my hand. Zach tightens his grip on my other hand.

"Magical plane," he reminds me.

The shelf of bottles and jars on the opposite side of the wall smashes. They shatter, glass breaking across the floor in a tinkling symphony. I know what's coming, know the beast lurks right out the door. As the wooden slats explode in, the hidden room no match for the pull of the mark, an overwhelming fear threatens to paralyze me.

There's no cage this time. Just our small group and the Rougarou.

It stands in the doorway, its towering frame gigantic in the enclosed space. Its mouth dribbles, long strings of drool hanging. The sharp toe claws click on the floor, reminiscent of Baba Geaux and his scratching nails. But these ones are ready to pierce and shred.

Pushed by panic, I leap into my plane, the horizon

materializing faster than ever before. My feet splash into the reflective pond, and my view changes from stark concrete to aqua sky. The physical world disappears, and I view everything through the lens of magic.

Zach glows next to me, a comforting warmth that radiates. The bonded Portia and Simone sparkle in a colorful aura. As I take in Luc, the sigil from La Siréne blares so bright it hurts my vision. And poor Zula. Her body dulls to almost invisible, a sickly gray. Her spirit oozes in a slow, upward drip, her time running out.

Around my finger, the strand of silvery moonlight pulses. I can't see where it leads, but a trail of it shimmers on the floor.

The curse swirls around Chance, ropes of storm cloud coiling like a boa constrictor. And though I can't see him through the thick haze, flashes of lightning offer me small peeks of the man hiding inside.

I also struggle to find the phantoms, and I look around the Rougarou, wondering where they went. No way they abandoned the curse they were summoned to defend.

The Rougarou takes a step forward and my vision catches hold of something, a hint of blackened gloom. As I stare, it comes into view, an optical illusion only visible at the correct angle. The ghostly figures are barely perceptible, their darkness so intense they blend into the shadows. Not just blend but become a part of them.

And now that I spotted them, I can keep the hovering phantoms in my sight. They move together, a hive mind flanking the curse, alert to everything, watching and protecting it from all sides.

Luc clutches the tranquilizer gun in his hand, slowly standing as he takes aim. The ticking noise travels through the phantoms, and the Rougarou spins, slashing a taloned hand. In a seamless move, Luc dives on top of Zula and rolls, protecting his sister from the claws, but the tranquilizer pistol slides a few feet away. He grunts and clutches his arm, blood seeping from between his fingers where the sharp talon struck.

"No!" Portia jumps up and plucks the bracelet, letting it snap on her wrist as she steps into the circle. "Look what I've got. I know you want it back."

The Rougarou's attention pivots to her, the red eyes glinting.

"Portia, what are you doing?" I fight to stay in my magical plane, to resist the urge to tackle my bestie and drag her out of harm's way. "Get out of the circle."

"I'm saving Luc. We need him to finish this."

The Rougarou paces in front of the circle, like a wild animal behind a pane of glass. The phantoms nudge it back, keeping it from crossing the salt. It snaps and snarls, strings of foaming drool flying, the glowing eyes focused on the bracelet.

Luc makes a move, pulling himself along the floor and closer to the tranq gun. A gushing fountain of blood follows him. He'll need stitches, probably a few hundred by the trail of crimson he paints on the concrete.

The scraping shuffle catches the Rougarou's attention, and it whirls, taking a giant step to stand over him.

"No, no, no." Portia shakes the bracelet. "Forget about him. Look at me."

The Rougarou ignores the bracelet Portia wildly rattles. Zach stands, releasing my hand to throw the jars, one by one, at the beast. The phantoms open their mouths, swallowing them all.

The Rougarou lifts Luc from the floor, digging its claws

into his upper arms. A pained cry leaves his lips as the beast brings them face to face.

Luc brandishes the knife. He must have grabbed it when he rolled with Zula, and he thrusts it into the beast's muscled chest. With him at close range, the blade sinks in. A deafening howl splits my eardrums, and the Rougarou throws Luc across the room. He crashes into the wall, and his body slumps in a heap.

The phantoms *tick, tick, tick,* and a surge of frantic energy weaves through them. They flicker like gas lanterns, whooshing to enclose the curse. The knife protrudes from the Rougarou's chest, and they direct its clawed hands to try and pull it out.

Zach grabs the baseball bat, ready to protect us. Portia runs from the circle to check on Luc, leaving herself completely vulnerable.

Panic screams inside me, our haphazard plan falling apart around us.

Time slows and the color disappears from my landscape, the turquoise sky dripping hue like a bucket of bleach pours over the top. The pink clouds drink ink until they turn stormy. Even the shimmering luster of the magic auras fade to a tarnished dullness.

I stand in this monochromatic plane, unsurprised when Grandma Lalin's ghost appears and takes my hand. After everything else dwindled to a lackluster sheen, her radiant beauty glares in a blinding splendor.

Leading the way, she walks me to stand in front of the phantoms. *Be careful,* she warns, and I understand what she means. The phantoms will eat the curse and disappear. We can't risk it. Zula struggles to hold on, her life waning. If we lose this opportunity, she won't make it through the night to try again.

What do I do? I ask her.

Whether it's her answer or a wonderful happenstance, I hear the hum of my cicadas. The distant buzz plays softly, and I focus on it, trying to bring it closer. What I'm supposed to do with the sound magic, I have no idea, but their familiar song soothes me.

And then I see. A memory from not long ago. A moment where Zach pulled me into his plane and his crows devoured Rivera's magic.

I'll need a lot more cicadas if that's supposed to happen here.

The phantoms rally to the Rougarou, closing rank around the curse. Even though time slowed and everything else stands in a near frozen state, the dark shadows remain unaffected. They twitch and move, keeping guard and preventing anyone from getting in close. They protect the curse first, and Chance second, reluctant to desert him. Willing to if needed.

They can't leave, though.

I call to my cicadas. Their buzzing dances on my skin like sunlight, an elusive brilliance impossible to hold onto despite basking in the warm glow. Gentle vibrations sing, peaceful waves lapping. But I don't want peaceful. I want roaring. Booming. *Come on!*

A dizzying rush nearly pulls me out of the plane, and my power fizzles like a wet match. Mom was right. I don't have the strength. The cost of rescuing Dad exhausted the magic. His life might be the only one I'm capable of saving tonight, but I have to try.

My great grandma and I take a step closer, and the phantoms *tick, tick, tick.* The sound passes through them. The curse slackens from Chance, stormy ropes uncoiling to expose the man beneath. *No!* The phantoms need to stay so Zula can take the curse back.

I stumble back, panic pounding in my chest. As the curse unwinds, dread crushes me, an all-encompassing fear that I messed up. Zula's life literally hangs in the balance of what happens tonight, no cure or medical care can fix the erupted wound. She needs to transform.

The phantoms fan out, and the stormy rope stretches. I don't know what to do. Don't know how to fix this. In desperation, I yank the string of moonlight on my finger, begging for help, pleading to a mother who tied us together. Of all the times I needed her, and she never showed—birthdays, school plays, mother/daughter days— this moment eclipses them all.

Please, Mom.

I tug the silvery strand, and a presence shimmers next to me. Faint at first, then more solid. A person with brown bobbed hair, dark eyes, who stands the same height as me. As soon as she materializes, Grandma Lalin flees. Her disappearance makes me question calling on my mom, and I worry this could be a huge mistake. I need help, though. Fast, desperate support to stop the phantoms.

"I warned you not to use magic," Mom says, a Cheshire cat grin stretching across her face.

Flashing electricity dances along the curse, the swirling storm spiraling. The snaky cloud locks into place, spanning in front of the phantoms. Their ticking grows louder and faster. Their mouths drop open, a slow widening that extends on the entire surface of their faces.

"We have to stop the phantoms." I point at them, as if Mom hadn't immediately noticed the eight ghostly black holes ready to eat the curse.

"The bigger riddle is what will happen to the curse if the family doesn't reclaim it?"

"If we don't, Zula will die." We ran out of time to philosophize an hour ago, and I ignore her question. "Please. Can you help me?"

"Of course. But this means you'll owe me a favor." With that, she slams her hand on the floor and a heavy silence shrouds us. Like a noise-canceling dome plopped over the top of the room.

Suddenly I understand. My mom's sound magic is silence. *Wow.* Totally cool, and totally frightening.

Without the ability to communicate through their pen clicking language, the phantoms pause in their motion, the gaping black hole mouths closing. The curse spins in front of them, a recoiling spring swirling.

Now what? I try to ask. But the quiet is so thick, no communication passes. No verbal asides, no internal conversing. Total, complete silence.

The silvery thread tautens on my finger, and unlike my ghost who I perfectly understand, Mom's meaning escapes me. She walks to Zach, who stays frozen with the baseball bat in his hands. *He's off magic,* I want to tell her. No use. The hush holds.

She reaches for him and draws him forward, his essence joining us on my plane. He's so beautiful to look at in this space, an added layer of warmth and light that pulses with each heartbeat.

His gaze takes in everything, and I wish he saw the colorful aqua and pink vista I created instead of this black and white sketch. But as he looks at me, the affection and love flowing from him fills my world with unseen color, making my plane vibrant and alive.

Don't do this, I try to tell him, worried about him using magic. But the thick silence swallows my concern.

By some unspoken signal, he turns to my mom. She spins her finger in a circle. He nods. They both face the shadows and lift their hands, completely in sync. The way they communicate confuses me, and a small flare of jealousy ignites at seeing them work together. This seamless symmetry makes it obvious they've partnered up before.

But more than that, it guts me to watch him dive back into using magic. Just like that. My anger burns at my mom for dragging him into this. But the real fire's aimed at myself for inviting her here in the first place.

Zach closes his eyes and darkness rolls in, a light switch dimmer turning down, down, down. My plane fades to twilight, and when I look up, I realize why.

Crows. Because of the silence dome, their caws stay quiet. But they fly overhead, the wings blocking any shards of light from piercing through their cover. The first one swoops, surveying the row of phantoms, and then a second follows.

A vibration skims along my arms, and I look to see my cicadas crawling around me. Their iridescent wings shimmer, and though they're small in number, they're here to help.

I send a pulse of my magic through their ranks, showing them what they need to do. Seeing it in my mind. Along with Zach's swarming crows, they join in to remove the phantoms. Bird after bird swoops, their beaks pecking pieces from the shadows. And my cicadas' wings vibrate, the gleaming blues and greens shaking apart the ghostly forms, erasing whole fragments of them.

The fluttering rattles inside me as well, an inner earthquake threatening to break me apart.

And Mom looks on, smiling tenderly. The affection and love flow from her, filling me with dread, knowing I pulled her further into my world even as something in me screamed not to.

CHAPTER THIRTY-TWO

BLACK WREN VOODOO: THE ROUGAROU, REPRISE

The cicadas and crows wipe out the phantoms, removing every trace. My energy depletes, the effort to hold my plane an astronomical task. Magical hunger pains attack my body, a rumbling emptiness that gnaws my insides and begs me to surrender. Sweet oblivion calls, an escape from the endless battle, a promise of relief. But a flicker of fortitude reminds me this fight isn't over. An angry Rougarou waits on the other side.

And I'm still marked.

My cicadas crawl around where the phantoms used to stand, and their wings take flight, lifting them higher and higher until they disappear. Zach's crows also glide above, fading into the monochrome clouds.

It's strange to observe them without any sound. No comforting buzz of insect wings or shrieking caw. Just utterly pin-drop quiet.

Exhaustion weighs me down, dragging me under, and

the landscape flickers, pieces of the physical world peeking through. A shard of concrete floor, a panel of wood. Even my clouds turn wispy, stretched black cotton balls of patchy fog.

Time also picks up speed, still super slow, but a visible difference. The Rougarou's clawed fingers find purchase on the knife's handle. Portia leaves her back exposed as she hovers over Luc, shaking his shoulder.

My mom dips her head, and Zach nods. They both turn to me and lift a hand. In sync again.

The string of moonlight glows on my finger. Little blue droplets travel down the thread and gather on my skin to absorb into me.

Zach picks up the silvery light and wraps it around his finger.

No, I try to tell him. *Don't connect to my mom.* But the silence dome still covers us, and I watch as the string winds tighter, linking the three of us together.

Aunt Lucy is going to kill me when she finds out.

Yellow droplets join the blue. Each pearl of color thrums with power, warm, cool, warm, cool. It builds, expanding with each drop, bursting in my core with a dose of strength, until the aching pangs subside.

As the magical Red Bull IV flows, I wrestle to maintain my control of the plane. The Rougarou pulls the knife from its chest, an incremental centimeter of movement every few seconds. The train of time rushes at us, a collision inevitable.

The trickling energy slows, and the moonlight thread loosens. Mom lifts her eyebrows in inquiry. I assume she's asking if the magical energy paint balls revived me, and I nod.

She slaps her hand on the ground, shattering the silence dome. My ears pop, and the hum of ambient noise seeps back into the world.

"I knew we'd make a great team." Mom walks backwards, fading with each step. "I'll be in touch."

She disappears. Not that I expected anything different.

Zach moves to me, and his hand hovers near my face. The almost caress ripples through my spirit, sending soft quivers of warmth. In this space, where the tangible becomes less substantial, his soft brush resonates like an echo.

Then he gently cups my cheeks, his energy mingling with mine.

He's got this touching on the magical plane thing down.

I desperately want to stay here with him and forget about everything else. But that's not how life works. At least not our lives. "I'm so sorry. I tried to tell my mom you're off magic."

"Hey, it's okay." His hands slide to the back of my neck, his fingers sending lingering waves of power that connect us. "I wanted to help."

"But now you're tied to my mom. What are we going to tell Lucy?"

For some reason, this makes him laugh. "I'm tied to you."

"And my mom—"

A reverberating clatter interrupts my impassioned speech as the bloody knife falls to the floor, at the Rougarou's feet. Its clumsy, clawed hands managed to pull the blade free.

"You're losing your hold," Zach says.

"I know." Pieces of my sky crack and fall, revealing more

concrete and wood paneling. "We have to face the Rougarou."

"The phantoms are gone. Luc can tranquilize it."

I try to patch my plane, replacing the holes, bringing the color back. All to no avail. "Is he going to be able to?"

We both turn to see Luc in a heap on the floor. Zach blows out a breath. "Maybe not."

If the etched circle was a clock, the Rougarou stands at eleven. The passed-out Zula and the tranquilizer gun at one and two. The crumpled Luc and hovering Portia at three, with Zach and me at the opposite side of the room at seven.

Somehow, in this cramped space, we need to collect the gun and shoot the beast. Add in dodging the lightning-fast attacks and razor-sharp teeth while we wait a few minutes for the tranquilizer to kick in, and our chances of survival: slim.

If I could walk over and pick up the gun, I would. But without it being infused with magic, I can't move it in this plane.

Our options: limited.

The reflective pond trembles, a huge chasm opening. Sections of glassy water spill into the gorge, uncovering more of the casting room.

"I can't control it." Panic flares in me. We have nowhere to run or hide.

"CeCe, it's gonna be okay. We have the bracelet too." Zach leans in, his lips hovering over mine. "I love you."

And then he kisses me.

As he presses in, I feel his energy. The kiss flutters through me—electric and weightless. Our magic dances, blues and golds and reds splashing across a canvas we create.

He's *really* got this touching on the magical plane thing down.

And it's over far sooner than I want.

"I love you too," I say, right as the last remnants of my plane fall and the physical world comes rushing back.

A loud howl bursts my eardrums, such a startling contrast to the silence dome. The Rougarou paws at its chest, whimpering at the gaping knife wound. Thick blood dribbles down its torso and matts in its dark fur. Its ear hangs lopsided, but already more healed than I would have expected from the close-range shot.

"Portia, is Luc awake? We need the tranquilizer." Zach clutches the baseball bat and puts himself between me and the beast.

"He's in and out." She swivels her head, noting the gun. Noting the Rougarou.

I watch the deliberation on her face, the way she bites her lip, her eyes darting from eleven, to one, to two, and back. The beast huffs, giant breaths like the big bad wolf. Its anger builds. The hackles rise, fur lifting on its neck.

No, Portia. Don't do it.

Resolve hardens her features, and she focuses on the gun again.

And then she goes for it, diving across the floor.

The Rougarou's glowing gaze locks on her. It squats low into its back legs, the muscles coiled springs ready to launch. The air stills, everything inside me stills, as the werewolf surges toward my best friend.

My feet carry me several steps before Zach grabs me around the waist, holding me. I fight him, screaming, needing to get to Portia. Prepared to go down with her, because I can't do the life thing without her.

"Stop!" Portia yells. She holds up her hand, palm out, a

barrier between herself and the Rougarou. The bracelet glows, a fierce red shining like emergency beacons, each stone a warning.

And the Rougarou listens.

The snout snorts right in Portia's face, wet exhalations blowing slimy spittle to string in her hair. She stays firm, unintimidated, and the carnelian blazes. Somehow, she commands the beast, the bracelet alive. Maybe because the phantoms were destroyed, or maybe she got the hang of it. Either way, the creature lowers its head in submission, and for the first time, I truly believe she controls it.

"Stay." With her other hand, she slowly reaches for the tranquilizer. Keeping her eyes on the Rougarou, she blindly feels, her fingers crawling along the floor. A metallic scraping sounds as she bumps it, and she clutches the gun in her hand.

"Lay down." She pulls the trigger, and a dart shoots, hitting the beast in the neck.

It roars, the rancid breath gusting over her, and then it does what she says, sliding back to rest on its side.

My mouth literally falls open, my terror turning to disbelief.

Luc stirs with a loud groan and pushes himself up. His noise signals the werewolf, and it starts to rise, but Portia stops it with a command.

The Rougarou blinks, eyes growing increasingly heavier. Its loud grumbles fill the room, and I stay frozen, afraid to alert it, scared to break the spell. All of us watch as the werewolf curls into itself, falling asleep.

"I do not believe my eyes." Luc laughs as he gets to his feet, wobbling unsteadily and using the wall for support. "Now Zula's up."

"We did it." The impossible lays before me, and I shake

my head, not quite believing. "*You* did it." I point to Portia. "But how?"

"I realized it's just a big dog and I treated it like one." Portia clutches the bracelet close to her chest, and I notice the stones frosted over. Her poor wrist must ache with the bitter chill.

"CeCe was ready to kick and scream that thing away from you." Zach's shoulders sag, the weight of worry and swing of relief showcasing his exhaustion.

"No! C'mon Zula!" Luc kneels in front of his little sister and shakes her shoulders. Her listless head flops from side to side. "You have to wake up. It's time. The Rougarou is here. Zula!"

Portia moves over to the girl, feeling for a pulse and shaking her head. *No, no, no,* she whispers and chokes on a sob. She runs a hand over Zula's curls. Straightens her purple pajama top. "Oh, sweetie, I'm so sorry."

Luc picks up the blade from the ground, forcing it into her lifeless hand. "She has to stab it. That's all. Take the knife, Zula."

The sorrow in his voice cracks, and the cold stillness of her body tells the story.

Though the grief sharpens to a bitter taste of loss, something deeper stirs in me, my thoughts moving in a different direction. "I might be able to save her," I say.

Luc whirls around so quickly I worry for the well-being of his neck. "How?"

"Necromancy." The chill of death magic presses in, and I know the price of calling on that power again. Not just for me, but for him. "It'll throw the moon even further out of balance, and we won't be able to make it right. You know what that means?"

Luc nods once, a solemn dip of his head. "Yeah. Seven years. Do it."

Portia pinches her eyes closed but stays quiet. Luc takes her face between his hands and waits until she meets his gaze. "It's always been for Zula."

Her chin wobbles, and she bites her bottom lip. It takes her three tries to finally speak.

"For Zula," she says.

CHAPTER THIRTY-THREE

THE MAGICAL PLANE: THE NECROMANCER

Zach gathered the supplies, and it takes me less than a minute to set up. Portia ripped the bottom of her shirt to tie an improvised bandage around Luc's arm, and the four of us sit on the concrete floor, inside the carved circle. The lifeless Zula lays at one o'clock. The medically sleeping Rougarou at three.

Normally, in talking to the dead, I search for a murderer. This will be different; it's to stop Zula from going to the other side.

"What should I do?" Luc taps his steel-toed boot against the floor.

"Be our lookout. If anyone shows up, take care of it." I worry with Aubree MIA and Grandpa Hijacker unaccounted for that we might get a surprise guest. "And don't touch anything. Especially Zula."

Luc nods, and grabs both the baseball bat and the tranq gun, loading it with another dart he pulls from his pocket.

As I begin, I feel directed, the occasional traces of my

great grandma whispering like a gentle breeze. Here and gone so quickly, it makes me wonder if I imagine it.

"Zula Mae Etienne." I usually ask the dead to show me their killer. Which...not what we want to accomplish. I settle for, "Come back to us."

The moon pulses, a tangible brightness that pounds in my heart. A fierce cold dips me in a frozen bath, my fingers going numb, the chill trembling through me. The intense shivers wrack my body.

I wish I had a jacket.

"Put a hand on CeCe's back," Zach tells Portia.

At their touch, an added energy flows through my spirit. Life magic and voodoo creating a circle with my moon power. The rightness of our connection, the completeness of our sphere echoes inside me. A truth that resonates across any time or plane. This is how magic works. This is how it's meant to be.

Forget black magic, the real power lies in balance. And not the kind my mom manufactures. True magic thrives in unity, blending each source to create something greater than any lone effort.

With the added boost from Zach and Portia, I answer the of call the moon. Death magic races through me, starting in the fingers of my right hand and traveling all the way to my left, leaving a trail of ice behind.

With a quiet whisper, I say her name.

"Zula Mae Etienne. It's not your time yet."

Let me go! Her wail echoes in my mind, as clearly as if she spoke it out loud. I feel her emotions too, which contradict her words. A yearning to live pulses loud and clear.

I see her life, not as a specific moment, but a collection of memories floating around me like cinematic bubbles. Love flows inside her, for her older parents, unequipped to chase down a rogue Rougarou in the heart of New Orleans. For Luc who readily stepped into the role. I see the heartbreaking goodbye as they prepared to leave for the city.

Her love for Luc blazes like a million stars condensed in a tiny space. She understands the sacrifice he made to help her, and more intensely, the seven-year sacrifice he plans to make. *Just let me go,* she says again, her desire to live dulling under thoughts of Luc. Her love for him strong enough to forfeit her existence in return for his freedom.

"Come back to us." I reach out with a tendril of magic. It unfurls and gently runs along her body.

The moon crackles with a burst of energy. Static before a lightning strike that charges the air. Portia and Zach both gasp as some of the excess energy passes to them from where their hands rest on my back.

And then...

A low cough echoes. Zula blinks open her eyes. Luc leaps from the circle to lift her into his arms, and she moans in response. Her wound still seeps, ugly and infected. Hushed whisperings string from his mouth as he presses his forehead to hers.

"I love you, Zula Mae." Luc coils her fingers around the knife's hilt. "But it's time now. We have to finish this."

"I can do it," she rasps.

The heavy blade trembles in her grip as Luc carries her to where the prone Rougarou lies. He gently sits her down and wraps his hand over hers. "*We* can do it."

Together they strike, the knife sinking into the furry flesh of the Rougarou's belly.

Portia glances between Zula and the beast. "Did it work?"

A beat of silence holds before Zula groans through clenched teeth. Wiry black fur sprouts from her arms in sparse patches. Her nose extends, the sound of crunching bone and wet, stretching skin causing my stomach to roil. She screams, the violent shifting painful to watch, let alone experience.

Luc stays next to her, even as sharp claws break through her fingertips, stretching into pointed weapons. Her whole body builds in mass, muscles bulging, clothes popping.

"It's okay now, Zula Mae. I know this hurts, but you'll heal."

"Be careful, Luc." Every muscle in Portia clenches tightly. Just one giant, coiled nerve.

Luc lifts his hands, showing he means no harm to his transforming sister. "It's me. I'm not gonna hurt you. I'd never hurt you."

Ever so gently, he checks her wound, his fingers stroking over her belly. She stays still, curling in on herself and mewling, but allowing him to examine it.

"It's already a little better. I—" his voice breaks, cracking his words, and he turns to me, his eyes glistening. "Thank you for savin' her."

A loud noise from the shop startles me, the sound of someone coming in. Luc moves at warp speed, diving to pick up the tranq gun, and pointing it at the decimated doorway.

I honestly don't have the strength to deal with anything else. No more Aubree, no more Hijackers, no more fight. At this point, I'm ready to surrender. *Take my magic, just let me go to bed!*

A rusty wheelbarrow crosses the threshold, followed by a bare foot with gross toenails. Then jagged capri pants, up to the white, feathered shawl around his shoulders, and the top hat on his head.

Baba Geaux.

His layers of necklaces clatter as he navigates through the debris, and a small tote bag hangs diagonally across his chest. "Hoo hoo! Took me a minute and half, but I got here."

"What are you doin'?" Luc keeps the gun pointed at the witch doctor with an unwavering hand.

"Now don't go gettin' all trigger happy on me." Baba Geaux saunters in, casual as you please. "I'm here to take out the garbage."

"Garbage?" I ask. There's no way he came in as cleanup crew from the construction carnage the Rougarou left behind.

He nods his head at the unconscious Chance. "Him."

For the first time, I realize Chance is back to being Chance. And he's in bad shape. Luc stabbed him in the chest, and then Zula stabbed him in the gut. Injuries that will only heal if he can transform again. Which...not likely.

"What are you gonna do with him?" Zach asks.

"Now, now, that's not for y'all to worry about." He scritches his toenails on the floor, and I cringe. "But I do have somethin' that is your concern. A gift."

Gift?

Digging in the tote, he pulls out two small sachets. One he throws to me. "Rub this over that Rougarou mark and then dump it in a warm bath. Soak in it for at least thirty minutes. It'll clear things up nice and tidy."

"Thank you...?" I say it more as a question, wondering what he wants in return. It's Baba Geaux, he always wants something.

"And for you. Well, for that bracelet, anyway." He tosses another sachet at Portia. "Fill a bowl with cold water and dump that in. Dip the bracelet at least six times. It'll clear the magic right up."

Luc plops to the floor, propping his arms on bent knees.

"No money or favors. We're not interested in your games tonight."

"No games." He crosses the room and picks up Chance, awkwardly lugging him into the wheelbarrow. "But one teeny-tiny favor."

"No," Luc says.

Baba Geaux ignores him and turns to Portia. "Tell Simone I miss her. That's all." He clears his throat and looks at me. "Your mama sends her regards."

I wait for more, that she'll be in touch, or she expects another favor, but Baba Geaux heads for the doorway, rolling Chance and the wheelbarrow out of the shop.

CHAPTER THIRTY-FOUR

LE PETIT THEATER: THE GOODBYE

Five Weeks Later

Little has changed with the moon. Still overpowered, still out of balance. Every few nights, the silvery thread tugs on my finger, a call from Mom to work together. But she thinks black magic is the way to fix it. I'd endure the cold of the moon every night for the rest of my life to protect Zach from using again, so I ignore the call.

Amazingly, *Voodoo Bayou* still got its run. Jennifer Wren, Zach's mom, replaced Chance as the music director. Ian (the saxophone guy whose name I finally learned) brought in a drummer who picked it up quickly.

Luc played Beau, sharing the stage with Portia's gleaming star power in the role of Kate. La Siréne, the Loa of sea and song, granted him permission to finish the production, especially considering she used her gift to help him get the part. His parents came to watch, bringing a healed and joyful Zula with them. Seeing her bouncing around and laughing made me cry. Legit tears I blinked my way through when she ran over to say hi.

Voodoo Bayou was a roaring success. Pulling it off in the limited amount of time amid a supernatural serial killer took near supernatural ability. But the reviews proclaimed it, *a New Orleans triumph.*

As someone wildly familiar with the power of a stage kiss, I was left speechless by Luc and Portia's offering. Even from the orchestra pit, I felt their shared intensity. Kate's sorrow poured out as she broke things off with Beau, sending him back to the bayou. And he drew her in, his hands shaking as he brushed the tears from her cheeks.

A heavy hush fell over the audience, silent enough to hear his trembling breaths. The word *no* whispered from her mouth, and she shook her head, her fists beating on his chest in an aching denial. His arms wrapped around her, drawing her close before his lips met hers. The desperate kiss crackled with a sense of finality, and they refused to let go of each other, as if it could prevent the inevitable goodbye.

But time, the ever-cruel master, keeps ticking.

I find Dad and Gina in front of the theater waiting for me. After several nights in the hospital, two surgeries, and weeks of physical therapy, he's finally getting back to normal.

Of the three victims who were taken by ambulance that night, Dad seems to be doing the best. Verily works through weekly rehab after suffering two broken legs.

Julie remains in the hospital, still in a coma.

The guilt of it sits heavy in my chest, the worst sort of heartburn that flares every time I think of her. *Could I have done more?* The silence from her hospital bed feels like an accusation. A reminder of her words. *I know what you are. Evil.* I no longer look at her as my nemesis. I'd forfeit every role in every play if it meant she'd wake up.

"Great job, baby girl." The brace Dad wears on his arm gets between us as he gives me a hug.

"Thanks. I'm glad you made it." And I am. So glad to see him up. Overjoyed that he strolls around without the assistance of a walker anymore.

"Hey, CeCe." Gina came too, both as his chauffeur and his date. She keeps a stabilizing hand on Dad's back and rubs up and down. Kind of adorable. "I loved the show."

"Thanks for dragging him along." I always liked Gina, but now I appreciate her. More than that, I treasure her. The way she stepped up to help take care of Dad showed me her heart. In those quiet moments, when she shouldered the weight with me, she became more than just Dad's "friend." She became family.

"This was a big outing," Gina says. "I need to get him home."

"I'm right here. I can speak for myself." He starts coughing and almost bows over from the pain. Gina and I share a look, both of us biting back our smiles.

"Fine." He adjusts his brace, tugging where it tightens on his bicep. "We can go."

He gives his usual silent nod goodbye, and adds a grunt, which means, *be home by eleven.* Maybe he meant midnight. It's hard to say.

"Bye, Daddy." While watching him, gratitude swells in my chest. Every step he takes feels like a gift. A reminder of how close I came to losing him.

The last of the crowd leaves, and I join the others. They all gathered on the sidewalk, our little army that defeated the Rougarou. And Devin.

At least he has a shirt on.

"Where's the afterparty? Café Du Monde? The Gumbo Shop?" Portia bounces on her heels, the final performance energy flowing through her.

"I can't." Luc rubs his chest like it aches, his whole demeanor heavy. "It's time."

"Time? What do you…" Portia's smile falls, her motions stilling. "La Siréne."

He pinches his eyes closed and nods his head. "The sigil started burnin' about an hour ago, callin' me to her."

"No." Portia cries. "It's too soon. It's—"

"Time. It's time."

Portia takes a few deep breaths, fighting to compose herself, and Luc says goodbye to Zach and me. He shakes Zach's hand, gives me a long hug. "Thanks for all you did for Zula."

"I'm sorry, Luc. So sorry." I choke the words from my lungs, my emotions a threatening storm.

"Don't fret over me, honey." His faint smile almost feels genuine, and he looks at Devin. "Hey shirtless summer, take care of Portia for me?"

Devin offers a solemn nod. "That's a promise I'll keep."

"Good." He nods and turns, giving his full attention to Portia. Running his fingers through her hair, he cups her cheeks. "I'll think about you every day."

She scoffs, rolling her eyes, but a flicker of something softer shines, a need to believe him. "It's seven years!"

"I won't run out of things to think about." This time his smile is genuine, and he brushes his fingers along her jaw. "It was all worth it, every minute, I got to spend with you."

For her part, she stays strong, eyes dry, a determined jut to her chin. "It was worth it for me too."

He kisses her on the top of the head, grazes his fingers

down her neck. Then the lightest touch of his lips on hers. "Goodbye, Portia."

"Bye Luc."

He walks away, and I don't know how Portia keeps her emotions together. I'm a mess, tears unchecked, nose running. Zach hands me a tissue, where he got one from, I don't know, but I gladly accept and swipe my face.

Portia blows out a trembling breath. "I'm heading out, and — no offense — I need some me time."

"Are you sure? I don't think you should be alone." The ugly tears pour, my meager tissue insufficient.

"Please. Let me have tonight to figure things out." She leans forward, giving me a hug, her face buried in my neck. "I promise to call if I need anything."

"Okay." I bite my lip, getting the emotional jag under partial control. "But you have until noon tomorrow. Then I track you down."

"Deal." She straightens her shoulders and waves, heading down the sidewalk.

Devin follows right behind, and she whirls around, poking a finger in his shirted autumn chest. "I said I want to be alone."

"Yeah, I know. Nothing wrong with being alone together." He rubs the spot she jabbed.

"Devin. I mean it."

"Look, Woofy asked me to take care of you, and I promised I would." He softly places a hand on her shoulder. "Let me keep my promise."

The fight wilts out of her, and the tears she bravely held off leak from her eyes.

"Fine, but no talking." Her voice softens, a hint of vulnerability breaking through her tough exterior.

He mimes locking his lips and throwing away the key.

On the one hand, I'm grateful Devin will be with her. On the other, I worry she might rebound with the guy she rebounded from with the OG rebound guy.

Or something like that.

But maybe not. Portia's changed, and not just because of Simone and her magic. A new fortification of strength forged like armor. A new, resilience, replacing the "useless" feeling, ready for whatever challenge comes next.

Zach and I are left alone in front of the theater. Dusk sets in, the sky burning in deepening shades of tangerine as the sun falls closer to the horizon.

He lifts my chin, looking straight into my soul, his crystalline blue eyes searching. "Are you okay?"

"Yeah." Another tear rolls down my cheek, but this one brings a soft smile to my lips. "It's amazing, isn't it?

His head tips slightly, and so do his lips, his grin responding to mine. "What is?"

An echo of *When the Saints Go Marching In* plays from a brass band nearby, and I close my eyes, breathing in the essence of a healed city. No more curfew. No more rogue Rougarou. The pulse of the French Quarter beats a healthy, happy rhythm.

"New Orleans finds a way," I say.

He scans the block. People dash in and out of stores, the sidewalks bustling. A tour guide passes by with a group, his cane tapping on the ground as he declares this the most haunted city in the world.

"Yeah. It does." He winds his fingers in mine, and my magic dances at his touch. The clean vibration has no oily trace of black magic. Just him. And I squeeze tighter.

"Come on. Let's check out the shop." He pulls our attached hands and leads the way to Black Wren Voodoo.

The dust of construction hazes the shelves, the rebuild

not quite complete. Apparently, an angry Rougarou does a lot of damage. The hidden casting room looks good as new, the door repaired, the wood paneling fixed.

Blood bleached from the concrete.

But in the middle of the circle, there's a new addition. A checkered blanket spreads across the floor and two low-rise beach chairs are set out.

"Are we on a date? I thought we were just checking out the shop." I smirk over my shoulder as I step further in the room, lowering into one of the chairs.

He sits as well, leaning back with an easy grin. "Unpredictability is one of my best features."

I laugh. "So, what comes next in this unpredictable date?"

"Snacks." He lifts a big bowl stocked with my favorite munchies, Zapps Voodoo potato chips, Aunt Sally's Pralines, Ragin' Cajun Peanuts, and Red Vines.

"You thought of everything." I reach for the chips, popping them open, and he grabs a bag as well.

I kick off my black sandals. Since we played for *Voodoo Bayou* tonight, I wear the orchestra pit special of black skirt and black blouse. He dressed similarly in black slacks and a black button-up shirt, and he follows my lead, kicking off his black dress shoes.

We crunch on our chips, the windowless room and dim light overhead making me feel separated from the world outside. Just the two of us in our quiet sanctuary. It's a beautiful thing, having a person in your life you can be quiet with. No need to fill the silence. Just the comfort of companionship.

His foot wanders over to mine, brushing against the side, as if he needs the point of contact. And soon enough, my toe rubs against his.

My pinky toe, the shameless flirt.

After a few minutes, he crumbles his empty bag and sets it aside. "There is something we need to do. Another reason for being here." He straightens and turns to me, leaving my pinky toe abandoned. "Are you ready?"

The peaceful silence shatters as I contemplate his question.

I curl the fingers of my left hand into my palm, clutching the invisible string that ties me to my mom. For an unfathomable reason, I've been reluctant to break the link to a woman who lied, used me, and walked away.

You know I care about you, right?

Her words run through my mind, a spark of hope I struggle to extinguish. Yes, she tricked me into binding Portia and Simone, but she also pulled me into her oak grove, fed me energy in my magical plane, and hid me from a grandfather who wants to control my magic.

Who is she, really? The manipulative magician, or the mindful mother?

I also watched the way she and Zach worked together, the seamless movements, the communication without words. And, I admit, I'm jealous. Jealous he has more of a relationship with her than I do.

Which is stupid. Like being envious of someone who spent more time with a moderately docile alligator.

I release my fist, loosening my fingers. After the weeks I spent calling and texting, trying to get a hold of her—to no avail—I prepare to cut the link connecting us. "I'm ready."

"Good." Zach nods and takes my hand. "Then let's go."

He pulls me into his magical plane, the beauty of the mountain vista more incredible than I could have imagined. But rather than admiring the majestic peaks or the colorful panorama, I stare at the silvery strand on my finger. A matching one ties around Zach, and we both have a thread glinting in the distance, tied to an imperceptible person.

Mom.

"At first, I thought she was looking out for me. Constance always had a way of making me feel important. I would have done just about anything for the magical mafia." He pinches the strand between his fingers and lifts it to his eye line. "But they care about magic more than people. If I had no power, no ability, she would let me drown."

A spark of yellow arcs between his fingers, and the thread snaps, ringing like VanHellSing's strings.

His speech calms the indecision in me, not necessarily extinguishing the hope, but making it irrelevant. I have my family. Dad, Zach, Portia. Luc and Devin. Even Gina. Our fierce army. Loyal and courageous and sincere.

I send a pulse of my magic along the connection, severing the thread.

The silvery light dims, the glow dying and the string falling to the ground. I know Mom wants help setting the moon to rights, fixing the damage left from the Hijackers and fake Rougarou. But she'll be doing it without us.

We blink back to the physical plane, sitting in our beach chairs, holding hands in the casting room. Grandpa Hijacker and the rest of my "family" still want my magic. And who knows where Aubree might be hiding. But in this moment, peace settles over me. A sense that everything is exactly as it should be.

The snacks shuffle around, Zach looking for what he wants. He grabs a Red Vine for me and takes one for himself. "Would you rather never eat a beignet again or never hear another jazz band?"

"Zach! What kind of torturous question is that?"

He winks at me, and it warms my insides. All the organs. Heart pumps, lungs inflate, brain goes mushy. Even skin gets in on it, happy goosebumps dancing across my flesh. He has a tight hold on me, but he'd never let me drown. Because of him, I float. Fly. He lifts me higher, leaving me breathless in the best way.

And I love him.

THE END

ACKNOWLEDGMENTS

I am neck-deep in emotional IOU's for this book and the least I can do (aside from offering my first born—sorry Megs) is extend my gratitude here. First and foremost, to my family. I have the awesomest husband—and no one can argue with me about that, because it's in print now. Legally binding. Ryan, your support is everything—my sounding board, my safe place, the voice reminding me that Diet Dr. Pepper isn't one of the food groups.

To my kids: you are the best chaos I could ever ask for. You keep me laughing and keep me humble. Thank you for letting me write weird things and still claiming me. In all fairness, I still claim you too.

To Donna, who opened her house, fed me both food and encouragement, wiped my tears, and never let me give up, even when I felt *very* committed to giving up. Honestly, everyone should have a Donna, but you can't have mine. Go get your own!

A standing ovation for Marko, who shares custody of Donna with me. Our soda runs are always about more than soda, and I'm grateful for your friendship.

I am so blessed to be a part of the Monster Ivy team. Thank you to this exemplary publishing house, especially to Cammie Larsen, Michelle Carpenter, and Mary Gray. Your contribution deserves more than words. Probably a parade.

A huge shout out for my writers' group, Sunday's

Without Nick. Thank you for always turning a potential writing spiral of self-doubt into a weekly excuse for emotionally validating conversations. Thank you all for attending an expensive writing dinner with me, where I felt so uplifted by your support I nearly cried into the basket of rolls. For Barbara Lund who puts up with my antics, and only slightly cringes when I hit curbs or drive in reverse on one-way streets. And Adam Lund for researching mermen Christmas ornaments and joyfully naming "snacky time." Barbara and Adam, thank you for being Beta readers. We'll always have Galveston!

To the amazing Beta reader Miranda Moore. Thank you for being a part of my journey. And to Arlene Eck, who reminded me that sometimes characters actually have to *do* stuff.

To the city of Houma, Louisiana for hosting Rougarou Fest where it's perfectly acceptable to approach strangers and talk about werewolves.

Last but not least, to The Coop. Forever and always!

About the Author

Debbie Hibbert is an author, lover of chocolate, and finder of weird things. What kind of weird things, you might ask? There was that one time with the mysterious chimes. The porcelain doll in the woods. The plastic flamingo in the trees. The Hell gates...yes, plural.

When not writing, Debbie likes to explore old graveyards, drink Diet Dr. Pepper, and solve mysteries with her dogs, Sherlock and Watson. She also likes the beach. Sunny days. Blue skies. Toes in the sand... You get the idea.

She's a Texas transplant that resides in Houston. In a hurricane, during the apocalypse, or through an extended reading of bad jokes on Twitter, she would choose her resourceful hubby and talented offspring to guarantee survival.

CONNECT WITH ME

Stay connected by joining my mailing list. Find it at my website: debbiehibbert.com

With the abundance of books available to read, thank you for choosing mine. If you have a minute, please take the time to leave a review on Amazon. You will be rewarded with good luck and positive vibes.

Much love, Debbie